AWOKEN

A Djinn Wars Novel

CHRISTINE POPE

Dark Valentine Press

AWOKEN

Copyright © 2017 by Christine Pope

ISBN: 978-1-946435-05-7

Published by Dark Valentine Press

Cover design by Lou Harper

Book formatting by Indie Author Services

Chapter One

JORDAN WELLS CAME TO THE CROSSROADS AT Highway 84 and Highway 17 in Chama, New Mexico, and paused for a moment to rest her weary feet, her worried gaze—as always—scanning the area for any sign of djinn activity. She probably shouldn't even be standing out in the open like this, but in all the empty miles between here and Pagosa Springs near the southern border of Colorado, she hadn't seen a single soul, human or djinn.

The fingers of Jordan's left hand tightened around the strap of the backpack she wore, even while her right hand rested lightly on the revolver at her hip. Yes, djinn were supposedly immortal, but Jordan and her fellow survivors had discovered they could be wounded. And even though she'd never touched a gun before the Dying happened and the world she'd known had ended forever, Jordan now reckoned herself a good enough shot that she could empty the shiny Ruger into any otherworldly adversaries, thus buying herself enough time to get away and hide.

At the moment, however, she had to decide whether to take a brief detour into Chama to look for supplies, or whether to keep heading south toward her ultimate destination, Los Alamos. It was the only sanctuary for mortals that remained—or at least, she had to pray that outpost of humankind still existed, even though more than eighteen months had passed since her group's last contact with the survivors in the mountain town.

Jordan shifted the backpack, feeling its weight. During her journey here, she'd been able to scrounge some food, and water was plentiful enough, thanks to the various rivers and streams in the region, but even so, supplies were getting light. According to the map she carried with her, she still had almost a hundred miles to go, and she hadn't managed to average more than twelve or fifteen miles a day at best, simply because she had to expend so much energy zigging and zagging, hiding in stands of trees when she could, using the cover of abandoned homesteads and ranches when there wasn't anything else available, flat out running in the open areas between houses...and praying a djinn wouldn't see her during those horribly vulnerable moments.

But still, to head into Chama meant she'd be going out of her way. Maybe she'd be lucky enough to find a few places on her way to Los Alamos where she could pick up more supplies. There were several settlements called out on her map—Tierra Amarilla, Cebolla, to name a few—but she had no way of knowing whether they would have anything useful to offer, or whether they were basically wide spots in the road. She'd never had the chance to travel to this part of New Mexico and was basically flying blind.

There probably won't be much to scavenge, she thought, *except in Española, and that's almost to your destination.*

Once again she scanned the landscape around her. Far off in the distance, a hawk circled, but the bird of prey was the only visible sign of life. For all she knew, there were no djinn at all in this part of the world. It was beautiful here, true, with the rolling hills and their crowns of ponderosa pine and aspen, just now beginning to turn gold, and the far-off peaks of mountain ranges she couldn't even name, but was the beauty of the landscape enough to attract one of those vengeful immortal beings?

Jordan didn't know. There was so much about the djinn she didn't know. She did know one thing, however.

They were very good at killing humans.

The thought brought back unwanted memories, of her group's first flight from Colorado Springs nearly two years ago now, of everyone who had died at the hands of the djinn. And then the much smaller group who had survived that attack, and had taken refuge in the small resort town of Pagosa Springs in the southwestern region of Colorado, not too far from the New Mexico border. They'd kept a low profile there, so much so that they'd managed to live in Pagosa for the last year and a half without any kind of djinn interference. That had all come crashing to a halt five days ago, when the little colony was set upon by a group of djinn intent on making sure none of Pagosa Springs' current residents survived.

As far as Jordan knew, none of them had. Except her. She'd never allowed herself to relax the entire time she'd lived there. Not really. She had various escape routes planned out of town, and a "bug-out" bag stashed in the utility room of the house where she'd been living. As soon as the attack began, she ran to get her things. Cowardly? Maybe. But you couldn't fight djinn. About all you could do was wound them badly enough to give yourself a chance to escape.

She swallowed, and did her best to shove those memories back in the depths of her mind. There wasn't anything she could do about that now, except try to survive. If even one person lived to tell the story of the survivors from Colorado Springs, then they wouldn't be entirely lost. Someone would remain to let other survivors—if there even were any—know that the Colorado Springs group had persisted, had managed to live on when so many others had perished.

Jordan's stomach growled. It had been many hours since the protein bar she'd consumed when she woke up that morning; the sun was now midway down the western sky. She had maybe three hours until darkness came. Yes, she could walk pretty far in that space of time, but what if she walked and walked and didn't encounter anyplace that would be suitable to shelter her for the night? In a pinch she could sleep in the forest, using a carpet of fallen pine needles as her mattress and her pack as a pillow —it wouldn't be the first time, but she vastly preferred a bed or couch in an empty house or ranch.

There would be far more places like that in Chama. And more chances to find some food, even if it was just freeze-dried camping stuff from one of the area's outdoor supply stores, or canned goods that hopefully hadn't yet expired. She repressed a grimace at the thought of eating yet another prefab meal like that, but it was better than starving.

The possibility of adding to her dwindling food supply seemed to decide things. She glanced around once again and determined that the coast was still clear, then veered left and took Highway 17, moving toward the heart of Chama.

Abandoned vehicles were scattered along the roadway, some on its edges, and some right in the middle of the road, as if their drivers had succumbed to the Heat while trying to get out of town. Jordan was used to such sights, and threaded her way among the discarded metal hulks without paying much attention to them. Actually, she was glad of those forsaken cars and SUVs and pickup trucks, just because they provided some shelter, and allowed her to follow the road rather than being forced to veer far off the asphalt ribbon that made its way along the valley, just in order to have adequate cover.

Two restaurants faced one another across the highway, but Jordan would rather get her supplies someplace else. Anything that had been in those restaurants' freezers would have long since spoiled, and canned goods—especially the industrial-size versions used for food service—were far too heavy to make for good road food. No, what she really needed was a camping store, or, failing that, a house that looked as if it might still have some beef jerky or diet bars lying around. Anything that would fit in her backpack and keep her alive.

A crunch of a twig made her start, but when she whirled around, hand going to the Ruger at her hip, she saw that the noise had been made by a pair of medium-sized goats—one white, the other brindle, like a swirl of caramel and cream—who were wandering along the edge of the road, pausing now and then to nibble at the weeds growing there. Her heart, which felt as if it had lodged somewhere midway up her throat, resumed a somewhat normal rhythm.

"Goddamn it," she muttered. The goats gave her an incurious glance and continued along their way, apparently unruffled by the presence of a human in a place that should have been utterly abandoned.

She paused so she could get her canteen out

of the backpack, and took a long drink. The canteen had been full that morning, but now was half empty. That was something else she'd need to take care of. Not that big a deal, since the Rio Chama wound its way through town, running more or less parallel to the highway until it crossed under the 17 and continued its way north into Colorado.

After she stowed the canteen, Jordan kept walking along the edge of the road, making sure to stop every once in a while to get a good look around. The landscape remained empty; even the goats had disappeared.

Toward the north end of town, near the depot for the Cumbres and Toltec Railroad—a popular tourist attraction she'd always meant to try, but had never gotten around to—she did spot a fishing gear store. Good. She could load up there, and then find a likely house to hole up in for the night. After that, she'd cut back to the 84 and keep going toward Los Alamos. This little detour would cost her an evening, but it wasn't as if anyone in the mountain town was expecting her.

For all she knew, Los Alamos would be just as empty and dead as every other town she'd passed through.

Jordan pushed that thought aside and tested the door to the fishing store—"Angler's Alley," said the wooden sign above the entrance. Luckily, the door was unlocked, and she went inside.

And stopped abruptly in dismay. Whatever might have once been here, it looked as if it had been looted long ago. The shelves were bare, packages of lures and fishing line knocked to the floor. The section of the store that must have once contained the camping gear was now completely empty, the only things remaining a couple of cans of Sterno.

"Well, shit," Jordan muttered. She'd come across scenes like this before—sometimes in the most unlikely places—but she really hadn't been expecting it in sleepy little Chama.

The notion of getting some more camping food had apparently been shot down the tubes, which meant she now had to go with plan B, scrounging from one or more of the houses in the area. It wasn't as much of a sure thing, but if nothing else, she could maybe find some canned beans or tuna or something. If she ate the canned stuff here, at least she could save the freeze-dried food in her bag for the days when she found herself someplace that didn't even have an abandoned ranch nearby.

She poked her head outside and looked around. The coast was clear.

Of course it was. There were no djinn around

here. Jordan didn't know where they holed up when they weren't murdering the world's last few survivors, but clearly, that place wasn't anywhere near Chama, New Mexico.

The murmur of the river drew her. She crossed the highway and went through the gravel-paved parking lot of the railway depot, using the cars and SUVs left behind by dead tourists as cover—and then the abandoned railway cars themselves—until she could get to the trees. Here the cottonwoods grew thick and tall, nurtured by the water from the Rio Chama. Once she passed into their shade, Jordan allowed herself a small sigh of relief. She always felt better when she was among the trees, surrounded by their sheltering greenery.

That cover didn't last forever, of course. After a few minutes, she came out to the river bank. At this time of year, it wasn't running too high, since it was far too early for snow melt—or late, depending on how you looked at it—and the monsoon rains that came on schedule every summer were almost gone, with October now here.

Jordan didn't really want to think about it being October. For now, the days were still mild, perfect walking or hiking weather, actually, but the nights had grown chilly. Snow usually didn't arrive until around Thanksgiving, but you couldn't count on that. True, she'd grown up in Colorado Springs, not northern New Mexico, but the climates weren't all that different. You could still get hit with snow as early as Halloween if you were unlucky.

It was fine. She could make it to Los Alamos in less than a week. Even as crazy as the weather had gotten right before the Dying, it hadn't snowed in early October.

She'd been hoping for a footbridge to cross the river but didn't see any evidence of one, even though she could just make out the roof line of a house on the other side of the Rio Chama, maybe a quarter mile away. At least there was a house; she'd start her search there, and only move on if she couldn't find anything of value.

After contemplating the depth of the water for a moment, and watching the flow of the river for another minute more, Jordan decided that she should be able to wade across. She found a large, smooth boulder and sat down so she could remove her hiking boots and socks, and then rolled up her jeans to her knees. The socks she shoved in her backpack, but there was no room for the boots; she knotted the laces together and hung them around her neck. Almost as an afterthought, she removed the gun and its holster from her belt and stuck them in her backpack near the top, leaving it unzipped. Just in case.

All right. Time to get moving.

The water was colder than she'd thought, and she had to grit her teeth at the shock of it against her bare skin. Under her feet, mossy rocks moved uneasily as she began to make her way across, but the footing was just stable enough that she managed to keep going, propelling herself from spot to spot as she forded the river. In the middle, she hit a deep patch and sank down to her waist, the icy current immediately striking a chill through her entire body.

Although she wanted nothing more than to let out a small shriek at the shock of the cold water engulfing half her frame, she bit her lip and kept going, telling herself that it was just water, and she'd dry off soon enough once she got to the other side and found some shelter.

Wishful thinking, since jeans weren't exactly known for their ability to dry out quickly. But she was more than halfway across, and she certainly wasn't about to stop now.

A minute or two later, the water grew shallower, and she struggled her way up to the rocky shore. When she reached around to check, it seemed that her backpack had escaped unscathed, and so had her hiking boots. It was just those damn jeans that were completely soaked, making it feel as though her legs were encased in lead.

Nothing for it. She paused long enough to put her socks and hiking boots back on. Then, mouth set, she kept moving, and wound her way through more cottonwoods and the occasional pine and aspen, until she came out into an open grassy area, clearly the backyard of the house whose roof line she'd glimpsed from the other side of the river. Seen up close like this, it was a much more impressive structure than she'd thought, two stories, with a steeply peaked dark green tin roof and a porch that appeared to wrap around most of the building. Set off to one side was an enormous solar panel, the kind powered by a motor so it could be angled toward the sun no matter the time of day. Right now it was tilted slightly toward the west, but that didn't mean much. It could have been frozen in that position for the last two years.

Jordan looked around, attempting to see if there were any noticeable signs of habitation. The grass in the backyard looked fairly level, although weeds grew along the edges of the culti-vated area. Still, its manicured state could simply be due to those wandering goats—they did tend to eat everything they came across, and for all she knew, the two goats she'd seen were part of a much larger herd. The dark beige paint on the house's wooden siding appeared faded, but she didn't detect any obvious flaking or cracks.

Inconclusive. But she was here, and she knew the odds of anyone surviving in this little out-of-the-way spot were less than one in a million, so she figured she might as well go inside.

The back door was closest. It opened on a utility room that looked as though it hadn't been touched in years. Dust coated the tops of the washer and dryer, and also the plastic laundry basket that sat on the floor. Otherwise, the room was empty, although when Jordan opened the cupboard and looked inside, she saw detergent and a box of fabric softener sheets, along with a bottle of bleach. Clearly, someone had lived here once. You could never be certain when you came across big houses like this in places that didn't seem able to support the kind of lifestyle their size suggested, since a lot of the time they were owned by people with enough money to maintain a second residence that they only used a few weeks out of the year, when they would come to remote towns like Chama to hunt or fish or just get away from it all.

She moved on from the utility room into the kitchen, which was up to date and spotless, with granite counters and stainless appliances, and a black-painted wooden island in the center of the room with a dazzling array of copper pots and pans hanging from the rack above it. To her surprise, the refrigerator was humming, clearly still working.

The solar panel, she told herself. *It would just keep going, even without someone here to maintain it.* Or at least, she assumed that was why the appliance appeared to be operating. All that electricity being generated, with no one around to use it.

When she opened the refrigerator door, she saw that the shelves inside were nearly empty. A few bottles of wine, white and rosé, all from New Mexico wineries. What appeared to be blocks of cheese, wrapped in plastic. The sight of them did make her frown, because she didn't think cheese could possibly have survived for two years without going moldy, even if it was refrigerated.

Maybe someone really did live here. Someone who, against all odds, was another Immune, just like Jordan herself.

A quick peek inside the freezer revealed packages of what she thought were meat, all neatly wrapped in brown paper. It seemed that someone had been doing some hunting around here.

Although she wanted nothing more than to get out of there, she was also aware of how her wet jeans clung to her legs, how uncomfortable they were. If nothing else, she needed to change into the spare pair she had in her backpack.

And what then? she asked herself. *Stick a pair of soaking-wet jeans in with the rest of your stuff? That's a great way to ruin everything.*

Well, hell. Maybe she could hang around for a little while, just long enough to spread the jeans out on the front porch so they could catch some afternoon sun before it set behind the hills to the west. She didn't see much alternative.

Even so, she went out into the living room, a sturdy, "guy" sort of place, with its dark brown leather sofa and chairs, and heavy oak furniture and a stone fireplace and an enormous Navajo rug on the floor. At least the walls weren't adorned with trophy animal heads, but rather oil landscapes of places that had to be located in New Mexico and Colorado—mountains and rivers, jagged cliffs topped with monsoon storm clouds.

"Hello?" she called out, feeling both scared to death and like a complete idiot.

Only silence answered her.

No one seemed to be home. Good. She slid off her backpack and set it on the floor next to the couch, and removed her boots once again, then awkwardly wriggled out of her wet jeans. They hit the wooden floor with a splat, and she winced. She had to get the gun out of the way— at least she'd kept her powder dry, so to speak— so she could reach her extra pair of jeans and a fresh set of underwear, but soon enough she was dressed again and feeling much better about life.

After picking up her discarded jeans, Jordan went to the front door and walked out onto the porch. The afternoon air was warm and friendly, playing with the damp ends of her long hair, which hadn't completely survived the dunking. She brushed off a spot on the porch floor as best she could, and laid the jeans out flat. There. The sun was still high enough that it touched the damp fabric, and she hoped the jeans would dry out enough so she could pack them away. Maybe she should have tried the clothes dryer, but since she'd spotted a propane tank out back, she guessed that particular appliance wasn't electric.

Instead of going back in the house, she lingered on the porch for a moment, letting her gaze sweep the backyard. Aspen and cottonwood leaves fluttered in the breeze, and the grass, now starting to turn yellow, shimmered in the sunlight, but that was the only movement she saw.

Satisfied, she headed inside, then paused long enough to pick up the Ruger and slip it back in its holster. There. That way she felt a little better about going upstairs to check things out. She hadn't seen too many signs of habitation on the ground floor, except for the mysterious food in the fridge, but you often could tell a lot more about that sort of thing by checking out bedrooms and bathrooms.

At the top of the stairs was a landing that overlooked the combination living room/dining room. Branching off from that landing was a short hallway, with two doors to either side and one at the end of the hall. Jordan chose the door immediately to her left, which appeared to open on the master suite. Her eyes widened as she took in the decor, which wasn't the sort of thing she'd been expecting in a house that, on first appearance, looked like a glorified hunting lodge.

At the center of the master suite was a large canopy bed of dark carved wood, maybe cherry or mahogany. From the canopy hung shimmery, gossamer-thin silks in jewel tones. Sari fabric? Maybe, or something similar. The same kind of fabric framed the windows, and moved slightly in the breeze.

Jordan took in the sight of the open window and frowned. Surely if that window had been open to the wind and the rain and the snow for the past two years, ever since the Dying, then the silk hanging there should have been tattered and stained, worn by exposure to the elements. And yet it looked fresh and brand new. The same with the large Persian rug that covered almost all of the wood floor.

Frowning, Jordan crossed over to the large wardrobe that dominated one wall and opened it. Inside were long robes of heavy silk, most in shades of blue and teal and green, some bordered in gold, some in silver.

Her heart seemed to stop in her chest. She recognized those robes.

Djinn wore those robes.

She had to get out of here.

She whirled away from the wardrobe...only to see a tall man blocking the door to the bedroom. His dark hair hung loose to his shoulders, and his deep blue eyes narrowed as his gaze met hers. He crossed his arms, and the dark turquoise silk robes he wore shimmered with the movement.

"What," he said, voice calm but still edged with menace, "are you doing in my house, human?"

Chapter Two

HASAN AL-ABYAD SUPPOSED THAT SOME MIGHT have enjoyed this day. The sun was high and bright in the sky, the sky as blue as if it had been carved from one enormous sapphire, and the fish were biting as only fish did on days such as this. He didn't need to fish, of course, but it was a pastime he'd always taken pleasure in, quiet and reflective, his own skills pitted against the wiliness of the fish.

And yet....

He did not want to allow the word to take up space in his mind, but despite his best efforts, it made its way to the surface anyway, like bubbles of black tar rising from an otherwise clear pond.

And yet...he was lonely.

Irony of ironies, when he had always prided

himself on his ability to thrive on his own. His liaisons with djinn women were brief, only lasting long enough to satisfy the urges of his body before he went back to his solitary habits. Not once had he ever questioned why none of those women seemed terribly saddened to see him go; he had always thought that they were as he was, glad of the chance to reclaim themselves and their lives once the tryst had ended.

This afternoon, though, he had been thinking of Danya, who had been given the lands near the southern border of what used to be Colorado. A while back, they had shared a few weeks of passion, but they had both moved on, happy to focus their energies on the demesnes that were now theirs, the promise of an earth owned entirely by djinn now come true. No doubt she had already built herself a grand palace of marble and stone, for Danya was an earth elemental, better suited to shaping such things than one such as he, who had command of the air.

For himself, he had taken the biggest and grandest house in the region that he could find, but, other than decorating the largest bedroom to his tastes, he had done nothing to change it. Why bother? The place suited him well enough, and he had no wish to be like the humans his kind had worked so hard to eradicate. He did not see the point in remaking everything in his image, or into something it was not.

Once he had a string of fine trout, he deemed it an afternoon well spent, and headed home. Not in the usual djinn way, of blinking himself from one place to another, but walking along, letting the fine breeze blow in his hair and the warm, heady smell of dry grass fill his nostrils. Soon enough the snows of winter would return, and he would not be able to enjoy the landscape as he did now. True, djinn did not feel cold and heat in the same way that frail humans did, but something about winter made him feel less free, less inclined to explore the territory which was now his. That was one thing to be said for the otherworld, the place where the djinn had been exiled for millennia before finally reclaiming the earth as their own. In that other plane of existence, there was no real weather, no seasons. It was constant, unchanging.

When Hasan reached his property and mounted the front steps to the porch, he came to a halt, gazing down at one of the last things he had ever expected to see there, spread out against the faded paint of the floorboards.

A pair of those unattractive trousers the

mortals called jeans, laid down carefully so they might catch the rays of the afternoon sun.

Where in the world could they have come from? Hasan turned and looked all around, but saw no obvious signs of life, other than a pair of jays scolding one another far off in the distance.

He returned his gaze to the jeans. They did not appear all that large, which meant they probably belonged to a female.

Eyes narrowing, he went to the front door and let himself in. At first glance, nothing appeared to have been disturbed.

But then his gaze moved toward the unfamiliar backpack that sat on the floor next to the couch. The pack was made of some heavy synthetic material in a shade of dark green, and had been left partially unzipped, as though whoever it belonged to had been in a hurry the last time she—or he—had taken something from it.

From upstairs he heard a floorboard creak. He stiffened, while at the same time experiencing a small twinge somewhere at the back of his neck, the kind of twinge that told him a human was nearby.

What temerity! To invade his house, to act as if the notion of personal property meant nothing!

At the back of his mind, he had the thought

that whoever this human was, they probably had no idea anyone even lived here. Hasan had not left very many traces of his presence. This house looked deserted, no doubt. But still....

Anger flared along his nerve endings as he made his way up the stairs. This human would soon pay the price for their lack of respect.

When he reached the doorway to his room, however, he stopped in his tracks, suddenly unsure as to how he should proceed. For standing there, staring into the open doors of his wardrobe, was a young human woman. Her long brown hair hung nearly to her waist, although it had been pulled back and tied into a long ponytail with brown leather cord. Since her back was to him, he couldn't see her face, but he could see that she was slender and not terribly tall, the jeans she wore clinging to her legs and rear end, clearly showing off the shapeliness of her figure.

Then, as if suddenly sensing his presence, she spun around. Wide blue eyes, blue as the summer sky, met his.

Tone quite even, considering the circumstances, he asked, "What are you doing in my home, human?"

Her eyes widened even further, filling with fear. He took in the graceful oval of her face, the straight little nose, the full mouth. That was all he had time for, because he realized that a silvery gun hung from a holster at her hip, and that she was reaching for it.

Foolish girl. Didn't she know that a bullet couldn't stop a djinn?

Apparently she didn't know, or was so desperate that she was willing to try anything. In the next second—far more quickly than he had thought, given the obvious fright in her expression—she pulled the gun out of its holster and pointed it at him.

"Get out of the doorway," she said. Her voice was lower than he'd expected, belying her delicate appearance, almost throaty. Or possibly it was merely rough with weariness. "I don't want to hurt you."

"You needn't worry about that," he returned, "because you can't."

"Yes, I can." Her finger twitched on the trigger, but she didn't pull it back. "Maybe I can't kill you, but I can still hurt you. I've done it before, to other djinn."

Interesting. So she'd encountered others of his kind and lived to tell the tale. Had they also hesitated when confronted by her, unsure whether they should harm a thing of such beauty?

Ridiculous. A human was a human, whether

or not she was beautiful. And yet, although Hasan knew his hands were far from clean when it came to killing mortals, he had never taken the life of a woman. Somehow that was a line he didn't wish to cross, even though he had come close a few times.

"Then you were lucky," he told her. "Because even with a gun, a human cannot prevail against a djinn."

Her hands shook, and Hasan tensed. He knew she was very close to firing the weapon, whether on purpose or because her nervousness would cause the gun to discharge. Perhaps he should see if he could get her to put the weapon back in its holster. Being persuasive was not one of his talents, but he thought he had better try.

"I won't hurt you," he went on. "I simply want you to put the gun down."

Her jaw set. "You think I'm that stupid? A djinn, promising that he won't hurt a human?"

Well, she had a point. Yes, there were some humans who had been spared, but only because they were Chosen, were protected by the djinn who had become their lovers. The rest of the survivors, however, had to be hunted down and eradicated, for the good of the world. "I can see why you would not believe me, but—" He stopped there and decided that the best thing to do would be to blink himself next to her, so he might pluck the gun from her hands before she could do any damage.

The human never gave him the chance. Perhaps he shifted slightly, or his expression changed—Hasan wasn't sure what set her off. But renewed fear flared in her eyes, and in the next second, her finger pulled back on the trigger.

It wasn't the first time someone had shot at him, but never before had it been in such close quarters. The shot rang in his ears. Indeed, the sound of the gun's blast was so intense that a few seconds had passed before he became aware of the sharp pain in his left arm. He looked down and saw blood welling up through the silk of his robe, and staggered backward a pace, away from the door.

That seemed to be the only encouragement the young woman needed, because she immediately bolted through the now open doorway and headed for the stairs. Grimacing, he tore away the sleeve of his robe so he might see the damage she'd inflicted. The bullet had gone through his bicep without hitting the bone, and so he knew he'd heal quickly—probably far more quickly than the human would have liked. Even as he glared down at the wound, the flow of blood started to slow, and the hole began to knit itself closed.

Good. He took the torn-off sleeve of his robe and knotted it around his arm, creating a makeshift bandage. Then he blinked himself down to the ground floor of the house, which he found empty, the front door standing open. The young woman's backpack was gone.

So, too, were her jeans, and Hasan had to allow himself a brief moment of admiration for her resourcefulness, that she would pause to collect such a thing even while running at full speed. And yes, there she was, already halfway across the yard, her long ponytail bouncing against her back as she fled for the safety of the forest.

Not that its cover would provide her any real sanctuary. These were his lands, and he knew them intimately. He could transport himself wherever he needed to go in the blink of an eye.

And so he did, materializing directly in front of her when she was only a few yards away from the edge of the cottonwood thicket. She pulled up sharply, her movement so sudden that she stumbled, clearly thrown off balance by the heavy backpack she carried. Hasan took advantage of her disorientation to close on her and tear the gun from its holster, then fling it far away.

She let out an incoherent cry and attempted to flee toward the weapon so she might reclaim it, but he reached out and tackled her, the two of them falling onto the short-cropped grass, with her caught beneath him even as the backpack slipped off her shoulders and fell to the ground.

He wouldn't let himself think too much about the feel of her body beneath his, the way her breasts rubbed against his bare chest as she struggled in his grip. "Stop it," he growled. "Do you really think you can escape me?"

For a moment she went still, her slender frame taut as a harp string. Then her eyes shut, and her jaw clenched. "Do it, then," she whispered. "Get it over with."

A second or two passed before Hasan realized what she was saying. She expected him to kill her.

He should kill her. She had shot at him, had surely meant to hurt him, even if she'd known that such a puny weapon could never mortally wound a djinn.

But he had yet to kill a woman, and he didn't intend to start now.

"If you wish for death, you will have to find it from someone other than me," he said.

Her eyes opened. They were filled with disbelief. "Isn't that what you djinn do?"

"Some of us," he replied. Ah, there was a prevarication, for of course he had the blood of many on his hands. For some reason, though, he didn't want to tell her the truth. Not yet, anyway. "But now is not your time."

She was silent then, clearly attempting to digest his words. Her hair had come loose from its leather cord, and fanned out around her like a cloak of brown silk. Yes, she was beautiful, even by djinn standards. He wondered why no one had selected her as his Chosen. Surely she was young enough.

Even as he noted her beauty, however, Hasan also realized that her cleanliness left something to be desired. The long hair could use a washing —as could the rest of her, judging by the faint odor of perspiration that clung to her clothing.

"I am going to get up now," he said. "Do not attempt to flee."

Her mouth twisted. "I think you've already proved that running away really isn't an option."

"No, it is not," he agreed, and pushed himself up to a standing position.

A moment later, she rose as well, brushing at the grass that clung to the knees of her jeans. Now they were badly stained, a detail that didn't escape her, because he could see the way she frowned as she took in the damage to her trousers. She shot a wary look at him up through her thick lashes, then asked, "So what now?"

"Now, you come back to the house. And bathe," he added. "You're filthy."

Traces of pink tinged her cheekbones. "Sorry if I offend," she retorted. "Most people aren't exactly at their best after being on the run in the wilderness for days."

He wondered how long she had been running...and what had precipitated her flight in the first place. From the way her mouth had tightened—wounded pride, or fear, or a combination of the two?—he could tell this was not the best occasion to ask. He would wait, then inquire at a more opportune time.

If she had any secrets, she would not keep them from him for long.

Just six inches to the right, Jordan thought bitterly as she followed the djinn back to the house. *Just six inches, and I would have gotten him in the heart. I doubt even a djinn could have bounced back so quickly from that kind of wound.*

As it was, she'd hit him in the arm, and although he'd wrapped some of the silk of his robe around the affected area, he certainly looked none the worse for wear. She supposed she should be glad he hadn't snapped her neck in retaliation. He certainly had the opportunity... and the justification.

In grim silence, she let him lead her back into the house, and then up the stairs to one of the rooms she hadn't explored yet, clearly a secondary bedroom, not as large as the one he'd taken as his own. However, it had its own *en suite* bath, making it more private than the other two bedrooms upstairs, which had to share a bathroom.

"You will use this room," said the djinn.

If she'd found this house on her own, she would have been thrilled to find someplace so comfortable to crash. The bedroom had a queen-sized bed and a spectacular view of the mountains. However, since the djinn obviously expected to use the room as a makeshift prison cell, Jordan found herself less than thrilled by the accommodations.

"I need my backpack," she said. "My spare clothes are in there."

"You have no need of that," he returned, not blinking. "I will provide something."

"But—"

"You will bathe, and you will remain in this

room. Don't bother trying to escape. I will sense you, human, wherever you go on my lands. Do you understand?"

All Jordan could do was offer a sullen nod. Where did he think she would go—out the bathroom window?

Actually, if he hadn't already proven that he was more than capable of catching up to her, she might have considered squeezing herself out the window and somehow making her way down to the ground. But she had a feeling such an attempt would be beyond futile.

"I will be back to check on you," he offered as a final warning, then went out into the upstairs hall and closed the door behind him.

Because she had to prove to herself that she truly was trapped in here, Jordan went to the door and tested the knob. Sure enough, it didn't budge, even though it looked like a typical interior doorknob and therefore didn't even have a lock.

Some kind of djinn trick, apparently. She frowned and went into the bathroom, turned the taps in the shower. At once water shot forth from the showerhead, strong and gloriously warm.

As horrible as the situation was, Jordan couldn't help feeling a rush of anticipation at the thought of a hot shower. She closed the bathroom door and locked it, then quickly climbed out of her dirty clothes and got in the shower enclosure, let the water beat down on her head. Oh, the feeling of having all those weary miles washed away, of getting truly clean for the first time in God knows how long. In Pagosa, they'd used the hot springs to bathe in the summertime, and queued for five-minute showers at the houses that had solar water heaters during the winter, but it had never really felt like enough.

Where was all this water coming from, though? Did the djinn's house have a well? Probably, just as it most likely had a solar water heater to supplement the huge solar panel that provided the electricity here. Whoever had owned this house clearly had been into off-grid living.

They also believed in high-end toiletries, since the shampoo and conditioner that sat on the shelf in the shower enclosure were an expensive brand that Jordan couldn't have afforded back before the Dying had forever changed the landscape of the future. She washed her hair twice, let the conditioner do its magic while she soaped the rest of herself, used the razor to get the scruff off her legs and away from her underarms. By the time she was done, she felt like an actual human being and would have been almost optimistic about the future—if it weren't for the djinn who waited for her downstairs.

Jordan got out of the shower and wrapped one towel around herself and one around her hair. A quick survey of the cupboards didn't turn up a hair dryer, but she did locate some moisturizer and some serum for her hair. It should dry just fine on its own anyway, since it was fairly straight and didn't tend to frizz.

You're trapped here by a djinn and you're worried about your hair frizzing? she asked herself as she hung up the towel she'd used to blot her hair to near-dryness. *I think you need to reexamine your priorities.*

Actually, she knew her priorities were just fine. Right now, she was only trying to distract herself by focusing on trivialities. To have survived this long, to have escaped not one, but two djinn attacks, only to walk right into a house owned by one of those bloodthirsty supernatural beings...well, she could only conclude that the universe had a fine sense of humor.

She kept the other towel wrapped around her as she went out into the bedroom. The djinn had said he would provide clothing, but he could have been lying. He might have told her that just to see if she'd walk out of the bathroom stark naked.

No, that was crazy. Djinn might look like humans—extremely perfect humans—but the ones she'd encountered sure as hell didn't have sex on their minds. Murder, yes.

The bedroom was empty. Or rather, the djinn wasn't there, but the clothes he'd promised her lay on the bed. Jeans identical to the Levi's she wore, only clean and dark and new-looking. A dark green cotton top, a sort of Indian-looking garment with embroidery around the neckline. Black leather flats. It was the sort of ensemble she might have worn to class back at college, or for a casual Friday night. How the hell the djinn had come up with it, she had no idea.

And there was also a stack of women's panties, lace and satin, and several matching bras in various colors. Jordan wondered where the hell the djinn had gotten the lingerie—until she went closer and picked up a pair of pale blue bikini underpants, and saw the Victoria's Secret tag still attached. So, what...had he simply snapped his fingers and summoned these things here from the closest abandoned mall? Wasn't that the sort of thing genies were supposed to do? She didn't know a lot about the djinn, because communications with the Los Alamos group had been cut off before much information was exchanged, but she'd learned enough to know that djinn were basically the same thing as the genies from folklore and fairytales.

Jordan had to admit, however, that the djinn who'd captured her was a lot better-looking than the Mr. Clean type of genie you usually saw in cartoons and illustrations.

Then she wanted to mentally beat herself up for harboring such a thought. What difference did it make whether he looked like a Greek god? He was evil, just like all the other djinn.

Once she was done getting dressed, she slipped into the flats the djinn had provided — which fit perfectly, as did the rest of the clothes; she didn't quite know what to make of that—and then finger-combed her hair one last time. She hadn't worn any makeup except lip balm for the past two years, so it wasn't as though she precisely missed it, although she guessed the outfit would look better with a face that was a bit more polished. Like it mattered. Even back before the Dying, she'd only bothered with anything more than mascara and clear lip gloss when she had to go to work at the bar and grill.

Now what? The djinn had said he would be back to check on her, but when Jordan put her ear to the door and listened as hard as she could, she didn't hear anything. Maybe he'd only said that to put her on edge. She didn't have too much trouble imagining one of the evil elementals engaging in those kinds of mind games.

Fine. The last thing she wanted was for him to appear just as she was attempting to listen at the door, so she stepped away and went over to the window seat, where she sat down and stared out at the view, trying her best not to be scared out of her wits. She hugged her arms to herself, suddenly cold, although the room was warm enough, the sunlight slanting through the windows helping to make it comfortable. If anything, the place felt a bit stuffy. No point in trying to open the window, however. She had a feeling the djinn would be up here in a heartbeat if she tried anything that remotely resembled an escape attempt, and at the moment she was feeling too shaky to attempt anything drastic.

What did he intend to do with her? Surely it would have been easier for him to kill her outright rather than make her his prisoner. But if he wanted her dead, why bother with the shower and the clean clothes? So she could make a better-looking corpse? From what she'd seen of djinn on the attack, they weren't too worried about the damage they caused, as long as all the humans in their immediate vicinity ended up dead.

Those memories only increased the chill in

her body. A harsh shiver went through her, and she wrapped her arms even more tightly around herself, wishing she could somehow do over this afternoon, could go back in time and tell herself to stay far, far away from the big house and its falsely welcoming porch. How could she have been so stupid?

No matter what the djinn had said, Jordan couldn't help thinking that her foolishness would surely cost her life.

Chapter Three

ALL WAS SILENT UPSTAIRS. HASAN KNEW THE GIRL must be there, because he could still sense her presence. He wasn't quite sure what he should do next. Interrogate her, attempt to discover who she was and where she had come from? Possibly.

She had looked hungry, though. Perhaps he should give her something to eat.

As soon as that thought passed through his mind, Hasan wanted to shake his head at himself. Why on earth should he care for her comfort?

Because if you were going to kill her, you should have killed her quickly and cleanly. Starving her is beneath you.

He should check to see what she was doing, though. Yes, he could tell she was still in her room, but as the water in the bathroom had stopped some time earlier, he was somewhat at a loss as to what she might be up to at the moment.

Well, that would be simple enough to discover. He would not knock and wait for her to respond. No, the easiest thing to do was employ his djinn talents for some discreet surveillance.

He blinked himself outside, and then took to the air. To be safe, he wove a faint glamour around himself, just enough to hide his presence, turn himself into only a faint shimmer in the air. Djinn could not make themselves completely invisible, but they were very good at directing the eye elsewhere, at making it seem as though an onlooker's gaze caught only the moving glint of sunlight on the leaves of a tree, or the subtle shadow of a bird flying high overhead.

It was a good thing he had taken the precaution, though, because he saw at once that the young woman was sitting on the window seat. She did not appear to be looking outside, however, even though the view was quite lovely, with the pine-covered mountains in the distance and the warm flame of the aspens closer at hand. No, she had her arms wrapped around herself, as though attempting to ward off a chill. Her lovely head drooped, and he thought he saw the glimmer of tears behind her long lashes.

At the sight of her obvious dejection, he experienced an odd pang somewhere in his midsection. Hasan could not precisely identify what he was feeling, only that he knew he had never experienced it before. For some reason, what he wanted to do then was go inside, reassure her that he had no intention of hurting her.

Take her in his arms and offer her what comfort he could.

No, that was madness. Why on earth would he want to console this wayward human, this trespasser? Had he forgotten that she had put a bullet through his arm not even an hour earlier?

As if to remind him of her belligerence, the wound twinged slightly. It was healing well enough, and would soon be gone, but he could not forget that she had had no compunction about shooting him, even though he had done nothing to antagonize her.

Well, except tackle her to the ground. But even that action had been born purely from the need to stop her before she shot him again. Surely no one could blame him for doing what he must to protect himself.

And yet...she looked so forlorn. What had she gone through, to reach this place alone, with no one to help her, no one to protect her from the djinn he knew must still be patrolling the area?

Not as many as there had been, true. So few humans were left now, and most djinn had retired to the lands they'd been given so they might start their new lives here on earth. Even so, some of the most dedicated still kept watch...just in case.

He wanted to know how she had managed it. He realized then that he didn't even know her name.

A blink took him back inside so he stood outside the door to her room. He knocked once and waited.

After a long pause, he could hear her fumbling with the doorknob. He realized then that the charm he'd laid on it to prevent her from opening the door was still active. A wave of his hand, and the charm was removed.

The door opened inward. The girl stood there, a startled expression on her delicate features. No doubt she'd tried to open it before and had been thwarted, so Hasan thought he could excuse her surprise now.

She looked much improved. Although her hair was still damp, it already appeared much shinier, and the road grime was gone from her face. The clothing he had given her wasn't terribly revealing, but he could still see the curve of hip and thigh in the trousers she wore.

Her eyes were so very blue. Like mountain lakes reflecting the sky.

Hasan had to clear his throat. "Are you hungry?" he asked.

Those eyes widened slightly. "Am I what?"

"Are you hungry?" he repeated. He would have liked to call her a simpleton for not understanding what he had asked, but he knew she probably did understand. She simply couldn't figure out why her captor would be concerned about such a thing.

"I—I suppose I am," she allowed.

"Then I will bring you something."

He closed the door on her startled eyes and found some relief in doing so. This was the most interaction he'd ever had with a human, and he was annoyed with himself for how he had reacted to her. What did it matter that she was lovely, or had looked so very sad when left to herself? Her people had almost destroyed this world. She did not deserve any pity from him.

The trout he had caught earlier were stored in the refrigerator. Although some of his kind enjoyed preparing food from scratch, Hasan did not count himself among them. It was so much easier to visualize the meal he wanted, and to have it appear. Yes, if he had the raw ingredients at hand, then the process did not require quite as much of his power, but he never let that restraint stop him. He used the fish because they needed to be eaten, but the rice and the vegetables to accompany them came from much farther away, as did the small loaf of bread and a pat of butter.

When he sat down to consume his own version of this same meal, he would have wine, but he saw no reason to extend that kind of largesse to his prisoner. A glass of water would do well enough; he assumed she must be thirsty as well, though she could have already gotten herself some water from the tap.

Although it might have been simpler to blink the tray of food into her room and have done with it, Hasan found himself loath to do so. He didn't quite want to admit that he wished to gaze upon her again, but....

Instead, he took her meal with him and ascended the stairs once again. Holding the tray with one hand, he lifted the other to knock at the door. This time, there wasn't nearly as long a wait for her to open it.

Again, a startled look passed over her face as she took in the food he carried. He hoped she had never attempted to earn her living by playing cards, because she would have been woefully hampered by the obvious expressions displayed on her features.

"Here is your dinner," Hasan said.

She took the tray from him, being careful not to touch his fingers. "Um...thank you."

Perhaps he should have told her she was welcome and left it at that, but it seemed foolish for him to hold her here and not even know her name. "What are you called?" he asked.

An obvious hesitation. Then she replied, "Jordan."

She didn't offer anything more than the single word, and his mouth compressed slightly. "Surely there is more to your name than that."

Her fingers tightened on the dinner tray. They were pretty enough, slender and graceful, even with the nails kept severely short. An angry red line cut across the back of one hand, as though she'd wounded herself at some point in the recent past. Well, if she truly had been running through the wilderness for the past few days, he could see why she might have had ample opportunities for minor scrapes and cuts and bruises. Her lips pressed together, and then she let out a small breath and said, "Jordan Marie Wells."

He wasn't sure the name suited her. It sounded too brisk, too matter-of-fact. But then, humans weren't always known for their mastery of aesthetics. "Well, then, Jordan...enjoy your dinner."

Her mouth opened, as though she intended to inquire as to his name. Hasan supposed he would give it to her at some point, but he did not want to delay her any longer, for her food would get cold.

At least, that was the excuse he provided for himself.

Before she could speak, he shut the door and set the charm upon the knob once again. He could not trust her not to attempt to escape, despite his warnings. And really, she now had everything she might need—food and water, a bed to sleep in, a private bath for her own use. No doubt his fellow djinn would say he was being far too lenient with her.

He did not want to analyze his precise reasons for that particular indulgence.

———

Jordan stared at the door with some mystification, then lifted her shoulders and went over to the bed so she could set the tray down on the nightstand. There really wasn't anyplace else to put it, except the dresser. At least here she could sit on the bed while she ate.

The food smelled good, even though she'd probably be happy if she never ate trout again, considering how much of that particular fish the group in Pagosa Springs consumed. However, there was fish...and there was fish. This one looked as if it had been pan-fried in a coating of pistachio. Very gourmet. And there was rice pilaf and green beans elegantly garnished with slivered almonds.

Where the djinn had gotten it all from, she had no idea. He certainly wouldn't have had the time to whip up this meal during the short period he'd been downstairs. Then again, he was a djinn, a supernatural creature. Maybe all he had to do was snap his fingers and make whatever food he wanted appear.

Despite the delectable smells rising to her nose, Jordan couldn't help hesitating. What if he'd drugged the food, or poisoned it? After all, she had no real idea as to what he might be capable of. No, that was ridiculous. If he'd wanted to kill her, he could have done so when he tackled her as she was trying to escape. All he would have had to do was put his hands on her throat and squeeze. But he hadn't. For whatever reason, he didn't seem inclined to murder her.

At least not yet.

Resolutely, she reached for the fork and

picked it up, then scooped some rice onto it. A cautious mouthful.

Oh, that was good. Buttery and rich, better than anything she'd eaten in a long while. Although the desire to start shoveling in food was almost overwhelming, Jordan made herself wait for a moment to see if she suffered any adverse effects. Nothing, as far as she could tell. No strange twinges or stomach aches or sudden onset of nausea. About the only thing that happened was a very loud stomach growl, which she could understand. One small bite of rice wasn't enough to sate the hunger that had been gnawing at her all day.

Another forkful, and then another. Some fish, then the green beans. She put down the fork and broke off a piece of bread, and smeared some butter on it. God, that was good, too. They'd made some bread at Pagosa Springs, but the supplies to make it had run out months ago. Jordan had forgotten how good those sinful bread-y carbs could taste.

She ate everything on the plate, and drank down the glass of water that had come with it. Too bad there wasn't more, but she knew if she overstuffed herself after being on lean rations for so long, she really would get a stomach ache. The food the djinn had provided was enough.

The djinn. Why the hell hadn't he given her his name? Had he determined that she was beneath him, and so didn't deserve even that minor courtesy?

Who knew? Jordan knew she'd drive herself crazy if she sat here and tried to ascribe human motivations to someone who wasn't human at all. She needed to remind herself of that fact, because for some reason her mind kept wanting to dwell on the unearthly perfection of his features, the deep lapis blue of his eyes. She'd never gotten close enough to any of the other djinn to notice whether they were as handsome as the one who currently held her captive.

Handsome? She wanted to scold herself. What the hell difference did his looks make? He was a murderer. Or at least, she assumed he must be.

Frowning, she got up from the bed, then took the tray and set it down on the floor next to the door. That seemed to be the most she could do, since she knew if she tried to turn the knob, she'd only be thwarted, just as she had earlier. When a djinn wanted a door to stay shut, apparently, it stayed shut.

By that point, the sun had dipped far enough to the west that the room was growing dim. Jordan went to the lamp on the nightstand and turned the switch, more out of instinct than because she thought anything would actually happen. To her surprise, the light did come on, providing a warm, friendly glow that did a good deal to chase away the shadows in the corners of the bedroom.

Well, she'd heard the refrigerator downstairs humming away, so she supposed she shouldn't be so startled to see that there was electricity throughout the house. She hadn't bothered to turn on the overhead lights when she was taking a shower, since the bathroom had a large window. Covered by curtains, true, but they were pale and filmy, serving as a privacy barrier and not much else.

It felt odd to have electric light again, though, almost as if the Dying had never happened, and she was back in her old life, getting ready to go to work or out for the evening. Then again, if this were really her old life, she wouldn't be locked in here, wouldn't have an enigmatic djinn just downstairs, making sure she didn't get away.

Although she'd just eaten and the hour was still very early, probably not much later than six-thirty, Jordan wondered if she should just go to sleep. What else did she have to do with herself? The room didn't have a single book or magazine in it; in fact, it was so devoid of personality that she wondered whether it had been a guest bedroom back when it was owned by a human being. No TV, no internet. Of course, she hadn't had those electronic distractions to amuse her for more than two years now. But at least in Pagosa Springs there had been other people, and books in the library and in the empty homes there.

Not quite sighing, she went into the bathroom and brushed her teeth, then washed her face and put on some of the moisturizer she'd found in the drawer. All very civilized, again like something she would have done back in the days before the world changed.

Nothing to sleep in except a couple of satin nightgowns. Jordan had never been big on lingerie, and she was even less thrilled to put on one of those bare gowns now, when she was completely at the mercy of the djinn downstairs. Of course, he hadn't shown any particular interest in her...at least, not that kind of interest. She supposed she should be grateful for that. Then again, why would he? Humans and djinn might resemble one another on the surface, but they were two completely different species.

Shivering a little, the skin of her shoulders bared by the spaghetti straps of the nightgown she wore, Jordan hurried over to the bed and slid under the covers. She had to expose one arm to reach out and turn off the bedside lamp, but as soon as she could, she shoved that arm back under the sheet and blanket and quilt, then pulled all three layers up to her chin.

The house was dead quiet, with not even a ticking clock in the background to break the silence. What was the djinn doing? Eating his own dinner? If that was what currently occupied him, he was being very discreet about it. She wondered what he did to keep himself busy. He hadn't been home when she first entered the house, which meant he must have been off somewhere far enough away that he hadn't even seen her approach the property...or sensed her presence. He must have realized she was there when he returned, then come upstairs to confront her. Anyway, djinn seemed able to tell when humans were around, but that ability wasn't infallible, or all-seeing. They couldn't sense you from hundreds of miles away.

Thank God. Otherwise, they would have been able to wipe out humanity's few survivors much more easily.

Jordan rolled over onto her side, still clutching the covers up to her chin. No way was she going to fall asleep here, tense as she was. The house creaked slightly and she jumped, worried that the sound signaled the djinn's return. Stupid, really, since if he wanted to, he could simply materialize inside the room with her. He wouldn't have to walk up the stairs or come through the door.

All right, that wasn't at all reassuring.

She made herself breathe in through her nose and out through her mouth, the way her friend Ella back in Colorado Springs had told her to do when she needed to relax. It didn't seem to be helping much at the moment.

Maybe she should try counting sheep.

Maybe you should count all the mistakes you made since you got up this morning, she thought in some annoyance. Clearly, going to bed this early had been yet another mistake. She hated to admit defeat and get out from under the covers, though. It was warm and comfortable here; the bed had a very good mattress.

And maybe....

Sleep came along, and claimed her for its own.

Jordan would have said she was too tired to dream, and yet she did find herself falling into dreamland, bits and pieces that didn't make sense —standing in the kitchen of one of the resorts in Pagosa Springs and watching her friend Suzanne make pancakes. No one had consumed a single pancake the whole time Jordan had lived there, but dreams didn't care about such things. Maybe her subconscious was telling her that she really wanted pancakes, though. If she asked nicely, would the djinn make some for her?

Crazy. She should count herself lucky that he'd fed her at all.

The dream shifted into darkness for a while, as dreams often did. When Jordan swam up out of it, she was conscious first of only an overwhelming sense of well-being, of warmth and safety. Someone's arms were around her, and her head was cradled against his shoulder. She couldn't see his face, but his embrace was strong and yet gentle at the same time, soothing. A tender hand moved over her hair.

She let out a small sigh and shifted her position, burrowing closer to the person who held her. This had to be Liam, her boyfriend from college. True, Liam had been pretty skinny, bones sticking out whenever he held her close, whereas this person felt solid and firmly padded with muscle, but who else could it be?

A lock of dark hair brushed against her forehead as he bent down to kiss her on the cheek. At last she opened her eyes, looked up to accept the caress.

A dark blue gaze met hers.

Dark blue.

The djinn's eyes.

In her sleep, she sucked in a gasp of air. No, wait, she had done that in real life, because now she was shoving against the pillows where she lay, pushing herself up to a sitting position. Her heart pounded in her chest, and she clutched at the blanket that covered her, willing away the remnants of that terrible dream.

What the ever-loving hell?

She tried to tell herself it was only a dream. It wasn't as if she could control such things.

But why would her subconscious have even conjured that kind of dream? The djinn wasn't gentle, or kind. He'd tackled her to the ground, had locked her up in this room. He wasn't a friend, or a lover.

He was the enemy.

Damn it. Right then she wished she'd left a cup of water on the nightstand, because her mouth was dry and she could really use something to drink. But that would mean getting out from under the protection of these covers. She couldn't risk that, which she knew was silly. Those covers wouldn't protect her if the djinn showed up right now.

Breathe, she told herself. *Breathe, and go back to sleep.*

She didn't want to sleep. Who knew what other horrors lurked, waiting to emerge the next time she fell asleep?

Unfortunately, the only other alternative appeared to be getting out of bed and fetching some water, and she didn't want to do that, either.

Damn it again.

All right, she'd sleep. And she sure as hell wouldn't dream of *him.* She wouldn't allow it.

Now she just had to figure out how in the world she could face him the next morning.

Chapter Four

HASAN MADE HIMSELF IGNORE THE CLOSED DOOR across the hallway when he went to bed that night. And when he got up in the morning, he went about his preparations as he always did—a leisurely bath, followed by the selection of his garments for the day. As best he could, he tried to put from his mind the image of Jordan huddled in the window seat, trying to hold back her tears. The troubles of a single human should not concern him in the least.

All the same, he would have to decide what to do with her. Should he let her out, or bring her another tray of food?

Best to let her out, at least on a trial basis. If she proved to be troublesome, he could always confine her to her room again. Of course, that begged the question of his plans for the female on a long-term basis, but he thought he should start with the morning ahead and see what happened.

An offering of coffee seemed to be the best approach, for humans appeared to love the caffeinated drink as much as djinn did. After summoning a pot of the stuff, which he left on the dining room table downstairs, he went up to her room, then paused at her door and knocked. He'd heard water running earlier, so he guessed that he was in no danger of waking her.

Sure enough, the door opened a moment later. Jordan stood there, fully dressed, her long silky brown hair neatly brushed. There seemed to be something subdued about her, however, for she did not appear at all eager to look up at him.

"What is it?" she asked.

Her tone bordered on abrupt, but he decided to overlook that for the moment. "I have coffee," he said. "I thought you might like to come downstairs and have some."

"You're letting me out of my room?"

"For now, yes."

She appeared to weigh that reply for a moment, then shrugged. "All right."

Not the most gracious of replies. Perhaps she was one of those humans who did not fare particularly well in the morning. She certainly appeared rested enough; the shadows were gone from beneath her eyes, and her skin and lips looked rosier than they had when he'd first encountered her.

Hasan decided it would be best to maintain his silence as he led her downstairs and into the dining room. Her expression did brighten somewhat as she spotted the pot of coffee and the two mugs on the table, which seemed to lend credence to his theory that she was not a morning person and needed the stimulant drink to wake her up all the way.

He poured coffee for the two of them, then asked, "Do you require milk or sugar?"

"No, thank you. I drink it black."

As did he. Before he could reach down to hand one of the mugs to her, she'd grasped one by the handle and lifted it from the tabletop. Was she really that eager to get her morning dose, or did she simply not want to have him serve her?

A flicker of annoyance went through him. She would have to learn that he was the master here. It would be simple enough to send her back to her room if she overstepped her bounds. In the meantime, however, he wanted to learn what he could from her, and it seemed better if he at least appeared to be friendly.

After taking a sip of his coffee, he told her, "I am Hasan al-Abyad."

This revelation didn't seem to impress her overmuch. She watched him steadily, mug of coffee clutched in one small fist. "Should we shake hands or something?"

"I would consider ourselves already introduced."

Looking at her, Hasan could tell she was tense, wound up tight as a watch spring. He supposed he couldn't blame her for that, just as he guessed that the false bravado was her way of coping with the situation. It couldn't be easy, to be faced with the demon you'd been fleeing for the past several years, to be held captive by someone who had no reason to keep you alive.

Then he told himself he should not be so sympathetic. She'd outright told him that she'd shot more than one djinn, so her hands weren't precisely clean, either.

"What were you doing in Chama?"

A lift of her shoulders. She blew on her coffee, took a cautious sip of the hot liquid. "Passing through."

"On your way to where?" He already had an idea, but he wanted to see if she would admit to that destination on her own.

"South. I decided Colorado was too cold."

Ah. He should have expected as much. It was on the tip of his tongue to ask her if she was headed to Los Alamos, but he didn't want to give too much away. He preferred to see how much information she would provide on her own.

"I don't think that's the true reason," he said easily. Her fingers tightened on the coffee mug, but other than that, she didn't move. "Yesterday, you made it sound as though you've faced down djinn before. Is that what happened?"

For a long moment, Jordan didn't answer. Her gaze moved past him, to the window on the other side of the room. Bright morning sunlight flooded into the room, revealing faint scratches in the polished oak floor, sending dust motes dancing in the still air.

"Yes," she said at last, speaking so softly that he had to strain to hear her. "We were in Pagosa Springs for about a year and a half. We thought it was safe. But...it wasn't."

"The djinn found you there."

"Yes." Jordan appeared to want to look at anything in the room except him. "I ran. I escaped. I don't think anyone else did."

Hasan frowned. He couldn't claim to know the geography of the region all that well, but he thought that this Pagosa Springs was located in the region which had been given to Danya. Had she been involved in this raid? He found that difficult to believe—not because he thought that the djinn woman he knew would scruple at shedding human blood, given the opportunity, but simply because hers was a nature that enjoyed the material pleasures of the world, required luxury and comfort. Chasing down the last few stragglers on her land didn't seem like something she would bother to do.

Asking other djinn to do her dirty work for her, however...well, Hasan could definitely believe that of his former lover.

"Were there any female djinn among them?"

"No." The answer was immediate, and definite. "There were five, I think. Plenty of djinn to kill off a dozen humans. Overkill, really."

Jordan's tone was hard, but he could sense the brittle edge to it, knew she had adopted that tone to try to hide the pain beneath. It was, after all, a very transparent subterfuge. Her gaze was steady enough, although Hasan thought he detected the glitter of tears in her eyes.

Weakness, this propensity toward tears. He knew none of those people could have been kin to her, because immunity from the Heat was not genetic. It had been planned that way, so entire families would not be able to survive and lend one another strength. Humans were notorious for their lack of cooperation, their infighting. Possibly one of the things that rankled him so much about the Los Alamos stronghold wasn't simply that they'd managed to survive, thanks to those wretched djinn-repelling devices one of their scientists had created, but also that the people living there had, by all accounts, created a thriving community from the ruins of their civilization. Yes, they had some help from the human-loving djinn in Santa Fe and their Chosen, but still....

He realized that Jordan was now staring at him, her gaze bright and direct. Perhaps the coffee was beginning to take effect. "What is it?"

"Nothing," she replied. "That is, I suppose I'm just trying to get past how human you seem."

Human? Was she trying to insult him on purpose? He drew himself up and said, "I am far from human."

"Oh, I know. I mean, you're kind of too perfect to be a human. It's just that I didn't have the opportunity before now to really look at one of you up close. I was trying too hard not to die the last few times I've had a run-in with a djinn."

The "perfect" comment mollified him somewhat—but not enough. "I doubt a human could do this," he said, pushing up the loose sleeve of his robe to reveal his left bicep, where she had shot him. After having an entire night to heal, the flesh had knitted itself together. There was no remaining trace of her attack on him.

Jordan's eyes widened slightly. "That's...impressive."

"And the reason why such attacks will never succeed." He drank some of his coffee, then asked, "Where were you before Pagosa Springs?"

"Colorado Springs. It's my hometown." Her full mouth went tight again, as though she was trying to repress an unpleasant memory. "I was living there after college. Then the Dying happened." Her gaze shifted away from him as she added, "You djinn happened."

He wanted to tell her that it was humanity's fault. Perhaps the djinn would never have intervened if it weren't that the world they'd desired for so long had been teetering on the brink, so very close to the point of no return. Something about the pain in her lovely features stopped him, however. Ignoring her last comment, he said, "But you were driven from Colorado Springs."

"Yes. About two months after the Dying. It was around the beginning of December. A real great time of year to be slogging across Colorado."

The brittle tone was back. Well, if it helped

her to manage her emotions, then he would ignore it. Part of him marveled that the two of them were sitting here at all, having a fairly reasonable discussion. Then again, he hadn't given her many options. It wasn't as though she could simply get up from the couch and walk out of the house.

At any rate, what she'd just said was true enough. Winter could come early here in the high country. He wondered who he had angered to be given this spot, rather than a homestead somewhere in the tropics, or even along one of this world's many beaches. Yes, the area around Chama was beautiful—he could have been inflicted with an ugly cityscape such as Albuquerque, the way Qadim al-Syan had—but the environment here was also harsh, demanding much of its residents.

"Would you like some breakfast?" he asked her. He couldn't help wondering whether her slenderness had something to do with short rations. She seemed healthy enough, but there was a tautness to her throat and jaw line that spoke of too many days of privation, even after a good meal and a night's sleep in a real bed. Perhaps a few more decent meals would make her look less strained.

"I—" For a second, it seemed to him that she

might demur, might act as though she didn't require any more food from him, but then she seemed to shrug and said, "Breakfast sounds good."

Hasan wasn't sure why he should be so pleased that she had answered him with the truth, but, paradoxically, he was. "Then let us sit down, and we can continue with our conversation."

"Don't you need to get anything from the kitchen?" she inquired, a look of confusion passing over her face.

"Oh, no," he assured her. "Djinn have no need of kitchens."

It wasn't exactly like *I Dream of Jeannie,* but it was close. All Hasan had to do was snap his fingers, and there on the oak table in the dining area appeared, not the pancakes of her first dream, but a plate of fruit, and another stacked high with bacon, and bread so fresh Jordan thought she could see steam rising from the basket where it rested. She'd sworn off bacon back in the day, but the aroma was so tantalizing that she knew she wouldn't be able to resist it now. Her dinner of fish and rice and vegetables now seemed very long ago.

So all she did was utter a polite thank-you as Hasan deposited some food on her plate, then waited while he did the same for himself. The whole time, she had to do her best not to stare at him. Hard enough when she was sitting here next to a djinn—well, at his left hand anyway, since he sat at the head of the table and so they weren't right next to each other—and trying to pretend as though every instinct in her brain and body weren't telling her to bolt.

Did he harbor any ill will about the way she'd shot him? It didn't appear so. Then again, she'd be the first to admit that she didn't know much about djinn and their capacity for playacting. On the other hand, the wound had basically healed so you couldn't even see where the entry point had been. She'd done more damage to his robes, actually; she noticed that the ones he wore this morning were a dark sapphire, with a wide border of silver. He sat there and ate, seeming to ignore the way the sleeve on his one arm remained pushed up. Possibly that was intentional. Those hanging sleeves could definitely get in the way while you were eating. Jordan did her best to look away as well, but it was difficult. She kept wanting to stare at the place where she'd shot him, to see if she could find any physical evidence of the injury she'd caused.

Or maybe she was just trying to avoid staring at the arm itself, with its smooth brown skin and the impressive amount of muscle that flexed and unflexed as he lifted his mug of coffee, or picked up his knife to spread some butter on a slice of bread. All right, she'd seen guys with those sorts of muscles when she was still at college, but she had to admit there hadn't been any particularly impressive specimens among the survivors at Pagosa Springs.

That was an uncharitable thought. They'd all been doing what they had to in order to survive. Several of the town's resorts had exercise rooms, but no one seemed too interested in using them. It seemed an indulgence when they had to work so hard just to find enough to eat, to wander all over town to find the houses with solar water heaters, or with propane tanks that hadn't yet been depleted so they could cook a hot meal. At first they'd tried to stick together at one of the hotels, since some had argued it was safer that way, but it hadn't taken long before everyone had begun to drift off to their own places. Not too far —there were sufficient available houses in one neighborhood that they all ended up living fairly close to one another—just enough to retain some semblance of privacy. Jordan wondered if her choice of a house at the edge of the occupied zone was what had saved her. It was easier to run when you weren't in the thick of things.

She realized Hasan was watching her, and she quickly reached for her own coffee to cover up her distraction. Both the coffee and the food were crazy good, better than she would have had in a restaurant, just like what she'd been given the night before. How the djinn had accomplished all this food prep with only a snap of his fingers, Jordan wasn't sure. Magic, she supposed.

Did she dare challenge him for staring at her? Maybe he hadn't spent much time around humans. Probably not, except to hunt them down and kill them.

At least he hadn't been one of the djinn who'd committed the massacre at Pagosa Springs. She was sure of that. Those five had been big and brawny, built like bouncers. Hasan was well muscled, but he didn't look like someone who knocked down brick walls in his spare time. Jordan knew he was strong, though; the hot water of the shower had kneaded away some of the soreness, and the excellent mattress had helped as well, and yet her muscles still ached from the way he'd tackled her the day before. This morning while getting dressed, she'd found a whole new complement of bruises to add to the ones she'd accumulated on her journey down here.

"How is your food?" he asked.

So polite, as though he'd asked her to have breakfast here in his isolated hunting lodge, rather than making her a prisoner in everything but name. However, since she wanted to go on breathing, she knew now was not the time to make snarky comments. "It's excellent," she replied. "Better than anything I've had in a long time."

"You had no cooks among you in Pagosa Springs?"

"Not really. We had to scrounge everything we couldn't hunt, or get from the river." The hunting hadn't been so great, either. Jordan would have thought if you gathered together a dozen or so people who'd spent most of their lives in Colorado, you'd have at least one or two who knew how to kill and dress a deer. Not so much. The first attempts had been bloody messes, to put it mildly. Over time, they'd gotten better, but theirs wasn't exactly what you could call a well-oiled survivalists' encampment.

And they couldn't take the risk of cultivating food, fearing that even small cleared areas might attract the djinns' attention. Jordan's botany classes had helped in that at least she knew which plants that grew in the area were edible and which were not, but it wasn't the same thing as growing fields of squash and beans and corn. By the end of each summer, even she had been sick of dandelion greens.

Hasan nodded. In the bright sunlight, she could clearly see the deep blue glint of his eyes, almost the same sapphire color as the robes he wore. Such a contrast to his warm-toned skin, and the black hair that fell back from his brow and hung to his shoulders. If she hadn't known better, she would have said he must be part Native American, with those high cheekbones and that long, sculpted nose. But he wasn't.

He wasn't human at all.

She shivered, and set down her coffee mug so she could pick up another slice of bacon. It was warm enough inside the house, but the food would get cold if she didn't eat it in a timely manner. And as weird as it was to be sitting here with a djinn, Jordan knew she had to eat the good food, keep up her strength. Hasan had warned her about trying to escape, but that didn't mean she wouldn't make the attempt if the opportunity presented itself.

"Do you know why it happened?" he asked then, and she blinked at him. Handsome features almost expressionless, he added, "That is, why you would be set upon now, when your group had lived in that one location for so many months."

It was a question that had plagued her ever since she grabbed her bug-out bag and headed south, knowing she couldn't help the people who'd become her friends over the past eighteen months, that the only thing she could do was get away as quickly as possible, and pray the djinn were too preoccupied to notice her fleeing into the cover of the trees. Why Hasan was asking her about it, she didn't know. Stockpiling ideas in case he wanted to go on his own human-killing spree? She doubted he'd find many victims to help him fulfill such a plan; she hadn't seen a single person—except the djinn himself—since she'd left Pagosa Springs.

"I'm not sure," she said slowly. Should she lie, or attempt to be truthful? It was so hard to know what to do when you were dealing with a being of unknown powers and abilities. Could a djinn detect a lie? Probably better to tell the truth, just in case. She'd only seen the smallest hints of his anger and didn't want to know what he would be like if she truly upset him. "A few days earlier, some of the guys in our group had ranged farther west than they usually did when on their hunting trips. I suppose they might have gotten out of our 'safe zone' and stumbled into a spot where a djinn might see them. I just don't know. Everything was fine...and then it wasn't."

She hadn't been looking for sympathy in Hasan's face, which was a good thing, because she sure as hell didn't detect any. His head tilted slightly to one side, as if he was considering a simple logic puzzle and nothing more. "Perhaps," he said. "It depends on how far west they traveled. But they might have stumbled into Danya's territory."

"Danya?"

"A djinn woman. She was given the lands in the southwestern part of Colorado. I can imagine that she might not have been pleased to have humans entering her demesne."

Did Jordan dare ask exactly who had "given" this Danya her new stomping grounds? Clearly, the djinn had settled themselves around the area —and around the entire globe, for all Jordan knew—but who was calling the shots?

Probably better not to risk it. At the moment, Hasan's expression was mild enough, but she had a feeling he wouldn't be very happy if she started asking too many questions. Maybe later.

No, there wouldn't be a "later." She had to get out of here, head toward Los Alamos. And if that promised refuge turned out to be a mirage, no more a haven than Pagosa Springs had been, well...she'd deal with that when the time came. Anything had to be better than being trapped in a house with a djinn out in the middle of nowhere. "So Danya had her brute squad come after us?"

Hasan shrugged, then reached for the carafe so he could pour himself more coffee. "We do not have servants here, as you can see. No need, when we can do everything we require for ourselves. So it is not as much that Danya would have a household guard to protect her and her lands, but that she might have called in a favor from some friends."

"I guess she didn't want to get her hands dirty, huh?"

"No, Danya is not the sort to exert much effort, not when she can have others do it for her."

Something about that reply made Jordan sit up a little straighter in her chair. "You know her?"

"We are acquainted, yes. The djinn community is not so large that most of us don't have at least a passing acquaintance with one another."

His reply was innocuous enough, but something about the way he looked away from her, was almost too casual in how he lifted his mug of coffee, made Jordan think that Hasan and this Danya had a closer relationship than mere acquaintances. Not that she would have cared one way or another—which djinn was sleeping with which djinn didn't matter to her at all—except if Hasan and Danya were close, maybe he'd think Jordan was a bit of unfinished business that his lover would like taken care of.

Her heart gave a nervous thump, and she also reached for her coffee, taking a larger swallow than she'd intended. The hot liquid caught at the back of her throat and made her cough.

Hasan sent her a curious glance. "Are you all right?"

"I'm fine," she replied. "Just swallowed wrong."

"Ah." He drank again, then put down his mug. Something seemed to occur to him, and he shifted in his seat so he could look at her more directly. "I will not tell her, if that is what worries you."

"Tell who what?" Jordan asked innocently.

"I will not tell Danya that you are here. We have not spoken in some time."

"Oh. I—I really hadn't thought about that."

His blue eyes glinted at her. "Perhaps. I just wanted you to know that I will not speak to

Danya, whether or not she was the one who insti-
gated the attack on your camp."

"Well, um...thank you."

They lapsed into an awkward silence after
that as Jordan looked down at her plate and did
her best to finish off the fruit and bread that
remained. Yes, she was very glad she'd somehow
survived this so far, but she couldn't quite figure
out what Hasan's game might be. Was he simply
curious about her? Or did he have some nefar-
ious plan up his sleeve?

As soon as she had finished, he said, "You
are done?"

She nodded.

"Good. Then you will go back to you room. I
have business to manage."

What that business might be, Jordan had no
idea. As much as she dreaded the thought of
being locked up in that room again, the last thing
she wanted was to antagonize him. And besides
—if this "business" required him to leave the
house, then maybe she would have a chance to
escape. It was a long drop from her room to the
ground, but she'd risk it.

She pushed her plate away and stood, and
Hasan rose from his chair as well. Clearly, he
intended to go with her upstairs, although she
knew there was no way she'd be able to give him

the slip while he was anywhere nearby. The whole time she was walking up the stairs, she was uncomfortably aware of his presence behind her—the soft, heavy tread of his footsteps, the rustle of the silken robes he wore, even what seemed to be a faint drift of cologne or incense or something sweet-smelling that hung on the air like the ghost of a scent. Against her will, she recalled her dream from the night before, of his arms around her, the warmth of his body next to hers.

No. She needed to tell her brain to leave that memory viciously alone. It didn't mean a thing. The man following her up the stairs wasn't a man at all, but an elemental, fey and dangerous. She could never let herself forget that.

As soon as he opened the door, she practically fled inside. Hasan didn't speak, and she was grateful for that. She had no idea what on earth she could say to him.

Even though it was still unfamiliar to her, the room she'd been given now felt like a sanctuary. She closed the door and briefly contemplated tucking the ladder-back chair that stood off to one side of the room under the doorknob, then realized that flimsy piece of furniture certainly couldn't hold back a djinn.

Instead, she went to the window and pushed

the curtains open, letting in a flood of sunlight. There. That was better. It was a lot harder to be afraid with a cheerful sun beaming in, sending its warm glow over the oak floor and the rustic pine furniture and the diamond-pattern quilt on the bed. When she went to the window seat and looked outside, all seemed calm enough, with only a light breeze whispering in the tops of the aspens and the cottonwoods, and rustling in the dry grass.

Of course it was calm out there. Who would come to disturb the peace on Hasan's homestead? This was his land, and although Jordan still didn't know how all this worked, it sounded as though the djinn were fairly territorial and tended to keep away from one another.

She didn't think anyone would be coming after her...unless Hasan had a change of heart and reported her presence here to this Danya person, the one whose land had been inadvertently trespassed upon. For some reason, though, Jordan thought he would keep his word.

Still....

With a lift of the shoulders, she climbed onto the bed, then hugged her knees up to herself. He had left her alone...for now. She knew she should be inspecting the window, trying to see if there was some way to pry it open, although she had a feeling it was as locked down as the door.

What did Hasan want from her?

And would she ever be able to get away from here without his consent?

Chapter Five

HIS TALE OF "BUSINESS" HAD BEEN A LIE, OF course. Hasan had nothing to occupy himself. If she were not here, he would have gone out hunting, or fishing, or perhaps even finally embarked on his project to redo the house, starting with the grounds, but he did not quite dare to leave her alone here, even though he knew she had no way of escaping the room he'd provided for her. The charms would hold on the door and the windows until he released them. Still....

He did go out to the porch to survey the yard and the woods surrounding the house. All was serene, as he had expected it to be. Perhaps at the back of his mind he had feared that whoever had destroyed the settlement at Pagosa Springs might have tracked Jordan here, but that didn't seem to be the case. Whatever her other human faults, she did seem to be quite good at eluding pursuit. How many mortals had the determination, talent, and luck to evade a djinn not once, but twice over?

As he stood there, letting the fresh morning breeze tug at his loose hair, Hasan wondered if he had done the right thing by banishing her to her room. Loath as he was to admit such a thing to himself, he realized he enjoyed speaking with her. A weakness, he thought. It was only that he had spent so many days alone, even the company of a human felt better than no one at all. She was uneasy around him, though. Most likely, she could not stop wondering what in the world he was up to, why he hadn't dispatched her when it would have been his right.

Good question. He still wasn't quite sure, either, except that his own limited scruples wouldn't allow him to kill a woman, even if she also happened to be a human who'd tried to put a bullet in his heart.

The day passed slowly. He wrestled with whether he should let Jordan out to share luncheon with him, but decided against it. Better to be somewhat unpredictable, so she wouldn't know what to expect. Instead, he summoned a meal of soup and bread, and sent it straight to her room. All was silent within, so he had no idea how the food was received. However, when he blinked the tray back into the kitchen, the bowl of soup was empty, as was the plate that had held a roll and butter.

And when dinnertime rolled around, he felt even more compelled to have her come down to share the meal with him...a compulsion he made himself ignore. She was a human, and his prisoner. He needed to resist this ridiculous desire for her company. At the back of his mind, he acknowledged the truth that he must decide at some point what he was to do with her, that he could not keep her a captive forever, but he also didn't want to choose between two equally unappealing options. Either he could send her on her way, and wash his hands of her forever, or he could let the other djinn know she was here. They would not scruple at killing a woman, that was for certain.

The roast elk he'd just eaten seemed to turn over in his stomach. Hasan had opened a bottle of cabernet to go with the meal and the wine bottle was now empty, but he knew he wanted more. He tapped a finger against the side of his wine glass, and at once it refilled itself. That was better. Another glass of wine, some breaths of night air before he retired for the evening.

Perhaps the oblivion of the nighttime hours would allow him to clear his head, and decide what he wished to do about Jordan.

He went to the front door and opened it, then stepped out onto the porch. The night wind was fine and cool, catching at his hair and fluttering in the silken robes he wore. Quite dark, with such a thin moon, but that was all right, since it gave him a better look at the stars, shimmering in the blackness. As he gazed up at them, however, he didn't see Orion's belt or the Big Dipper, but instead the graceful oval of Jordan's face, the rosy fullness of her lips, the clear blue of her eyes.

If only she was a djinn....

Better to push that thought away. He raised his glass of wine to his lips and sipped, then wondered if perhaps he should have summoned a drink more appropriate for the hour, some sauterne or muscat or possibly even port, rather than the red wine that currently filled the glass. No, this wine was sufficient. Anything sweet would have been too much, would have overpowered the memory of the elegant meal he'd just consumed.

This was better. He must have been more tense than he'd thought, because he could feel his muscles begin to relax as he continued to drink and watch the great wheel of the stars above his head, now in subtly different positions than the ones they'd occupied when he'd first been born, more than a thousand years earlier. At some point he would have to make a decision about Jordan, but that could wait a day or so. If nothing else, she needed some time to get her strength back, to sleep under a roof for a few nights. Even though she hadn't told him where she'd been headed, he could guess well enough. Only Los Alamos could possibly offer her the refuge she desired.

A blight on the landscape, as far as he was concerned, a citadel of those who shouldn't have survived and yet, against all odds, were still there more than two years after the Dying had scoured the earth of their kind. He and his other compatriots who'd settled in this region had discussed the problem many times, hoping they could discover some way to circumvent the devices the humans in Los Alamos had deployed to keep away the djinn, but there didn't seem to be any answer. To come within the field of effect of those machines was to become weak and ineffectual, one's powers stripped away, the very strength within one's muscles and sinews sapped to the point where it was an effort to simply put a single foot in front of the other. No successful attack could be mounted under those conditions.

As far as Hasan knew, there were no other human survivors on the continent beyond the Chosen and those who sheltered in Los Alamos, and a few stragglers here and there like Jordan, who'd somehow managed to escape notice. But those isolated few were not enough to worry about. It was the very existence of that former citadel of science that rankled so much, which cast back in their faces every day that Hasan and his djinn fellows had not quite succeeded in making the former territory of New Mexico as free of humans as it was supposed to be.

There was nowhere else for Jordan to go. And if he let her leave, then he would only be contributing to the very thorn that had been piercing his side for the past two years.

Scowling, he drained the rest of the wine in his glass, then turned to go inside. In that moment, however, a strange scuffling sound met his ears, followed by a high-pitched scream that sounded almost as if it had come from a woman's throat.

Jordan? he thought for a second, until he realized that the cry had come from the edge of the property, where the lawn met the trees, and not from within the house. He could still sense her presence there, and so he knew she was safe.

All the same, he set down his glass on the

porch railing and hurried out into the darkness, intent on discovering the source of the sound. As he approached the stand of aspens, he saw a pale blur, a blur that now made piteous bleating noises.

One of the goats that sometimes wandered onto his lands, the young one with the mottled coat. The animals did him the service of cropping his grass, and so he'd never tried to keep them away. Now, though, the goat kicked out with its hooves, striking at a dark shape that was trying to get at its throat.

A wolf, Hasan realized. He had heard their howls in the night, but they did not usually venture down from the hills. With mankind gone, and the land gradually returning to its wild state, the predators had grown bolder, had increased in number. Recognizing that a predator more dangerous than they lived in the house here, they had stayed away. But perhaps the goat was too much of a temptation, and the hungry wolf had finally decided to take a chance.

He raised a hand, even as he heard a shocked cry from somewhere off to his left. Pausing for the barest trace of a second, he glanced over one shoulder, saw Jordan running toward him. How had she gotten out of the house?

Because you were careless during dinner and

forgot to refresh the ward on the door, he thought in disgust, and wanted to shake his head at himself. No time for that, however.

The air was his element, and so he had no trouble making it his servant. With his right hand he made a pushing motion, and immediately a gust of wind swept out and caught the wolf, shoving it away from its prey. The wolf let out a yipe but regained its balance and began to move toward the goat once again, clearly undeterred.

Well, if gentle persuasion was not enough—

Hasan raised both his hands. Winds swirled around him, coalescing into a dark funnel that moved toward the wolf. Its eyes glared at him, baleful yellow, just before the tornado engulfed the animal and lifted it away. He still didn't wish any harm to the wolf, however, and made the tornado move a good quarter-mile away before it deposited the predator on the ground and disappeared. Clearly defeated, the wolf loped off into the darkness, limping a little.

Just as Hasan lowered his arms, Jordan approached, panting from her haste. She wore some of the human garments he had provided for her, but she obviously hadn't stopped to put on any shoes; her feet were bare against the faintly yellowed grass.

Her mouth opened, as though she intended

to ask him a question, but then she let out a sound of dismay and darted past him, went to where the wounded goat had fallen to the ground. Ignoring the blood that dripped from the bites in its throat, she put her arms around the animal, holding it close. "He's still alive," she cried out. "You have to help him!"

Hasan had already intended to do that very thing, although she'd forestalled him. Mouth set, he went to where Jordan sat on the grass, the injured goat cradled in her arms. Blood streaked the pale blue of the shirt she wore, and her worried eyes met his as he approached.

"Let me see," he said, crouching down next to her.

She lifted her arms slightly. Yes, there was a series of bites and claw marks on the goat's brindled coat, although none of them appeared mortal. Still, the animal needed to be tended to.

"We'll have to bring him inside," Hasan told her. "Let me pick him up."

Teeth clamped worriedly on her lower lip, she nodded and then got to her feet. She watched without speaking as he bent and took the goat in his arms. It should have struggled, but Hasan could tell the animal was too weak for that. Instead, it allowed its head to loll against his chest as he headed back toward the house, Jordan only a few paces behind him.

Because of his inborn djinn strength, the animal's weight was not an issue, although Hasan was all too aware of the way its blood was now also streaked across the breast of the robe he wore. Ah, well. It could join the one that had been ruined when Jordan took that shot at him. Luckily, new clothes were easy enough to summon.

However, because he didn't want to drip blood all the way across the living room, he headed for the back door to the house, the one that entered through the now unused laundry room. Once inside, he took the injured goat into the kitchen, where he laid it down on the floor. A snap of his fingers, and thick blankets appeared on the tile next to it. Seeing what he was doing, Jordan hurried forward and leaned down next to the animal, then tucked the blankets in around it. The wounded goat leaned its head against her arm, as if it could tell it was in the presence of a sympathetic soul.

"Here," Hasan said, handing her a damp cloth that he had also summoned. "Use this to clean its wounds."

"'His,'" Jordan corrected him as she took the

cloth and shot a quick glance at the goat's under-side. "He's a billygoat."

Male, female...it didn't really matter one way or another to Hasan, who considered an animal's sex unimportant. But humans were close to their pets in ways that djinn were not.

He watched as Jordan carefully blotted the blood away from the goat's wounds. "It's not as bad as it looks," she said. "But we'll still need something more than water to clean him up. Did this house have any antiseptic—hydrogen perox-ide, or betadine, or Neosporin?"

"I have no idea," Hasan replied. "Djinn have no need of such things."

Her gaze flickered to his arm, which now bore no trace of the wound she had caused the day before. "No, I suppose you don't. But this little guy doesn't have your power of healing. We don't want these wounds to get infected."

"I'll go look in the bathroom."

"Thanks."

She went back to attending the wounds on the goat's neck as Hasan left the kitchen to inspect the one bathroom on the ground floor of the house. He'd never really looked in the medi-cine cabinet, or under the sink, except when he first took up residence here and wanted to determine that the house didn't contain any items that might spoil or otherwise cause a problem.

The medicine cabinet was empty except for a small bottle labeled "Zyrtec." He didn't know what that was, but he knew it wasn't any of the things Jordan had asked for. Bending down, he opened the cupboards beneath the sink to see what he might find in there. A bottle of toilet cleaner, and extra toilet paper, and then a long yellow box. Hasan picked it up, saw that it said "Neosporin" in large green letters, and nodded in approval.

Bearing his prize, he returned to the kitchen. Jordan was leaning up against the cabinets, the goat in her lap, its head burrowed against her chest. She was stroking it behind the ears and humming, her voice soft, pretty.

For a second, Hasan could only stare down at her, an odd sensation he couldn't quite identify stirring in his breast. He didn't know if he'd ever seen anyone look so gentle and yet fierce, as though she intended to will the goat back to health through sheer force of personality.

He cleared his throat. "I found some of what you called Neosporin."

She looked up, her expression brightening. "Oh, good. The hydrogen peroxide would have stung like hell, and I know this little guy wouldn't have liked that at all."

"Then this should be much better." He began to open the package and extract the long tube inside, only to have Jordan interrupt him.

"Can you check the expiration date? We'll have to use it regardless, but it couldn't hurt to know how old it is."

"Expiration date?" Hasan inquired, turning the tube over in his hands. He couldn't see a date anywhere.

"It's usually stamped on the crimp at the bottom of the tube."

"Ah."

No need to squint, when one had djinn eyes. "It says 11/2018."

She smiled. "Then we're safe. They must have just bought it when...." The words trailed off there, and she wouldn't quite meet his eyes.

Hasan could understand her reticence. The owner of this house would have purchased the medication not too long before the Heat tore through the world's population, rendering such over-the-counter remedies useless for anyone except the few who remained. Deeming it better not to say anything, he quietly handed her the tube.

In silence she took it from him, then unscrewed the cap and squeezed out a thin thread of translucent ointment. Deftly she applied it to the animal's throat; the goat didn't struggle, but appeared to take its medicine with some meekness. Or perhaps it didn't even understand what she was doing, and only thought Jordan was stroking its neck.

"There," she said, once she was done and had screwed the cap back onto the tube. "Can you get me a towel or something? I'm all sticky, and I don't want to use the other cloth you gave me, since it has blood all over it."

"Of course," Hasan replied, and went to the drawer where he knew such things were kept. He extracted a cheerful yellow dishtowel and gave it to her, and she used it to wipe the last of the Neosporin off her hands. During all this, the goat remained where it was, its head pillowed on her breast. In that moment, Hasan experienced an odd stab of jealousy.

It would be pleasant, he thought, to be where that goat was right now.

But since he didn't want to acknowledge such a notion any more than he already had, he cleared his throat and said, "So what do we do with this fellow? This property has a barn, but I haven't inspected it lately to determine whether it's solid."

"Oh, no," Jordan replied at once. "I'm not putting this little guy out in the barn. Not yet, anyway. He can sleep in here tonight."

"In the kitchen?" Hasan asked, not sure whether he was more taken aback by her peremptory tone, or the shocking demand she had just made. True, he didn't actually prepare his meals in the kitchen, only stored the components in the refrigerator and the pantry, but still....

The young woman seemed to understand that little detail as well, for she said, "Do you plan to come in here tomorrow and make bacon and pancakes?"

"Well, no."

"And can't you wave your hand and clean up everything once he's well enough to go stay in the barn?"

"Yes, but—"

"There you go," Jordan said, her tone brooking no argument. "We'll see how he's doing tomorrow and decide what to do. And we'll also need to find his friends."

"Friends?"

"I saw a couple of goats in town yesterday. Lord knows how many of them are wandering around, just waiting to be wolf bait." Her blue eyes looked very bright under the kitchen's track lighting. "Do *you* know how many there are?"

"No. I fear I haven't paid much attention."

"You should really have rounded them up and kept them in the barn. I know they've come around and kept your lawn short, but they could have done more weed clearance if they hadn't been wandering far and wide and had been kept on your property. Besides, goats make awesome cheese."

"I know that," he said, somewhat waspishly. Did this girl expect him to spend his days as a cheesemonger, when all he had to do was wish for something, and it would appear? "How do you know so much about goats?"

"I don't, really," Jordan replied. "But I studied using them for weed abatement in one of my classes. Much more environmentally friendly than using chemicals or heavy equipment."

This answer startled him somewhat, because Hasan's experience had taught him that humans in general didn't seem to have much concern for the world they lived in...which of course was the reason why the djinn had seen fit to take it away from them.

"Well, we shall worry about his 'friends' tomorrow," Hasan said. "For now, I think it is best if we all go to sleep."

Blue eyes glinted up at him through a fringe of thick lashes. "Do djinn sleep?"

He didn't know if she was teasing or not. After all, she must have heard him come up the stairs and retire to his room the night before. "Yes...but much more lightly than humans." He hoped she got the warning. Yes, he needed to get his rest, but he would also be able to tell immediately if she tried to get away.

"Ah." She stroked softly between the goat's ears; its eyes closed, and it let out a hoarse breath that sounded very close to a snore. "Well, good night, then."

At first Hasan wasn't sure what she meant. Then, as she carefully settled herself against the cupboards, he realized that she planned to stay down in the kitchen with her new pet. "You can't possibly intend to sleep in here."

"Oh, yes, I can. I don't want to leave this little guy alone."

"But you need your rest as well—"

"Then get me a pillow."

Scowling, Hasan snapped his fingers, and one of the pillows from her bed appeared in his hand. "Will this do?"

"That's perfect." She extended a hand, and he gave the pillow to her. Moving with care so she wouldn't disturb the sleeping goat in her lap, she tucked the cushion behind her head.

Hasan wanted to argue with her, but realized such efforts would be futile. And really, if she wanted to stay down here with that damnable animal and give herself a sore back, then that was her prerogative. At least if she was being so protective of the goat, then she probably wouldn't try to run away. He knew he didn't dare bar the doors against her, in case she needed to let the animal outside to empty his bowels and bladder.

"Then good night, Jordan," he said, his tone stiff with disapproval.

"Good night, Hasan."

He turned and left the kitchen, wishing to shake his head but managing to refrain from doing so. Right then, he wondered if he was completely mad for letting this woman into his house.

The first thing Jordan noticed was the massive crick in her neck. She'd fallen asleep with her head tipped to one side, and so her neck was stiffer than hell, worse even than the nights when she'd had to use tree roots as a pillow. Well, another hot shower should take care of that problem.

Morning sunlight peeked past the curtains at the window. As soon as she stirred, the goat was up and out of her lap. He wobbled to his feet and gave a little shake, as though trying to get rid of a few kinks of his own. Then he let out a bleat and headed toward the back door, his hooves clip-clopping on the kitchen's tiled floor.

Could goats be house-trained? Jordan didn't think so, but it was pretty clear what the goat wanted. Or maybe he was just hungry. She climbed to her feet, trying to ignore the various aches and sore spots she'd given herself from sleeping on a hard surface like that. Yes, she'd had to resort to more than one makeshift bed during her flight from Pagosa Springs—and before that, when the group had run away from Colorado Springs—but this was the first time she'd had to sleep on a bare floor.

Chosen to sleep on the floor, that is. She could've followed Hasan's advice and put the goat out in the barn. However, she would never have forgiven herself if something had happened to the little critter while she slept safely in the bed the djinn had provided for her.

Ignoring the way her back was groaning, she went to the door in the laundry room and let out the goat. At once he gamboled off into the grass before picking a likely spot and getting down to some serious grass munching. Watching him, she realized she could use a pick-me-up of her own. Only one day back to drinking coffee, and she was already hooked all over again. Before that, it had probably been at least four months since she'd had a real cup of coffee. They'd done their best to ration the stuff, but even so, the Pagosa Springs group had run through their supply much more quickly than they'd planned.

As they had with a lot of things, actually. Plans and lists had been drawn up with the intent to make their meager supplies last for as long as possible, but the sad fact was that none of them had any experience actually calculating how much a person might consume in a given day, and so their numbers had always been off. Jordan remembered how she'd worried whether they'd be able to make it through the coming winter, whether some of the weaker members of the group might end up dying from malnutrition or one of the diseases that preyed on the body when it was weak.

She also realized, as she stood there and watched the goat move to another spot on the lawn, that the back door hadn't been locked. If she'd wanted to, she could have gotten up some-time during the night and attempted to escape.

Maybe. Hasan had said the djinn slept lightly. He might have noticed her trying to get away.

Had he left the door unlocked as a sort of test? Or had he simply thought that the goat might need to go outside to do his business? Hasan had seemed concerned about the cleanliness of the kitchen. But the door to her own room hadn't been locked, either, which she'd discovered as soon as she tried to run outside and see what was going on.

"I see your friend has survived the night," came the djinn's voice from behind her, and Jordan startled, then turned around. Hasan looked impeccable, slightly damp hair brushed away from his forehead, his robes a smoky blue-gray color banded in silver.

Whereas she—Jordan had to resist the urge to wipe at the blood that stained the front of her shirt, even though she knew it was long dried and was only coming out after a long presoak in a washing machine. If the washer even worked; everything in the laundry room looked as though it hadn't been touched in months.

"Yes," she said, glad she sounded so normal. It was hard to look at him, with the expanse of hard, flat stomach and well-muscled chest that those robes exposed. She'd thought she'd put her discomfort over his appearance behind her, but apparently not. Why did djinn have to be so physically beautiful, anyway? "None of his injuries looked like they wanted to start bleeding again, and his energy seems good."

"That's for certain," Hasan responded, his tone dry. Out in the field, the goat was frisking about, jumping from place to place as if in search of the most succulent patch of grass he could find. If it weren't for the reddish splotches on his throat, you'd never be able to tell that he'd been attacked the night before. "I thought you could use this," the djinn added, and handed her a heavy mug of coffee.

Where that solicitude had come from, she didn't know, but she wasn't going to argue. "Thank you," she said, and wrapped her hands around the heavy mug and took a sip. Ah, that was perfect—dark Italian roast, fresh as if Hasan had just ground the beans himself. Another sip, and Jordan began to feel almost human, despite her night on the floor.

"I see the kitchen is more or less intact," he said.

"Yes, I think he slept all night."

"Did you?"

His eyes were intent on her, and Jordan could

feel color rise to her cheeks. Stupid, she knew, because he wasn't giving her *that* kind of look. More like he was just trying to see how much worse for wear she was after her night on the kitchen floor.

"I've had a better night's sleep," she said lightly. "But I don't think I took any permanent damage, if that's what you mean. And I did sleep. I have plenty of energy to go looking for our little friend's herd."

"You're still intent on doing that."

"Well, yes." Jordan sipped some more of her coffee, partly because she needed more caffeine, and partly because by doing so she didn't have to keep looking up into Hasan's face. Spending the night here hadn't erased any of the strangeness of the situation, that was for sure. Sometimes he seemed impatient with her, sometimes almost amused. He certainly hadn't shown any signs of wanting to hurt her. Did his behavior mean that she needed to change her ideas about djinn, or was it only that something about him was different from the others of his kind? And why had he kept her locked up all day, only to leave the door open that night? "I probably need to get cleaned up first."

"That would be wise." Before she could say

anything, he went on, "I'll gather up some breakfast while you take care of that."

He seemed very mellow this morning, so she felt emboldened to comment, "Also, the clothes you've conjured for me are nice, but they're not very practical, especially for rounding up goats. Could I have my T-shirts back?"

His mouth twisted in a half-smile. "I'll think of something."

It wasn't a yes, but since Jordan thought her situation precarious enough as it was, she only nodded and said, "Thank you." A few more sips of the coffee in her mug, and then she murmured an "excuse me," set the mug down on the kitchen counter, and headed upstairs.

The room where she should have slept looked much the same—with the exception of the missing pillow, which still sat on the floor downstairs. On the bed were a pair of faded jeans and a long-sleeved peasant blouse embroidered in blue and green. Not a T-shirt, but she could compromise. Something about wearing jeans that looked brand new made her want to keep them looking brand new for as long as possible. These broken-in ones would be much better for traipsing around outside.

Her shower this morning was much faster than the one from the day before. She scrubbed her face and hands, washed her hair quickly, and was out before even ten minutes had elapsed.

When she was done getting dressed, she ran a comb through her damp hair once again and faced herself in the mirror. Maybe a few shadows under her eyes from the rough night she'd just spent, but that was all. She could have fared much worse.

As to what the day would bring...she honestly didn't know. So far Hasan had seemed friendly enough, which in itself was a twist she hadn't expected. She couldn't trust him, though. About all she could do was try to take her cues from him, and avoid upsetting him or making him angry.

And if she was very lucky, she might be able to survive this.

Chapter Six

HASAN CONJURED A BREAKFAST FOR THEM—NOT OF pancakes, as Jordan had jokingly suggested the evening before, but of fruit and bread and cold ham. When she descended the stairs, her gaze moved to the spread on the dining room table, and she smiled slightly.

"How is our friend?" she asked.

"See for yourself," he replied, and pointed toward the living room window, where he'd pulled the curtains aside to give an unobstructed view of the front lawn. There, almost in the middle of the space, was her damnable goat, chomping away at the slightly dry grass as if it didn't have a care in the world. Perhaps it didn't, now that it knew it had someone around who wished to watch over it.

Her smile widened. "He doesn't seem any the worse for wear, that's for sure."

"And yourself?"

"I'm fine," she said. "A hot shower cures all ills."

Hasan was forced to admit that showers were one human invention he could wholeheartedly praise. And Jordan did look much better than she had when she'd gone upstairs. Now her hair was sleek and brushed, albeit still slightly damp, and the cheerful embroidery on the top he'd provided for her brought out the blue in her eyes. Also, while he in general thought modern American clothing drab and unattractive, one couldn't deny the way well-fitting jeans showed off the female figure.

He shouldn't be looking at her figure, however. With a deliberate effort, he moved his gaze away from her and toward the table. "Shall we?"

Jordan nodded and went to take a seat at the dining room table. As she settled her napkin in her lap, she said, "I was kind of hoping the goat's friends would have come looking for him, but it doesn't seem that way."

"Perhaps they are fine where they are," he said mildly as he put some bread and fruit on his plate, and speared a piece of ham with his fork.

"After all, they have been ranging wild for quite some time."

"I thought about that." Jordan helped herself to some food. "But the wolves are getting bolder. I don't think the goats are safe."

Hasan had observed that change in the wolves himself, although he was somewhat surprised to hear Jordan commenting on it. "You had problems with wolves in Pagosa Springs?"

She'd just popped a grape in her mouth, and had to finish chewing it before she answered him. "Not the first winter. Things were very quiet...almost like the world was in shock or something. The next winter, though—the wolves came through several times, and we wasted a lot of ammo driving them off. We were also worried that all the noise would bring the djinn down on us."

She stopped there, not quite looking at him. Was she concerned that her comment about the djinn might upset him? Possibly. He found nothing in it to bother him, mostly because she was only being matter-of-fact. Pagosa Springs was not in his territory, and so he had never gone on any "cleansing" missions there, but he thought it entirely possible that the djinn in the area had done a sweep early on, deemed the settlement cleared, and never returned to see if a group of refugees from elsewhere in Colorado might have made their way there.

As for the wolves, well, their only true predator had been removed from the world. No wonder they were ranging farther and farther afield these days. Yes, they knew better than to go up against a djinn, but with only a little more than twenty thousand of his people spread across the entire globe, Hasan guessed the probability of wolves squaring off against djinn was fairly low.

"Their population is increasing," he said as he poured himself some water from the pitcher he'd set out. "As are the populations of deer and elk. Balance is being maintained."

Jordan appeared troubled by that statement, but she didn't try to contradict him. Had she noticed those shifts in population, or had her group's hunting efforts more or less wiped out any such gains in the immediate area around Pagosa Springs?

"Well, I suppose the deer and elk can take care of themselves," she said. "But the goats are domesticated animals. They're used to being watched over."

"Perhaps," Hasan allowed. "On the other hand, they've had two years to adapt to the alteration of their circumstances. From what I've seen, they appear to be doing quite well. However," he went on quickly, noting the way Jordan's lips had parted, as though she intended to protest that particular observation, "last night's attack does show that they need to be watched over. Wolves have never come to Chama before now."

His words appeared to mollify her, for she settled back against her chair and reached for another piece of bread. "Have you used the barn here at all?"

"No. I had no need to. But if it requires any sort of repairs, I can manage that." Which he could. All djinn had the ability to construct their own homes—although the earth elementals were best at it—and he assumed that ability would extend toward any outbuildings on his property. As he'd told Jordan, before now he'd ignored the barn because he had no use for it. He'd fished in the river and hunted deer and elk, and also gathered fruit from the trees in the area, but at the same time, he'd conjured other items to expand his pantry, or simply because he didn't feel like physically obtaining the food he required.

"We should go look at it."

"Now?"

"Well, after breakfast. Then we can go try to find the rest of the goats."

It seemed as good a plan as any. "Of course," he said, and watched her smile again, light touching those big blue eyes of hers.

Hasan reflected that a man might do a good deal to earn one of those smiles...and in this particular instance, a djinn was no different from a mortal man.

The morning breeze was brisk and cool, but the sun bright and warm, making the conditions just about perfect for a walk out to the barn. Hasan moved a few paces ahead of her, leading the way. The sunlight glimmered on the silk of his robes while the wind blew his hair away from his face. Right then he did look very godlike, and Jordan had to make sure she kept her gaze locked elsewhere.

The whole situation was positively surreal. Now they were acting like...well, maybe not exactly friends, but people who were friendly enough with each other. He was the enemy, though. She knew he must have far too many deaths on his conscience. She shouldn't let her breath catch when his eyes met hers, or when he turned to look at her. This wasn't junior high, and he wasn't the most popular boy in school.

No, this was the real world. She could never let herself forget that, or forget the people she'd lost. Her own family—such as it was—had died when the Heat swept over the world, but the group at Pagosa Springs had become her new family, sturdy Frank and pretty Suzanne and Suzanne's boyfriend Cole, who'd once been a pharmacist. And Lisa and Tom and Drew and everyone else. Now that she wasn't running to save her life, she found her thoughts returning to them, recalling little details about their lives and their personalities, as if trying to give them the memorial service she knew they'd never have.

By that point they'd reached the doors to the barn, which were shut, although one of them had cracked open an inch or two. Hasan paused there and turned back toward her. His eyes narrowed slightly as he appeared to survey her features.

"Is something wrong?"

"No," she replied at once. She knew she couldn't talk to him about her losses, because it was his kind who'd been responsible for those deaths. Not Hasan himself—not in this case, anyway—but the notion of guilt by association was something she couldn't entirely put aside. "I'm fine. Let's see what we've got here."

He sent her a final curious look, but then gave a slight lift of his shoulders and grasped the handles of the barn doors, pulling them outward. From within came a fetid odor, and Jordan wrinkled her nose.

"What the heck is that?"

"Damp straw that spoiled. We'll have to remove it."

She had a flashback to the time in junior high when she'd helped a friend, who was in 4-H, muck out her henhouse. It was not an experience she wanted to repeat anytime soon.

Hasan must have noted her obvious lack of enthusiasm, because one corner of his mouth tugged upward. "It is not such an onerous task when you have a djinn to help out."

His hands lifted, and a wind came out of nowhere, blowing into the barn with such force that the doors on the opposite side of the building were pushed open. At once all the straw inside began to swirl with the wind, making its own little tornado, before it moved out of the barn and disappeared over the rise that backed up to the structure. Once the straw was all cleared away, and only packed earth remained, the wind disappeared.

"That is handy," Jordan remarked. More than handy—she'd seen a small demonstration of

Hasan's powers the night before when he drove off the wolf, but this just proved to her once again that he was no one to be trifled with. Also, the djinn attacks in Colorado Springs and Pagosa Springs had been so chaotic, so frightening, that she hadn't retained a lot of detail. This latest display showed her what a single djinn could do. No wonder her human compatriots hadn't stood a chance.

As to why she'd somehow managed to survive...Jordan couldn't begin to say. Luck? It had to be, since she knew she wasn't any stronger or smarter than the ones who didn't make it.

"Yes," Hasan said, his tone almost absent. Clearly, he wasn't impressed by his own powers. He went inside the barn, and Jordan followed.

Now that the fetid straw had been cleared away, she saw it was a large, airy space, with six stalls for animals and a larger feeding area at the far end, with troughs hanging from the wooden walls—troughs that were now filled with fresh fodder for the goats. Off to one side a door stood open, revealing a small room, obviously used for storage and tack, because she saw a bridle hanging from a hook on the wall. She wondered what had happened to the horse, or horses, that once resided here. This wasn't a true horse stable, and so she guessed that whoever had once owned the house had either converted the space for horse use, or had kept several different kinds of animals in here.

"I don't know how many goats are wandering around Chama," she said. "But it looks like we should be able to fit at least seven or eight in here."

After she spoke, Jordan realized she'd said "we." A slip-up, because this was Hasan's property, and he had the final say about what he did with it. Really, she was just doing what she could to help protect the animals she'd encountered. About all she could do now was hope that the djinn wouldn't find her words presumptuous and take offense.

Apparently, he didn't, because he only nodded as he moved farther into the barn, then paused to look into one of the stalls. "Yes, that sounds about right. Shall we see if we can round them up?"

He wasn't angry. In fact, he looked pleasant and relaxed, which were two words she'd never thought she could apply to a djinn. "Sure."

Hasan took a step in her direction and held out a hand. Jordan looked at it, confused. Why was he reaching toward her? She didn't think that touching him was a very good idea. Bad enough that she could still recall all too clearly the way it had felt to have his body on top of hers, pushing her down against the ground. All right, what he'd really done was tackle her so she couldn't get away, but still....

"I don't wish to walk into town," he said, his tone almost too neutral, "especially if I will have to herd goats on the way back. Likewise, I have no desire to attempt to drive the vehicle that was left in the garage here at the house. I can take us there in the blink of an eye, but you must hold on to me. Do you understand?"

Swallowing, she nodded. She'd seen how djinn could appear to blink themselves in and out of existence, moving from place to place almost instantaneously. The thought that she might travel in the same way scared the crap out of her, but she had a feeling that if she demurred, told Hasan she really wasn't into that kind of travel, he really would get angry with her.

It took more effort than she'd thought to put one foot in front of the other, to make herself go up to the djinn. When she laid her hand in his, all she could think was how human he felt. Shouldn't his skin have been too cold, or far too hot? Something to tell her that he was of a race terribly different from hers, even if they did look the same?

When he pulled her close to him, put both arms around her waist, she barely stifled a gasp.

Hasan raised an eyebrow, as though he'd noted her reaction. "Merely holding your hand is not enough," he said. "The forces that move a djinn from place to place could tear you from my grasp. I do not think you would want to be lost in the void between worlds."

No, she definitely would not. At the same time, being held against his bare chest like this was a level of discomfort that passed beyond excruciating into something she couldn't begin to describe. Her cheeks flushed with heat, but at least with her face nearly pressed into him, he couldn't see that she was blushing.

Although maybe he could feel it.

"No, that makes sense," she told him, wondering if she sounded like a complete idiot. Not that he would care. After all, she was just a human. She could already tell that Hasan didn't have a very high opinion of human intellect.

"Then we will go."

The world flashed away, dissolving into nothing. A strange pressure on her ears, as though she'd suddenly ascended a thousand feet in less than a second. Strange colors whirled around her for an instant or two, only to resolve into the not-quite-familiar but certainly prosaic main street of

Chama, with the depot for the Cumbres and Toltec railroad in front of them, and the bait shop across the road.

As soon as they stood on solid ground, Hasan released his grip on her, as though he didn't wish to continue touching her any longer than was necessary. Fine by Jordan, who was glad she didn't have to struggle to get him to release her.

She took a few steps away from him, shielding her eyes from the sun as she glanced around the street. There, that was perfectly normal, wasn't it? After all, they'd come here to locate the goats. He didn't have to know that she was glad of the excuse to not look at him. Bad enough that she couldn't quite ignore the way she could still somehow feel his arms around her. It hadn't been an embrace, nothing like that, and yet....

Okay, she needed to refocus. Maybe that crappy night's sleep she'd gotten while sitting on the kitchen floor had done something to addle her brain. That had to be it. Because the absolute last thing she wanted to think was that some small, crazy part of her had actually enjoyed being held by a djinn.

Hasan was also looking up and down the street. "There," he said after a moment. "Farther up the road."

Jordan turned to see what he was talking about. Sure enough, in a grassy area a few hundred yards past the railway station, stood several goats, chewing away at the weeds and looking as if they didn't have a care in the world.

"Well, then," she said, and began walking in that direction. What she'd actually do when they caught up with the goats, she wasn't sure. Although she'd taken classes in biology and botany, none of them had included much information on animal husbandry. She knew as much about herding goats as she did jet engine maintenance—in other words, nothing at all.

If Hasan harbored any doubts about their situation, he didn't show it. He strode along next to her, every inch of his frame purposeful, focused. Maybe he didn't know much about goats, either, but he wasn't going to let a minor detail like that slow him down.

Jordan had worried that the animals might scatter as she and Hasan approached. That didn't seem to be a problem, however, since only one of the goats even looked up when they drew near. The other two kept munching away, clearly not about to allow the presence of humans—or a human and a djinn—interrupt their breakfast. Did djinn smell different to animals? She had absolutely no idea, because Hasan hadn't smelled like much of anything when he brought her here, except a faint spicy scent that might have been cinnamon or might have been cloves, or neither of those two, just something pleasant and warm.

And there she was, thinking about being held by him again. Yes, it had been a very long time since she'd allowed anyone to get that close to her, but come on....

"I can guide them," Hasan said. "We will have to go the long way around, I fear, because while you might have been able to ford the river" — he paused there, as if recalling how she'd first trespassed on his land—"it will be too deep for them. There is a foot crossing about a quarter mile downstream from where you crossed."

"Well," Jordan replied. "It's a beautiful day, so if we have to take a long walk, it's certainly not the end of the world."

"True." He made a waving motion with his hands, but instead of summoning a wind as he had to clear out the barn, it was more like he had called something that would prod the goats along. They all stopped eating and, after letting out a few startled bleats, began to hurry down the road, back into town.

"What did you do to them?" Jordan asked as she began to jog along in their wake.

The djinn was tall enough that all he had to do was lengthen his strides, rather than actually run to catch up with the goats. "Gave them a gentle nudge. And I'll continue to do so until we get them safely in the barn."

That seemed to be the case, because every time it looked as though the animals were beginning to veer off course, Hasan would move his hands again, and the goats would immediately get back in line. They all headed roughly southwest on Highway 17, until he waved his hands to the left, pushing the animals between a feed shop and a Family Dollar, and cutting back toward the river.

As they came out from between the buildings, Jordan saw the crossing Hasan had mentioned, really just a shallow strip of sand that jutted out from the banks of the Rio Chama. They'd all still get their feet wet, but it would only be up to mid-calf on her at the most, a depth the goats could easily ford.

Not that they looked terribly eager to get in the water. This time the motion Hasan made with his hands looked almost like a shove, and with a few protesting bleats, the goats trotted out into the water and hurried across the sand spit, picking their way around any exposed rocks.

Within a few minutes, they had reached the other bank.

Jordan had to pause to remove her shoes and socks, but the djinn had no such worries. As soon as he came to the river's edge, he lifted himself into the air, hovering so he was a few inches above the water. As she sloshed across the sand, he drifted ahead of her, staying completely dry.

Another handy trick. Would he have carried her, if she'd asked him? Maybe. Since the last thing she wanted was any more close contact with him, she decided it was better to just get her feet wet. Grass grew thick on the bank, so she dried her toes as best she could, then slipped her socks and shoes back on. The goats didn't seem inclined to wait for her, and neither did Hasan, which meant she had to drop into another jog so she could catch up with them.

When she did, the djinn was walking along normally, both feet firmly on the ground. The goats ranged a few paces ahead, but not so far away that Hasan couldn't control them if they decided to bolt for some reason. Jordan came abreast of the djinn, who didn't even look down at her, but instead kept his focus on the small group of animals as they made their way across the field and up toward the barn.

Was he feeling slightly embarrassed, too? No,

that wasn't possible. Djinn didn't seem to be the type to be self-conscious, or unsure of themselves. At least, Hasan didn't. Jordan couldn't speak for the djinn she'd encountered elsewhere, since she'd been too busy running away to try to take a read on their personalities.

When they reached the barn, Hasan had to give the goats another "push" to go inside, since it seemed clear that they preferred to stay outside and try some of the grass in the immediate vicinity. Jordan couldn't blame them; if she were a goat, she wouldn't want to be trapped in a barn on a fine early October day like this one.

But in they went, bleating in annoyance. Hasan didn't try to force them into any of the stalls, however, but allowed them to range around in the open area beneath the hayloft. Once they realized there was fodder available inside, they settled down to eat again, and didn't give the people who'd brought them here a second glance.

"We'll have to find your friend," the djinn said as he closed the barn door behind them.

"I doubt he wandered too far," she replied. "I mean, if I were a goat, I'd probably want to stay near the place where I was fed and given water, and had someone taking care of me."

"I'm not sure goats are always that logical."

Something about Hasan's tone of voice as he uttered that reply made her want to chuckle. And that was crazy, too. She shouldn't find anything about him funny or interesting or, God forbid, attractive. Besides, even though he was allowing her to roam around the property with him, rather than keeping her locked up in her bedroom, he was still her captor.

And if you tried to get away, where would you go? she asked herself. *To some dream of Los Alamos, which may or may not even still exist?*

Well, that had been the plan. Even if Los Alamos had fallen, surely there must be places where people still lived, where they'd managed to keep themselves hidden from the djinn.

Or maybe not. If those vengeful elementals were now focusing their energies on ridding the world of tiny groups like the one in Pagosa Springs, then there must not be very much left for them to hunt.

"There he is," Hasan said, and Jordan shook herself out of her dark reverie to see her little rescue goat, only a few yards away from the front porch of the house, his head buried in a clump of dandelions.

"Told you he wouldn't go far."

"So you did."

That might have been grudging approval in

the djinn's voice. Hard to say for sure, since his face was impassive enough as he looked across the front yard to the spot where the goat cropped away at the greenery, apparently oblivious to their presence.

Now what? Jordan supposed Hasan could use his powers to shove the goat where they needed him to go, but that seemed like rough handling for an animal that was smaller than the others. Carrying him seemed so undignified, especially when he'd done such a good job of bouncing back from the injuries he'd suffered the night before.

"Come here!" she called out, and the goat lifted his head briefly before returning to his late morning repast. "Come on!"

This time Hasan did laugh, although he sounded more amused than mocking. "It is not a dog, you know."

"Yes, I know," she replied, her tone waspish. "Do you have a better idea?"

"Of course." The djinn extended a hand toward the goat, fingers outstretched.

This wasn't a push or a pull. Jordan wasn't sure exactly what Hasan was doing, except that the goat stopped eating and began to trot toward them.

"How did you do that?"

"We djinn have our ways."

That wasn't much of an answer, but she didn't want to argue with him. He still seemed remarkably mellow, and she wanted to keep things that way...at least until she figured out what the heck she herself was doing.

Anyway, that goat went trotting past, his coat of thick, short hair glistening in the sunlight. There wasn't much Jordan could do but follow him as he headed toward the barn, intent on his destination. This time, Hasan brought up the rear, as though he knew that he didn't need to do anything else but make sure the goat didn't veer off course at the last minute.

The door to the barn opened, apparently of its own accord, although Jordan guessed that must have been Hasan, using his powers in yet another subtle way. Was there anything he couldn't do?

She probably didn't want to find out.

Without looking back at them, the little goat trotted inside. Happy bleats from the others who were already there seemed to indicate that his compatriots were glad to have him back. The doors closed again, and Hasan looked down at her.

"I've provided them with water as well. They should be fine for a while, but you'll probably want to let them out sometime this afternoon so they can range."

"I'll let them out?" she repeated, somewhat mystified. "You trust me to come out here all by myself?"

"Safeguarding the goats was your idea," Hasan said. "Therefore, it should fall to you to watch them. As for the rest?" A small pause, and then he smiled. "I don't think I need to worry about you running away. As I told you, I can sense your movements. I would know. Besides" — and here he paused, his smile broadening slightly—"where could you possibly go?"

Chapter Seven

Jordan hadn't responded to his question, had only looked away, her full mouth set in a hard line. Hasan didn't think she would answer, but he could tell his words had upset her.

Did that bother him?

Not really.

He wanted her to think that she had no chance at refuge anywhere. His reasoning for this stratagem was somewhat murky, but he'd come to realize something in these few hours he'd spent with her, something he wasn't sure he wanted to admit to himself.

He enjoyed being in her company. There was something strangely pure and yet determined about her—the way she had stubbornly slept on the kitchen floor to make sure that the goat he'd rescued made it safely through the night, or the way she'd insisted that all the other goats in the area be rounded up so they wouldn't be prey for wolves. Her behavior contrasted with what he thought he'd believed about humans, that they only looked out for themselves, that even among those who pretended to be for the greater good was a tendency toward selfishness and self-aggrandizement.

It was refreshing. *She* was refreshing. If she'd been a woman of the djinn, he would have decided that she was worth pursuing. Because she was human, however, Hasan found himself torn. He was not one of those weaklings who claimed that humanity was worth saving, and who had shackled themselves to one of their mortal "Chosen" for all of eternity. No, he was not that great a fool.

And yet he found it difficult to keep himself from staring at her mouth, from recalling how her slender body had felt in his arms as he transported them into the heart of town. She had been uncomfortable, that much was clear, and yet at the same time he'd sensed a response to him from somewhere deep within her, a reaction she probably didn't want to acknowledge to anyone, let alone herself.

Which put them...where? When they got to

the house, Jordan said she was tired and wanted to go upstairs to lie down. On the surface, it sounded like a reasonable enough excuse. After all, she'd just passed a weary night on the hard kitchen floor, and then had done a good deal of walking. However, Hasan sensed that her real motivation was most likely a desire to get away from him, if only for a short while.

Although he experienced a flicker of irritation at this thought, he didn't try to stop her, only said that he understood and that he would provide a late lunch for her after she woke, if she so wished. She murmured a thank-you and made her escape, leaving him to go back out to the front porch, where he sat down on the bench and stared at the autumn-tinted landscape, trying to decide what he should do next.

A wise man probably would send her on her way. It would be easiest. She could go out into the world, and survive, or not. Hasan rather thought she would survive, given how tenaciously she had hung on to life so far. But that would be putting her in the way of the djinn who still roamed here and there, determined to find humanity's last survivors. If they found her, she would die.

Or worse. None of those involved would ever admit to such deeds, but he'd heard rumors among those dedicated to cleansing the earth that sometimes comely human women were taken and used before they were killed. Hasan had never stooped to such behavior, and so his fellow djinn kept quiet about their heinous acts, at least when they were around him. Still, the thought that Jordan might suffer such a fate only cemented his desire to keep her here, at least for a while.

Besides, if he did let her go, and she did somehow manage to reach Los Alamos, that would be one more strike against that wretched stronghold of humanity. They would have something he wanted.

No, that was ridiculous. He didn't want her. He only...

...only what? His thoughts were so muddled, he wasn't sure what to think anymore.

This had been so much easier when humans were only faceless prey to him, anonymous, flawed, a few steps above vermin such as mice and rats. Once one began to think of them as people, as individuals, then they became much more difficult to kill.

A pair of bleats made him focus on the source of the sound, which had come from off to his left. He saw a couple of goats approaching from the direction of the riverbank, more of the town's resident herd. Good. He could gather them up and put them with their fellows. The task would give him something else to think about rather than the admittedly thorny problem of Jordan Wells.

Hasan got up from the bench where he sat, extending his hands as the goats approached. They came up to him quite without fear, for all domesticated animals instinctively realized that the djinn meant them no harm, and instead wished to be their protectors. He had only driven off the wolf the night before because it would have killed that yearling goat. In itself, he would not have considered such a loss to be a tragedy, for prey succumbing to predators was part of the natural order of things.

But the attack had upset Jordan, and so Hasan had stepped in.

He was not sure he wanted to consider the ramifications of such an action. It would mean that he already cared about what she thought, what she wanted, after spending a short two days in her presence. That was not how he allowed women to affect him, even djinn women. He might permit himself to explore an attraction, to spend time with a woman, but he never allowed them into his heart. It was enough to enjoy the physicality of such a relationship without letting it grow any deeper. While he understood that it was necessary to continue his race, he had left it to others to find a partner they could spend decades with, to have a child with. He'd always moved alone through this life. He preferred it that way.

The goats followed him to the barn, as though they knew that the rest of their herd was already safely inside. He opened the door and watched as they trotted in, perfectly trusting, perfectly fearless. As well they might be. They knew they were now under his protection.

The odor of fresh hay had begun to mix with that of not-so-fresh goat, but Hasan didn't mind. They were safe here. This would be their place.

He closed the barn door and began to walk back to the house. For some reason, he liked the idea that Jordan slept within, that the place wouldn't be empty when he returned.

And that realization should have bothered him more than anything.

Jordan had told Hasan she wanted to sleep, but that wasn't exactly the truth. All right, she was tired enough that she knew she probably would have slept if she'd kicked off her shoes and lain down on the bed. However, she hadn't come up here to sleep.

She'd come up here to get some much-needed solitude.

Because she could feel herself slipping into an odd sort of acceptance. So what if he was a djinn? He hadn't retaliated, even though she'd *shot* him, for God's sake. He'd fed her, given her a place to sleep, even listened to her crack-brained ideas about rounding up all the goats in town. Were those the actions of a homicidal, vengeance-driven person?

Well, she supposed even Hannibal Lecter could be charming when he wanted to.

She sat on the window seat, head resting against the wall as she gazed at the landscape outside, the grass rippling with the wind, the aspens in the grove beyond showing a little more gold than they had the day before. She was so tired, she probably could have slept right here on the window seat. If nothing else, she could try to give herself a crick on the opposite side of her neck. At least that way it would be even.

Movement caught her eye, though. Jordan sat up a little straighter and watched as Hasan strode toward the barn, a pair of goats following him. One of them was white and one a sort of dark chocolate color, and they tagged along with the djinn like a couple of dogs taken out for their afternoon walk. As far as she could tell, none of the animals feared him at all.

He went inside for a few minutes, then came back out, sans goats. His head was lifted into the wind, dark hair blowing behind him like a banner of black silk.

God, he was gorgeous.

That thought seemed so traitorous, Jordan had to shove it to the back of her mind and pretend it had never existed. Problem was, Hasan was still there, walking along as though he was the king of the world or something, the same wind tugging at the heavy silken robes he wore, showing off even more of his muscular chest and a stomach so defined, she thought it might be an eight-pack instead of the usual six.

Because...damn.

Jordan turned away from the window. No point in torturing herself with his male perfection. He was a djinn, and therefore the enemy.

She closed her eyes and leaned back against the wall. The cushion for the window seat wasn't all that thick, and she knew she'd be more comfortable lying on the bed, and yet she stayed where she was. Trying to torture herself for having impure thoughts about a djinn?

Maybe.

It had been a horribly long time. More than two years, because she'd broken up with the boyfriend of her senior year of college just a month before graduation. He wanted her to stay in Boulder and try for her master's degree. She'd made it through four years with scholarships and grants and part-time work, and the thought of having to patchwork her financing for another two years was just exhausting. So she'd gone back to Colorado Springs, where she'd been forced to move in with her mother because she couldn't afford an apartment on her own. Colorado Springs, where no one seemed too interested in hiring a recent graduate with a degree in environmental studies, but were only too glad to have another pretty girl cover the night shift at the bar where Jordan's mother had worked for the past fifteen years.

Anyway, dating was not high on her list of priorities, and when the Heat hit some three months after graduation and the world changed, romance and sex had to take a distant back seat to survival. In Pagosa Springs, people had formed their attachments, but Jordan kept herself out of it. She wasn't interested, thought it was too risky, a belief only cemented when she'd had to hold her friend Suzanne's hand as she took a pregnancy test she got at the local pharmacy, Suzanne crying that she and Cole had used protection, but she was late and didn't know what to do....

The test had come back negative, thank God. Suzanne had only been late because of stress and a shaky diet that probably didn't provide everything her body needed, even though everyone in the group had also been taking supplements. But the incident only made Jordan more determined to stay aloof. Run the risk of having a baby in a world that had fallen apart? No way.

Her libido, which she'd thought safely dormant, appeared to have woken up, and for a djinn, of all people.

If only she hadn't taken that damn detour into Chama. She could have avoided Hasan altogether, could have kept going to Los Alamos. Maybe there she might have met a nice guy, possibly a former scientist or engineer or something, and together they could have worked on ways to maximize the colony's resources, something to make her feel useful. She certainly didn't need to worry about safe environmental practices now, when all of the world's industry had come to an abrupt halt after most of its population perished from the Heat. If nothing else, the Dying must have been great for reducing levels of CO_2, or helping to keep the polar ice caps from receding any more than they already had.

All right, maybe the safest thing to do was just admit that, even though she knew he was a villainous djinn, Hasan was also extremely hot. Acknowledging the fact would make it easier for her to stay on her guard. Besides, finding someone attractive didn't mean you had to act on that attraction. She could allow herself to admire him and leave it at that.

Easy for her to say. Jordan got up from the window seat and headed into the bathroom, where she washed her hands and splashed some cold water on her face. That helped a little. And although she looked tired, her walk earlier in the day had given her some color in her cheeks. She didn't look quite so much like an extra from *The Walking Dead*.

Should she go downstairs, or should she hide up here for a while longer? It would be easier to hide, but in a way, that felt like admitting defeat. She had to prove to herself that she could be around Hasan and act like a normal human being. He never needed to know that she found him attractive.

Attractive. What a lukewarm word. She knew he was the best-looking man...djinn...whatever... that she'd ever seen. But, as her mother had been fond of pointing out, looks weren't everything. Jordan's own father had been an extremely handsome man. He was also a man who brought her a new bike for her fifth birthday, kissed her on the cheek and told her to be a good girl, and then disappeared forever. No letters, and sure as hell no support checks. Bridget Wells had finally been able to obtain a divorce on grounds of abandonment, but it hadn't been easy.

So Jordan knew all too well that a handsome face didn't mean squat when it came to a man's character. Or a djinn's.

And she'd have to keep that sober fact in mind, no matter what.

Jordan came downstairs sometime after Hasan returned to the house. Her hair swung, shiny and sleek, down her back, and he couldn't tell if she'd slept and then made sure to tidy herself up afterward, or whether she hadn't lain down on the bed at all.

Something he shouldn't be wondering about, because the image of her asleep, her rich brown hair fanned around her on a pillow, made a surge of desire go through him. It was ridiculous, the way he'd begun to react to her. This was a human he supposedly wanted. Beautiful, yes, but not without flaws, like the light sprinkling of freckles on her straight little nose, or her brows, which were almost too thick for beauty and definitely in need of plucking.

Focusing on those imperfections made the heat in his body recede somewhat. As she came into the kitchen, where he'd been musing on the contents of the pantry and thinking of what he might like to summon for their luncheon, she offered him a hesitant smile.

"Was I asleep for very long?"

"Not too long," he replied. "I was just thinking of lunch—if you're hungry, of course."

"I am, actually. All that walking and fresh air, I guess."

She did look like she'd gotten a bit of sun, for her cheeks were faintly pink. He had to hope that she hadn't formed any new freckles.

Hasan didn't trust himself to inspect her face too closely, however, and so he waved a hand and produced several plates of sandwiches—another human invention that he'd acquired quite a taste for. These were modeled on a submarine sandwich he'd had in New York in 1967, piled high with deli meats and dressed with vinegar and oil.

Jordan's eyes widened slightly. "Those aren't subs, are they?"

"Yes. I had one once and enjoyed it very much. You like this kind of sandwich?"

Her gaze slid away from the plates of food, although a moment earlier it had looked as though she might actually start salivating. "I did when I was younger. But all that processed meat—"

Younger? He wanted to laugh at that comment. Humans had such a skewed perspective when it came to the passage of time. Voice casual, he said, "Eat it, or not. I doubt one such meal can cause too much harm."

He reached for one of the sandwiches and picked it up, and then took a rather ostentatious bite. Jordan hesitated for a moment before she gave a small lift of her shoulders and retrieved her own sandwich. Another pause before she bit into it. Then her eyes shut, as if she was experiencing a moment of pure ecstasy. Perhaps she was. How long had it been since she'd eaten anything remotely like that sandwich?

"Oh, my God, that's good," she said after she'd finished chewing. "Where do you even get the ingredients for something like that?"

Was it worth explaining to her that as long as the individual components existed somewhere, even if on a purely molecular level, a djinn could summon them and build them into anything he wished? Or should he simply pass it off as magic, which in a way it was?

"It is a skill of ours, to bring to us the things we need," he said. "That is all. However, with food, it has to be something we've once experienced, or we don't have the requisite information to re-create it. I never bothered to try sushi, and so I could not have any here to give to you."

"Too bad," Jordan replied. "Yellowfin sashimi was amazing. But this sandwich is also amazing."

"I'm glad you like it."

They were both quiet after that, eating in silence. For all her concerns about "processed meat"—whatever that might be—she ate the entire thing, barely leaving any crumbs on her plate. When she was done, she set the dish down on the counter by the sink. "Water?" she asked.

Another wave of his hand, and two glasses and a pitcher of water with slices of lemon floating in it appeared on the counter. This time Jordan's eyes didn't widen quite so much, but Hasan could tell that she still wasn't quite used to the way he could conjure things out of thin air.

She drank—quite a bit, more than half the glass—and then set it down on the tiled counter. "I'm going to check on the goats, let them out to forage a bit. If I need help rounding them up later—"

"I'll assist you," he said. "Don't worry about that."

"Thank you." For a moment it appeared as though she intended to say something else, but then she flicked her hair over her shoulder and disappeared into the laundry room. A moment later, the back door banged shut.

For a djinn, meal cleanup took only the blink of an eye. The plates disappeared, scrubbed and returned to their places in the cupboard, ready for dinner.

Hasan went to the back door and pushed the curtains out of the way. There was Jordan, making her purposeful way up the hill, long hair swinging behind her. Perhaps she should have tied it back out of the way, but he was glad she didn't. He liked to watch it blow in the wind, the sun picking out sparks of copper and dark gold within the warm brown.

With a frown, he let the curtains fall closed, then turned around and went back into the kitchen, and on into the dining room. He surveyed the table for a moment, trying to decide what he should conjure them for dinner. Something that would be a reward for watching over those goats.

Or at least, that was how he tried to justify it to himself. He had no doubt that the other djinn who'd assisted him in clearing this territory of humans would laugh at him now, amused beyond belief at the notion that Hasan al-Abyad, the inveterate mortal hunter, would be mooning over a human woman and trying to decide which meal would tempt her appetite best. And no one would probably laugh harder than Qadim al-Syan, who had taken a mortal woman for his own...especially when Hasan had been so adamant about how Qadim was betraying his kind by loving a human, albeit a beautiful one.

Well, Qadim would never have to know about Hasan's shame. Besides, this wasn't love, or anything close to it, but simply physical desire. What red-blooded male wouldn't have wanted someone like Jordan—assuming it was in his nature to desire women, of course? There was a great deal of difference between wanting to bed a woman and actually giving her one's heart.

It could become something of a game, he realized. To toy with Jordan, make her desire him. However, he would not use the djinn glamour to beguile her. While many of his people would not consider such a stratagem cheating, Hasan wanted to know he could entice her on his own, with no magical intervention. If he won and actually took her to bed, all the better. He could scratch the itch that had been building within him for some months, and then send her on her way. Perhaps he would finally reveal to her that Los Alamos did exist, that something more than a mirage waited for her at the end of her journey. Yes, that would be a magnanimous gesture. And no one would ever have to know that he'd sullied himself with a mere human.

That sounded like an excellent plan. Now all he had to do was put it in motion.

Chapter Eight

THE GOATS APPEARED HAPPY TO BE LET OUT IN THE sun. Since the grass extended all the way to the barn, they didn't seem inclined to wander very far, but got down to eating almost as soon as they were allowed to run loose. A weather-worn bench of faded gray wood that might have once been painted white had been set up against the western wall of the barn, and so she sat down there and watched her charges, although her mind was only half on what she was doing.

Her gaze kept shifting to the house. She couldn't see any sign of movement within, but that was to be expected. What did Hasan do with his time, anyway? It wasn't like he had to put much effort into cleaning up after lunch. Did he read? She'd gotten the impression that he liked to go hunting, to roam around the territory that was his, but she hadn't seen him leave the house, unless he'd done so while she was busy inside the barn with the goats.

The spot where she sat was slightly higher than the ground where the house was built. From here, she had a clear view past the river with its border of cottonwood trees and into town—such as it was. Chama really wasn't more than a wide spot in the road, with a few restaurants and stores, and a cluster of modest houses—and a few nice ones, although none of them as big and expensive as the home Hasan occupied. She wondered what the people who'd lived in Chama had done to support themselves. Worked on ranches in the surrounding area? There certainly wasn't any industry here, nor much of a retail presence. Maybe the scenic railroad had provided more employment opportunities.

She really didn't want to think about all those lives, now erased as if they'd never been. The whole time she'd been in Pagosa Springs, the survivors there had talked about what might be happening to the rest of the world, whether anyone else had managed to survive humanity's systematic destruction at the hands of the djinn.

Yes, they'd spoken to the people at Los Alamos during the weeks immediately after the Dying, had been told that there were also survivors in Southern California...but that had been years ago. Anything could have happened to them.

Cole, the pharmacist, had always argued that even with the Heat's insanely high mortality rate, there still had to be millions of people who were immune. Hunting down and killing millions of people just wasn't practical. But they'd seen what had happened in Colorado Springs before they fled. The djinn hadn't worried about whether something was practical or not. After all, they had all the time in the world.

Jordan remembered the cool, precise voice of Miles Odekirk, the scientist who'd first told them who their enemies were, that the people behind the world's destruction weren't truly human at all. He had been very matter-of-fact about the whole thing, which in a way made it easier to handle. He had a nice voice, not really a baritone, but too low to be a true tenor, calm and measured. She'd always wished she could know what he looked like. The other person who'd spoken to the Colorado Springs group a few times was a woman named Julia Innes. She also sounded good over the radio, never strained, her words spoken in a smoky contralto that had made the men within earshot stop to listen to what she had to say. Then again, they would've listened even if she'd sounded like a screech owl. The information she'd offered was too important to ignore.

They'd started discussing plans to escape to Los Alamos, since the group there had devised a way of keeping themselves protected from the djinn—some kind of device Dr. Odekirk had invented. Unfortunately, the djinn had descended before the Colorado Springs group had time to get much further than the planning stages. Of the hundred-odd people who'd gathered there, residents of the city itself, or refugees from Denver and Aurora, Pueblo and Alamosa, only twelve survived to flee into the mountains and forests, struggling their way west until they found a place to hide in Pagosa Springs.

Jordan crossed her arms and fought back a shiver, even though she really wasn't cold. The wind had died down a bit, and the sun was warm on her face. She knew she was—well, "safe" probably wasn't the right word. Hasan had been almost too friendly today, but not in a way that she could consider creepy or off-putting. No, it was a brisk, casual friendliness, which meant... what? That he'd gotten tired of being alone, and even having a pushy human around was better than nothing?

It seemed like a reasonable enough explanation. She just couldn't say whether it was true or not.

Because the goats took it into their heads right then to start moving away from the barn, headed upslope, she got up from the bench and followed them. If they got too ambitious about their wandering, then she'd probably have to go fetch Hasan to coax them back inside. As she'd told him, she didn't know the first thing about herding goats. Maybe waving her arms at them and yelling "shoo!" would be enough. Or maybe doing something that stupid would only make them bolt into the woods.

It was so quiet here, only the sound of the wind whispering in the grass, broken occasionally by a bleat from one of the goats. In the background was the murmur of the pines, and was that the cry of a hawk? Jordan squinted into the southwest, thinking that she saw a dark shape spiraling down from the clear blue sky, although she couldn't be absolutely sure. Pagosa Springs hadn't been this quiet; it wasn't as though anyone there made a lot of noise— actually, they did their best to keep the sound of their activities down in order to avoid attracting attention—but even so, you could usually hear someone talking in the background, or the ever-present murmur of the San Juan River.

From across the field, she spotted Hasan moving toward her. Since she'd been woolgathering, she really hadn't noticed when he'd left the house. For a moment, she wondered why he bothered to walk at all, when he could just blink himself to any spot on the property that he wished. Maybe he knew she still found that particular djinn talent a bit off-putting, and so had decided it was better to use his own two feet to get himself around. If so, that was very accommodating of him.

She waited as he approached, and then lifted a hand to give him a wave. He smiled, white teeth glinting in the sun.

Damn, it was so hard not to stare.

"It's been almost two hours," he said. "Do you want to bring them back inside now?"

Had it really been that long? She'd been so lost in thought, Jordan hadn't paid any attention to time passing. Funny how it became less important when you didn't have your phone to check every five minutes, when you didn't have anywhere you needed to be. Chores had to be done, but were accomplished much more fluidly.

"That's probably a good idea," she said. "I have a feeling they could do with some water."

"As could you, I would guess, after being out in the sun this long."

Yes, she was thirsty. And probably sunburned, too, although her burns never lasted very long, shifted over into a tan just a day after sun exposure. Still, she probably should have thought about that before she came out here without a hat or even a pair of sunglasses. If she was going to play amateur goatherd, she'd need to be more careful. With any luck, the Family Dollar in Chama would still have a few bottles of sunblock left around.

"Water sounds good," she agreed. "So let's get these guys back in the barn."

Hasan waved at the goats, and they immediately left off cropping the grass and began to trot toward home. Jordan fell in behind them, the djinn next to her. Already it felt strangely natural to have him at her side like that, even though she tried to tell herself that there was absolutely nothing natural about this situation...or about him.

"Do you eat duck?" he asked after they'd herded the goats into the barn, checked to make sure they had plenty of water, and then closed the door behind them.

"Yes," Jordan replied. Well, back in the day, her budget hadn't really allowed for too many meals of duck. She'd tried to avoid red meat, partly for health reasons, and partly because she knew that cattle production was really terrible for the environment. After the Dying, she didn't have the luxury of those scruples. She'd eaten what was available, even if it went against her personal principles. Not that the Pagosa Springs group had eaten any cattle. They'd come across a few cows and guarded them carefully, needing their milk—and the cheese and the butter they could make from that milk—far more than their meat. The woods had teemed with deer and elk, and the San Juan River was rich with trout. No one had wanted for protein, that was for sure. She glanced up at Hasan, who was looking forward, face impassive as usual. "Is that what you're planning for dinner?"

"I was thinking of it, yes."

"It sounds wonderful. I can't remember the last time I had duck." Which was true enough. Maybe it had been for Liam's birthday, the winter before the world changed? Everything had been a blur back then, life moving so quickly because of the rush to get things in order for graduation, to make sure she hadn't missed any necessary classes. It had all seemed so important, so life and death.

There was a joke.

"Good."

He was quiet then, as though musing on his dinner plans. Jordan knew she should ask him what exactly he intended by all this, whether he planned to keep her around until he got bored with her...but she just didn't have the courage.

She didn't know if she ever would.

———

Hasan had asked Jordan to change for dinner, and though she appeared surprised, she quickly hid her reaction by giving a not entirely convincing chuckle, then saying, "I suppose these jeans probably do smell like goat. And I need to get washed up anyway."

He had only thanked her, because agreeing with a woman that she did indeed smell like a goat was not precisely an auspicious way to start what he hoped would be an intimate evening. With any luck, he could get her out of his system quickly, and set his sights on a much worthier companion. Danya was out of the question, but he'd heard that Amina, who'd been given the area around a town named Vail, was quite beautiful, and not so far away that they couldn't form a temporary alliance. He would have to see.

As Jordan dressed for dinner, he set the table with a cloth of deep green brocade, and summoned plates of fine, translucent china, painted with gold around the rim. Goblets of gold as well, and a centerpiece of flowers that never grew in this northern climate—lilies, and orchids, and fragrant jasmine. He made the wax that coated some of the candlesticks disappear, so the brass gleamed as new. The curtains of heavy brown linen that hung at the windows were far too plain, and he whisked them away, replacing them with draperies in dark green, bordered with gold.

By the time he was done, the room seemed to shimmer, both from the candles he had lit everywhere, and the gold accents on the fabric and the dishware. The sun had gone down, but that was no matter, because here was an oasis of light and warmth.

Just as they had the day before, the stairs creaked, signaling Jordan's descent. Hasan turned so he might watch her walk down the stairs. He had conjured more outfits for her, but a djinn woman's garments of a close-fitting silken coat and filmy pantaloons rather than human clothes, and he'd wondered whether she would avail herself of them, or stubbornly cling to her jeans. To his delight and surprise, she had put on the silken coat in a warm wine color, trimmed in gold, and pantaloons striped in gold and wine and black. She'd pulled some of her hair away from her face so he could see the heavy gold earrings that swung back and forth, almost brushing her cheeks. As he'd gone about his preparations in the dining room, he'd also made a box of jewelry appear in Jordan's room, along with the clothing. He liked to see a woman adorn herself, although he hadn't been sure that she would dare to wear any of the jewels he'd provided.

Clearly, she hadn't shied away from helping herself to the jewelry, for as she came closer, he saw that she also wore a stack of thin gold bracelets on one arm, and a heavy ring of gold and tourmaline on the middle finger of her right hand.

It wasn't that she took his breath away. No, it seemed more as though he hadn't known how to truly breathe until he saw her.

Did he dare to compliment her appearance? Some women appreciated such things, while others were made uncomfortable by praise. Although he could not claim to know her well, Hasan thought that Jordan was probably one of the latter. Better to tame her slowly, rather than offer compliments that would embarrass her, and possibly make her uneasy.

"You found the clothes and the jewelry," he said, hoping that was a neutral enough subject.

The fingers of her left hand located the ring on the right and twisted it, while she brushed against the silken coat with the other. She did smile, but her expression seemed somewhat strained for all that. "Yes. The clothes are beautiful. And the jewelry...I've never—well, I don't think I've ever touched anything this valuable, let alone worn it."

"I'm glad you like it." He wouldn't mention that it was simple enough to summon these things, to have an image in his mind of what he wanted, and then to have it come to life immediately afterward. "Would you sit?" he asked, and pulled out a chair for her.

She looked around at the altered dining room, at the elaborate centerpiece that sat in the middle of the table. "This is quite a setup. Is it your birthday or something?"

"No. Djinn don't celebrate their birthdays."

"Why not?"

"Because we have so many of them."

Jordan seemed to absorb that reply, then nodded. "I suppose I hadn't thought of it that way." Without further comment, she seated herself in the chair he'd chosen for her, and was quiet as he pushed it closer to the table.

Once she was situated, he took his own seat at the head of the table and reached for the wine, a dry rosé from the Rhone region of what had once been France. After his people had exhausted the world's stores of wine, they would have to work on making their own, but that was no matter. That day was still a long ways off. And it would be amusing to put on the wine-maker's hat, to devote his time to that ancient art form. At least, as an elemental of the air, he would not have as much to fear when it came to ensuring that the fragile grapes survived. Any hint of a damaging frost, and he would be able to bring a warm, friendly wind to keep them safe.

"This is duck with a black currant reduction," he said as he set a portion on Jordan's plate. "And potatoes au gratin, and peas with butter sauce."

"You must have eaten in some amazing restaurants," she commented as she looked down at the food he'd given her. "That's how you know about these dishes, right?"

"Yes, I've experienced them for myself."

Something about her expression darkened. "So you spent time here in this world, enjoyed our food...and yet you still thought it was okay to exterminate the population?"

Of course he had thought it was fine. Just, even. A few well-prepared dishes couldn't negate the very real fact that if the djinn hadn't stepped in, this world might soon have become uninhabitable. Humans had been given a gift, and had squandered it.

He opened his mouth to say as much, then paused. Getting into an argument was certainly not how he wanted to begin this evening. After reaching for his wine glass and allowing himself a healthy swallow, he said, "It is far more complicated than that. Yes, I will admit that I—and all of my kind, really—have moved among humans, have experienced life in this world, even though we could not actually live here. It was denied us, and given to you. But because you did such a terrible job of being its stewards, we decided to take it back."

That comment seemed to hit home, because she didn't protest. Or rather, her jaw set, and Hasan could practically see the possible retorts swirling around in her mind. When she spoke, however, her words surprised him. "We did do a terrible job. Or rather, some people did. A lot of us tried to change things. I protested, I marched, I spent my summers planting trees. We're not all bad. Or at least," she added, her tone tinged with the sort of sadness he could barely comprehend, "we weren't all bad. There are so few of us left now that we can't really do any harm."

How he wished he could reach across the table, lay a hand on hers. He knew that she would only pull away from him, however, and so he forced himself to remain where he was. "The decision was not made lightly."

"Well, that's good to know." Eyes narrowed, she picked up her own glass of wine and swallowed. Then, deliberately, she set it down and began to push out her chair. "I'm not as hungry as I thought."

"Jordan," he said, making sure the note of warning was clear in his voice. "You will stay."

"Or what?" she flared. "You'll kill me, too? Lock me up in that room until I die?"

He hesitated, wanting to lash out but forcing himself to bite his tongue. Typical human exaggeration. He hadn't locked her up last night, or today. Hadn't he allowed her free run of his property, given in to her ridiculous demands about protecting those damned goats?

When he didn't reply, her mouth compressed. Voice shaking, she said, "You know what? I'm tired of being afraid."

This time she really did get up, and so Hasan

was forced to rise from his chair as well. He took a step toward her, and she flinched, but then stood her ground, her chin firm, as if daring him to do his worst.

Oh, no. He would not do his worst.

He hoped he would do his best.

Before she could move, he'd taken another step. His hands closed on her arms, and he pulled her close, bent his head to kiss her. Those full lips, so very soft, tasting of the sweetness and the tartness of the rosé, more exquisite than he could have imagined.

For just a second, her entire body went rigid. He sensed the unwillingness in her, the fear. If it persisted, he knew he would have to let her go, because while she no doubt believed him guilty of innumerable crimes, forcing a woman was not among those transgressions.

But then her mouth opened, and her tongue touched his. Heat arced through his body, and he stiffened at once, consumed with need for her. He took her face in his hands, kissed her over and over, felt her arms go around him and her full breasts press up against his chest.

Good God, he could take her right now, on the dining room table. Somehow he held back, though, knowing that a kiss was all she could allow herself to give for now, that a consummation would have to wait until she was ready. After one of the longest moments of his very long life, he lifted his mouth from hers, let her go so she might regain control of herself.

Her face was flushed, her chest heaving. Hasan had to force himself not to look at the enticing curve of her breasts, pushed to prominence by the tight silk coat she wore. Instead, he gazed down at her lovely features, at the slightly swollen curve of her lower lip.

At last she said, "I...wasn't expecting that."

"Did it displease you?"

"No, I—" She stopped herself there. After a long pause, she went on, her voice low, almost a whisper, "It should have displeased me, shouldn't it? I mean, there's got to be something wrong with me for wanting—"

"For wanting what?" he asked softly.

"For wanting you," she replied.

There could be no other response but to pull her close again, to kiss her once more, to experience her sweetness and her fire. He had thought that kissing a human must feel different from kissing a woman of the djinn, and yet he could sense no discernible difference, except that Jordan's kisses aroused him as no others ever had, perhaps because of their purity. She did nothing to hide herself, or her reaction to him.

He could think of no greater gift.

This time she was the one who pulled away. "I—damn. Damn it." She put a hand to her mouth, as though she somehow suspected it of being the source of her surrender. Then she looked up at him, confusion and fear and passion somehow all blending in her beautiful blue eyes. "What do we do now?"

"Nothing that you don't want to do," he replied. "For now, I would suggest sitting down and returning to our dinner."

Her gaze became disbelieving. "Seriously?"

"Yes, I am quite serious. I can prevent the food from growing cold for a while, but eventually it will become inedible. And," he continued, hoping he had not misjudged her, that his reticence would work for him rather than against him, "I was not sure you truly wished for matters to progress further than they have. At least not tonight."

"I don't," she blurted. "I mean—I don't know what I should do. But I think I need time to...to process all this."

"Then you shall have it. But I know I think better on a full stomach."

She offered him a watery smile at that remark, and seated herself once again. Hasan did the same, picking up his knife and fork and returning to his neglected meal. That seemed the best way to manage the situation—to go on as though nothing untoward had happened. As he'd said, he would allow her time to ponder this shift in their relationship, and how she intended to handle it.

In the meantime, they had a dinner to eat.

Chapter Nine

SOMEHOW JORDAN GOT BACK TO HER ROOM, BUT she couldn't exactly recall getting up from the table, or climbing the stairs. It wasn't that she'd drunk so much that she'd wandered upstairs in an alcoholic haze. In fact, she'd barely had a glass and a half, not enough to make her even tipsy. It wasn't the wine.

No, it was Hasan.

Granted, it had been a very long time since she'd kissed anyone, let alone done anything more. But Hasan's kisses—strong, passionate, intense—were so beyond anything she'd experienced before, she didn't know what to think. And that embrace had come out of nowhere. Nothing in what he'd said to her earlier that day, or how he'd acted around her, had given her any indication that he was consumed with desire and couldn't hold back any longer.

Jordan closed the door behind her and stumbled over to the bed, then sat down. Almost mechanically, she began removing the earrings she wore, then drew off the bracelets and the ring. She set them all on the nightstand, figuring she would move them to their jewel box in the morning. It wasn't as if she had to worry about anyone coming along and stealing them.

After she was done, she sat on the edge of the bed for a long moment. Dimly, she realized that her entire body was trembling. Shaking from the aftermath of those kisses—including the one he'd given her just before he said good night and went inside his own room—or from something else.

Guilt?

Maybe. No, probably.

How could she have let him kiss her like that? She was a traitor to her entire race. How could she have forgotten everything he was guilty of?

All right, to be perfectly honest, she didn't have an exact read of his crimes. However, she knew he had to have killed more than one person. Many people, probably, for no other reason than they were human and, according to the djinn, didn't deserve to live on this planet anymore.

The food she'd eaten at dinner flip-flopped in her gut, and she pressed her hands against her stomach, willing it to calm down. Throwing up right now was not an option—not because there wasn't a toilet handy, but because the last thing she wanted was for Hasan to hear her vomiting.

She cast a wary glance at the door. Yes, Hasan had assured her that he would not pressure her for more than she was willing to give—what a gentleman—but if he was capable of the crimes she thought he was capable of, could she allow herself to trust his word?

In his mind, those murders weren't crimes at all, no more than someone would think spraying for roaches was a crime.

Once again, her stomach roiled. How could he have such an opinion of other humans and still want to kiss her, want far more than that? Why was she different?

All right, she was pretty. Big deal. There had once been thousands—maybe millions—of women who were better-looking than she could ever hope to be. Even now there were probably survivors who could beat her in a beauty contest. And yet Hasan had zeroed in on her.

Only game in town, Jordan, she told herself.

He's probably just horny and figures you're an easier lay than some djinn woman.

She hated to think such a thing, but what else was she supposed to believe?

With an abrupt movement, she pushed herself off the bed and went into the bathroom, got down the silky nightgown Hasan had provided for her from the hook where it hung. Had he been plotting this from the very beginning, making sure she had sexy lingerie, or had he simply provided these types of undergarments because that was a stereotype of what human women wore?

Again, she had no idea. The nightgown wasn't as skimpy as it could have been, but it still had spaghetti straps and a long slit on one side. It probably wouldn't do much to keep her warm, once the weather really got bad. Not that she was planning to stick around that long.

But....

As much as she hated her weakness in succumbing to Hasan's kisses, she hated even more the thought of not being with him, of walking away. Which she knew was ridiculous. She'd never been the hopeless romantic type. She didn't believe in love at first sight—or at first kiss. Her parents' example had told her that chemistry didn't mean squat. Bridget Wells had been crazy in love with her handsome husband, and apparently he'd felt the same way, according to Jordan's Aunt Liz. And yet her father had still walked out. So much for a love for the ages.

No, she didn't love Hasan. How could she? She barely knew him. The most she'd allow herself to admit to was base physical attraction. Maybe if she'd allowed herself to unbend, to get closer to one of her fellow survivors in Pagosa Springs, she wouldn't be feeling so needy right now. That part of her had lain dormant for far too long, and now that Hasan had kissed her, held her in his arms, she realized how difficult it would be to snuff out the fire he'd kindled within her.

Difficult, but not impossible. She got in bed, turned off the lamp on the nightstand. Deep darkness filled the room, since the moon was still only a slender fingernail, nothing that could provide any real illumination. Even so, Jordan stared up at the ceiling, knowing that she should try to get to sleep, but not sure how she could accomplish such a task when her entire body felt so awake, she might as well have had a double shot of espresso with dinner, rather than a glass of wine.

You will sleep, she told herself. *You'll sleep, and then in the morning you'll figure out what to do next. Tell him you made a mistake, that you didn't really know what you were doing.*

She wasn't sure whether Hasan would buy that excuse. Her response to him had been just a little too enthusiastic. But she'd have to try. There was no way she could continue down that path, pretend that he was innocent, that his hands were clean. She couldn't live with herself if she allowed herself to be that weak. Not after everything she'd been through, all the people she'd lost.

And if Hasan didn't like it, well...he'd have to figure out a way to live with his disappointment.

All was quiet behind the door to Jordan's room. Hasan hadn't really expected anything else, but still he had to quell a stab of disappointment. Some part of him had hoped that she would leave her room and come to him, would continue what they had started. His body ached for her. If her kisses had been that sweet, he could only imagine what it would be like to feel her naked flesh pressed against him, to bury himself deep within her.

Perhaps such a thing might still come to pass, but he knew it would not be this night. He sat at the chair by the window and stared out into the darkness. His djinn eyes could see well enough, even though the night was nearly without a moon, only a thin sliver hanging low in the east to break up the starry expanse. Eventually he would go to bed and try to lose himself in slumber, but for now he only wanted to sit here and gaze at the dark landscape, and remember what it had been like to have Jordan Wells in his arms. Torturing himself? Possibly. Or rather, because he couldn't have the real thing, he might as well try to find what solace he could in memories of her touch, her taste.

He thought of her flare of anger at the realization that he'd found some things of value in her world, and yet still had no compunction about removing the very people who'd created the food and the art he'd admired. If he'd tried harder to explain himself to her, would he have succeeded? The djinn were a practical people— they had to be, to survive in the otherworld of their exile, barred for so many millennia from the world that should have been theirs. They saw no dissonance in enjoying a fine wine made by mortals, or a dinner prepared by a mortal chef. Some djinn collected works of art created by humans. At the same time, while admiring their creativity, the djinn also realized that humans could not be trusted. They could see beauty, and still think nothing of destroying it.

The same might be said for the djinn, he supposed. After all, the Heat did not spare the beautiful and the strong, but was egalitarian in its destruction. Being immune had everything to do with luck and a certain combination of factors in the blood, and nothing else. At least, that was what he had been told. Although he had assisted in cleansing the world after the djinn-created disease ran its course, he had not been involved in the mixture of alchemy and science that had given birth to the supernatural plague, for his skills did not lie in such things.

Just as well. The stains on his soul were bad enough without being one of the Heat's creators as well. No doubt Jordan would hate him if she knew everything he had done, all those he had killed. In the beginning, he had kept count, but the practice had begun to seem like vanity to him, notches on a belt rather than a necessary duty that must be performed. Although he had vowed not to rest until this territory was cleansed of every human soul, some part of him had been glad to be given land in such a remote corner of the world. He could come here and breathe in the clean air and watch the clouds passing overhead in a pristine sky, and try to forget the work that had consumed him for such a long time.

And then Jordan had come to him. Cruel fate, or the work of a whimsical God, one Who thought it was time that Hasan surrendered at least a small part of his heart? He couldn't say for sure. At any rate, he was not quite willing to admit that he cared for Jordan. Her company amused him, and her person excited him, and for the moment, that was as far as he was willing to go. It was enough.

Whether matters would stay that way, he couldn't begin to guess.

———

Awkward, Jordan thought as she came downstairs the next morning, drawn by the scent of coffee that emanated from the kitchen. She'd purposely put on jeans and a blouse and flats, ignoring the beautiful djinn clothing Hasan had provided for her. By wearing human clothes, she hoped she would send a clear message that she wanted to move on from the night before, that her allegiance was with her own people, no matter how passionate the kisses she and the djinn had shared the night before.

When she came into the kitchen, she found

him standing in front of the window there, staring out into the yard. That he faced away from her was something of a relief, because at least that way she had a little bit longer to gather herself, to tell her stupid heart to stop beating so quickly just at the mere sight of him.

"Good morning," she said, since she knew she needed to get that first dreadful moment over with.

He turned. His expression was somewhat somber, and he didn't smile when he saw her. Was that a good sign? Maybe it indicated that he wasn't going to push things.

"Good morning," he responded. "Coffee?"

"Yes, please."

Instead of using magic to fill a mug for her, he actually got one down from the cupboard and poured some coffee from a carafe into it. As he handed it to Jordan, she wondered why he sometimes used his djinn powers to accomplish ordinary tasks, while at others he acted just as human as she was. Pure whim? Maybe.

She took a sip of the coffee. It was strong and hot, and a good antidote to her muddled thoughts. Also, if she was drinking coffee, that meant she didn't have to talk.

Unfortunately, Hasan didn't appear ready to

let things go. "Are we going to speak of what happened last night?"

Jordan made herself look up at him. Those dark blue eyes—a shade she'd never seen in a regular human being—were fixed on her. A small shiver went through her body. "What's there to talk about?"

His eyebrows lifted. "I would think we have a great deal to talk about."

"I—" She drank some more coffee. The hot liquid burned its way down to her stomach, bringing with it a spurious sense of courage. "I think I made a mistake."

"A mistake?" His mouth twisted. "You did not appear to think you were mistaken last night."

"I know. I—" Again she had to break off her words, hunt for what to say. This had seemed so much easier when she rehearsed the exchange in her mind. Now, though, with Hasan in front of her, the mouth that had kissed her set and angry, the open robes he wore showing off way too much of his muscular torso—she found her resolve faltering. His presence was so very overwhelming. Desperately, she said, "It's just an attraction. That's all. Why would you want to have anything to do with me, anyway? I'm just a human. I'm beneath you, right?"

Hasan's hands tightened into fists, and the

muscles along his jaw line went hard. "Did I say that to you?"

"You didn't have to." Since he didn't respond, only stood there and watched her with narrowed eyes, she made herself go on. "Humans and djinn—how would that even work? It's impossible."

For the briefest moment, his gaze slipped away from hers. What was that about? She didn't know him very well, but it almost seemed as though he knew something she didn't.

Well, that wasn't so very unexpected. However, she didn't have the energy or the will to ask him what he was hiding. Better to walk away from this minefield.

"Anyway," she said, "I need to go check on the goats. I'm sure they want to be let out so they can have some fresh grass and sunshine."

"'Goats'?" he repeated, his tone disbelieving. "We have resolved nothing, and you're worried about goats?"

"I don't know what there is to resolve," she replied. "I just told you this whole thing is impossible. And yes, I am worried about the goats. They need us to help take care of them."

Having delivered that remark, she set her half-empty mug down on the counter and headed out the back door. His expression stormy, Hasan followed her. Clearly, he thought the matter was far from resolved, no matter what she might have to say on the subject.

The grass was wet with dew. Belatedly, Jordan realized she should have put on her hiking boots, rather than the flats she currently wore. Since there wasn't anything she could do about it now, she slogged grimly up the hill toward the barn, all too aware of the angry djinn who followed in her wake.

However, he didn't try to stop her as she went inside and greeted all the goats, who happily trotted out the door and into the field, kicking up their heels and bleating at one another before they settled down to filling their bellies. It was only after she'd shut the door that Hasan faced her, preventing her from heading out into the field to be with her charges.

"Tell me you felt nothing," he demanded, arms crossed.

That would be a lie, and she didn't want to lie to him. "Oh, I felt something," she said. "That isn't the point. The point is that you're lonely, and I'm lonely, and I suppose I would be naïve to think something like that might not happen. It doesn't change the fact that it probably shouldn't have happened. I mean, have you stopped to think past the two of us getting in bed together?"

Once again he frowned, the level black brows drawing together. "We did not get in bed."

"No, but that's sort of the next step, isn't it?" Perversely, Jordan felt relieved to get the topic out there in the world, rather than trying to dance around it. "Which is why I think it's better if we just stop now."

"And what about what I think?"

Oh, hell. From his somewhat arrogant manner, Jordan had already been able to tell that Hasan was someone used to getting his own way. It must really drive him crazy to have a lowly human telling him how things were supposed to go from here. On the other hand, she didn't want him to think that his own feelings or concerns didn't matter. They did—but they wouldn't change her mind, either.

"It's about what we both think," she said gently. "Of course it is. But if you stop to consider where this is going, where it possibly could go... well, then it's probably best if we both just walk away from it. I'm attracted to you, Hasan. You know that already, or I wouldn't have responded the way I did last night. But pure attraction isn't enough."

To her consternation, he reached out and took her hands, pulled her closer to him. She wanted to tear her fingers from his grasp, but she knew that would only anger him. Besides, she wasn't sure if she could even get away. He was so very strong.

"Walk away where?" he asked her. "Down an empty road to nowhere? You truly believe that is better than staying here with me?"

Right then, she didn't know what she believed. Los Alamos was a dream, a mirage. He was so very real—the grip of his warm fingers on hers, the dark hair ruffling in the wind, the curve of his lips, sensual even when he was angry with her.

"I don't know!" she burst out. "I don't know anything, except that you're driving me crazy! I should be vermin to you, shouldn't I?"

He went very still. "Oh, no," he told her. "Not vermin. Not you. Never you."

And oh, God, he was going to kiss her again, and she knew she wasn't going to stop him. In the next moment, his arms were around her, and he was pulling her close, his mouth on hers, hard, demanding that she open her lips to him. The richness of coffee touched her tongue as she tasted him. It was impossible to do anything except let him hold her, explore her mouth, make her more his with every passing second. Jordan knew she should pull away, but that was like asking light to escape a black hole. She couldn't do it. She was being sucked into him, and there was no escape.

A rumble of the earth. She thought it must have come from all the tremors passing through her body, but then a cool female voice interrupted them both, saying, "Really, Hasan? I had no idea you'd acquired a pet."

He pulled away from her. Jordan stumbled, then felt him put a steadying hand on her arm. She barely noticed. All her attention was focused on a woman who stood a few paces away from them, a hulk of a man—a djinn—immediately behind her. The woman was almost supernaturally beautiful, with long white-blonde hair that hung to her waist and ice-blue eyes. Her tight-fitting coat of blue and brown brocade showed off an impressive amount of cleavage, cleavage made all the more visible by the way she had her arms crossed under her breasts.

Hasan said something under his breath that sounded almost like a curse. Then he spoke aloud.

"Hello, Danya."

Chapter Ten

Of all the misbegotten timing....

Now that he was sure Jordan stood steady on her feet, he let go of her arm. A few yards away, Danya regarded the two of them, a smirk on her full mouth. Not smiling at all was her companion, whom Hasan vaguely recognized. Farid, that was his name, although Hasan could not recall his clan designation. He supposed it didn't matter.

Once again Danya's gaze flickered toward Jordan before returning to Hasan. "I see you've found something to occupy yourself in your solitude, Hasan al-Abyad."

"How I occupy myself is no concern of yours." Perhaps he could have found a way to be more politic in his reply, but truly, the djinn woman's uninvited presence set his teeth on edge. And for her to have appeared just as he was locked in such a compromising position with Jordan Wells.... He would not allow himself to groan in frustration, but Hasan did wonder why the universe would treat him so capriciously when there were so many other far more deserving recipients of its largesse.

"That is not true," said Farid, stepping forward so he was shoulder to shoulder with Danya. "Not when you are harboring a wretched human on your lands."

His baleful gaze fixed on Jordan, who pulled in a breath but stood her ground. Hasan was glad to see such courage in her, even if such courage was probably derived from having him standing next to her. Yes, they might have been arguing just before Danya and Farid appeared, but clearly the mortal woman thought of Hasan as her ally.

"'A wretched human'?" he echoed, matching Farid stare for stare. "Who she is and her presence in my territory are none of your concern."

"Oh, I know Farid feels otherwise," Danya said, one hand on Farid's wrist in a clear effort to restrain him. The hulking djinn subsided, even though he outmatched his companion physically. Watching the way Danya's fingers lingered on

Farid's flesh told Hasan all he needed to know about their relationship. He might have been acting as her bodyguard at the moment, but he was also far more than that. "You see, he's been hunting her ever since Pagosa Springs. He hated the idea that one of the humans might have escaped his cleansing."

"It was you!" Jordan burst out. Her eyes glittered with tears—whether of sorrow or anger, Hasan couldn't be sure. Possibly both. She turned toward him, face pale. "I thought I recognized him, but it was so crazy getting out of Pagosa that I couldn't be sure."

Hasan wished he could take her in his arms and comfort her. That would have to wait, however. Of far more immediate concern was getting rid of Danya and Farid. No doubt Danya was only trying to humor her companion, for she had never been the bloodthirsty type, but Farid presented a far more dangerous obstacle.

"She is under my protection," Hasan said, enunciating each word carefully so there could be no question as to his meaning. "And she is on my lands. You have no jurisdiction here."

"Oh, my," laughed Danya. "You are quite caught up in your little pet, aren't you, Hasan? Should I be offended that you went from me to...to *that?*"

Jordan bristled, but Hasan kept his focus fixed on Danya. "I have not 'gone' anywhere," he replied. "And she is not my pet."

"Perhaps. Do I need to remind you that harboring beings such as she is strictly forbidden? Any human who is not Chosen is fair game, after all." The djinn woman looked from him to Jordan, her gaze speculative, mouth slightly pursed. "And I can tell that she is not your Chosen, so really, your claim to be her protector is completely illegitimate."

"I will not comment on that," Hasan said, sensing how Jordan's eyes had narrowed at the term "Chosen." Of course she would have no idea what the phrase meant in this particular context, but she was an intelligent young woman. She would at least be able to tell that the term carried a good deal of significance. There would be questions later, he feared.

Right now, however, he had to do what he could to deflect Danya and her lap dog, get them away from here. The murderous glitter in Farid's dark eyes worried him. Hasan's erstwhile lover probably had him by the balls...literally...but that wouldn't mean much if Farid truly decided to finish the job he'd begun in Pagosa Springs. The other elemental controlled water, which could be tricky in a fight. Hasan thought he should be able to prevail—djinn battles had as much to do with wits as brute strength, and Farid did not appear as if he was overly burdened with intellect—but better to avoid a physical conflict at all.

"What I will say," Hasan continued, "is that I have offered hospitality to this young woman, and therefore she is protected, even if she is not Chosen. I believe the elders might have something to say about that, should you violate one of our oldest laws."

Neither Danya nor Farid seemed to care for that response; the big djinn made a low growling noise at the back of his throat, and Danya herself let out a huff of a breath, clearly exasperated.

"And I believe the elders will also have something to say about you harboring a human who is not Chosen," she said. "But I will leave that up to them. Unlike you, I have no desire to incur their wrath, and so I will leave your pet alone...for now."

"But—" Farid began, and Danya held up a hand, sapphire rings sparkling in the bright sunlight.

"Enough for now, my dear," she told him. "It is not our place to be judge and jury in this... although if the elders react as I think they will, you most certainly shall be the executioner. Let us go."

Another rumble of the earth beneath their feet, and the two djinn were gone as if they had never been there at all. Throughout the entire exchange, the goats had kept munching away at the grass as though they hadn't a care in the world. With that slight earth tremor, they looked up from their grazing and glanced around, then appeared to give the goat's equivalent of a shrug and returned to their meal.

Jordan, however, did not appear to be nearly that unruffled. Hands on her hips, she stared up into Hasan's face, consternation clear in every feature.

"What the *hell* is a Chosen?"

He led her back inside. Jordan submitted to his touch on her arm because, as much as she hated to admit it, her knees felt far too wobbly after that encounter with the two djinn. The way the one called Farid had stared at her—even now her heart gave odd little nervous thumps, as if it knew too well that the huge djinn had death in his eyes.

Hasan brought her into the living room and had her sit down, then made a glass of iced tea appear out of nowhere and put it in her hands.

How he'd known that iced tea was her comfort drink, she had no idea. She drank coffee in the morning to wake up, but it was iced tea she'd always turned to for the times when she didn't want water.

She definitely didn't want water right now. Actually, even though it was probably only nine o'clock in the morning, what she really wanted was a shot of something strong. Tequila, or maybe whiskey. Something to help with the shaking in her body.

"Drink," Hasan told her, and mechanically she lifted the glass to her lips and forced down a swallow.

"Will they come back?" she asked.

"Most likely," he replied, then went on quickly, no doubt responding to the panic she felt flare in her, "but not right away. I do not know if Danya truly intends to go to the elders, or whether she only said that to worry me."

"Who're the elders? Are they your government?"

"'Government' is too strong a term. The djinn do not have a government in the human sense of the word, for we mainly govern ourselves, following a code set up millennia ago. The elders step in when disputes cannot be settled between individuals or clans, or when that code has been egregiously broken, but only as a last resort."

Jordan absorbed that explanation without comment. *No government,* she thought. *The libertarians would've loved that.* Then she gave him a faint nod, and made herself drink some more iced tea. It did taste good, although when it hit her stomach, she realized she hadn't yet eaten anything this morning, that she was pouring all this caffeine on top of an empty stomach. Like that mattered. If she asked, Hasan would get her some breakfast. Later, though. Right then, she needed to again ask the question that had occupied her thoughts ever since she'd heard Danya utter the word.

"Hasan, what is a Chosen?"

He hadn't yet sat down, had hovered near her, as though he was a mortal man ready to run to the kitchen and fetch her something, even though of course he could just snap his fingers and get her anything she needed. Or maybe he simply wanted to be ready to bolt out of the room in case she asked something he didn't want to answer. Normally, he was so self-assured that it jarred her to see his hesitation, the way he stood there, hands at his sides, his eyes not meeting hers.

At last he seemed to decide that sitting down

was a better option. He didn't take a seat on the couch, however, but positioned himself on the edge of the armchair, fingers clenched on his knees.

For the longest moment, Jordan wondered if he was going to answer her at all.

Then he pulled in a breath, apparently a preamble to what would come next. Looking somehow past her, rather than at her, he said, "The Chosen are humans who were immune and saved from the cleansing that followed the Dying."

"'Saved'?" Jordan repeated. "Saved by whom?"

"By a group of djinn who did not agree with the majority of my people, who believed we were committing a great sin by ridding this world of the scourge of humanity. One thousand of them altogether. Each of them chose a partner from among the Immune."

"Wait...what?" She moved to the edge of the couch and set her glass of iced tea on the coffee table. The words Hasan had spoken were everyday English, but they didn't make much sense to her. If what he had said was the truth, then there was all kinds of precedent for djinn to be with humans. Maybe not *all* djinn, but definitely these conscientious objectors. "So they're lovers?"

His mouth tightened, but he didn't attempt to avoid the question. "Yes. They have settlements around the world, usually made up of approximately fifty to a hundred members of the One Thousand—the djinn who objected to the scourge—along with their partners. And their children, I suppose. I've heard rumors that they've begun to reproduce."

Holy hell. Djinn living with human partners, having families. It seemed impossible to her, but here was Hasan speaking of such things as though they were commonly accepted truths. Could he be lying? No, he had no reason to. Oh, he'd definitely sinned by omission, that was for sure. He could have told her of these Chosen earlier, when they were arguing and she'd said that humans and djinn couldn't possibly be together. He'd known the truth, even as he'd decided to keep it from her. For the moment, she decided it was probably better to ignore precisely why he'd made the choice to stay silent on that subject.

"Where?" she asked.

"The settlement here in New Mexico is in Santa Fe."

A nice place to end up, if you were lucky

enough to be among the Chosen. How had that happened? How had the djinn known where to find their partners? Was there some kind of lottery?

And, ticking at the back of her brain... *Why wasn't I Chosen?*

She wasn't sure if she wanted to know. Clearing her throat, she decided to follow a more neutral line of inquiry first. "Who are the Chosen? I mean, how did they manage to luck out when so many others were left to fend for themselves?"

"Most of them were between twenty and twenty-five of your years when the Heat swept over the world." Hasan paused there, as if he'd meant to say something else, then decided against it. "When the djinn selected their Chosen, they settled somewhat close by their human partners' place of origin. That is why the djinn in the Santa Fe community are there, rather than somewhere else—all their Chosen came from this part of the world."

"What about you?" Jordan asked. "I mean, you obviously don't have a Chosen, but you're still wandering around here in New Mexico."

His mouth turned down slightly at the phrase "wandering around," but his voice was even enough as he replied, "Although we didn't know right away precisely where we would eventually be settled, the elders did give us a general idea. That was how those of us who were not of the One Thousand ended up scattered around the world."

"The elders gave out the room assignments, so to speak?"

"Yes, they determined who would live where. Do not ask me how they made those decisions, because they did not share their deliberations with the rest of us. And it is not our place to question their judgment."

Jordan could tell Hasan didn't like speaking of any of this. His body was rigid, and he still wouldn't look at her directly. Well, fine. She didn't like the idea that a bunch of survivors had apparently been taken care of since the beginning of this post-apocalyptic nightmare, while she and everyone she'd known who was still alive had to fight and scrounge just to survive. And she supposed it didn't really matter why the elders had decided Hasan would be stuck here in northern New Mexico, while someone else might have been given a cushy setup in Malibu or Hawaii. That decision was between Hasan and the elders. For all she knew, he'd done something to piss them off. Considering what an arrogant bastard he could be sometimes, she didn't find such a hypothesis all that implausible.

"What about Los Alamos?" she asked.

"It is...separate from all this. The people who live there are ordinary humans, neither Chosen nor djinn."

"So it still exists."

"Oh, yes." His fingers tapped on the arms of his chair. Jordan was still learning to read him, decipher his reactions, but she could tell that the topic of Los Alamos didn't thrill him at all. "They have a way to keep djinn out of their territory, devices created by someone named Miles Odekirk."

"Dr. Odekirk?" The sound of his name cheered her up more than she'd thought it would. Since she herself had gone through so many travails over the past year and a half, she'd begun to wonder whether he had perished like so many others. But Hasan had made it sound as though the scientist was still alive.

"You know him?" Hasan asked, clearly surprised by her reaction.

"Well, 'know' is kind of a strong word. The group in Colorado Springs had some contact with the group in Los Alamos before we had to go on the run. I never talked to him directly, but I heard him speaking with the leaders of our group. I guess it's just nice to know he's still out there."

From the way Hasan frowned at this comment, Jordan got a distinct impression that the djinn was not nearly as impressed with Dr. Odekirk as she was. "As far as I know, he is there, along with the rest of the Los Alamos community. As you may have guessed, I would not precisely be welcome in that human stronghold, but word does get around nonetheless."

She supposed it would. No doubt the djinn had tried to come up with all sorts of schemes for destroying that bastion of humanity. It seemed that so far they'd been unsuccessful, however. That made things easier for her. If she left, she wouldn't have to worry about whether she was walking toward a mirage, a fantasy she'd built up in her head, because Hasan had just confirmed that Los Alamos and the people who lived there were very real.

Did she dare ask the one last question that preyed on her mind? She wouldn't bother to ask Hasan why he didn't have a Chosen; his comments about humans over the past few days told her exactly what she needed to know on that subject. Why he had seen her as a romantic interest rather than yet another human to be exterminated, she wasn't sure, but she knew that his overall opinion of humanity was extremely low. He had had no reason to be among the One Thousand, the djinns' conscientious objectors.

He'd been amazingly truthful with her so far. Maybe that encounter with his former lover and her thuggish new boyfriend had put the fear of God in him. Anyway, nothing ventured....

"Hasan," she began, then hesitated. This time he did look directly at her, his eyes so deep and dark and inky blue that she thought she might drown in them. Steeling herself, she went on, the words coming out in a rush, "Why wasn't I Chosen? I was the right age."

"I don't know."

"That's no answer."

With an impatient movement, he pushed himself out of the chair where he sat and went to the window. Outside, the day was sunny and bright, belying the slight chill carried on the breeze, the one that whispered of winter coming. "It is the only answer I can give you, Jordan. Where you lived—that was not part of my territory. I do not know the djinn who settled there, except Danya. I have heard that the settlement of djinn and Chosen is in Aspen—"

"Figures," she remarked, and Hasan raised an eyebrow.

"What figures?"

"Well, the djinn here are in Santa Fe, and the ones in Colorado are in Aspen. High-end vacation spots. Not exactly slumming, you know?"

"I suppose you have a point. That is neither here nor there. What I was about to say is that, if you wanted a true answer to your question, you would need to go to Aspen and make your inquiries there. Only they can provide you with the answers you need, because they are the ones who made that choice." His fingers played with the edge of the curtain for a second or two. "I will admit that I am rather surprised no djinn selected you. After all, as you pointed out, you would have been the correct age. And, in addition to that, you are intelligent and resourceful and beautiful. But, as you humans were fond of saying, there is no accounting for taste."

Beautiful. He thought she was beautiful. Oh, her college boyfriend Liam had told her that, and she'd heard more or less the same from her Aunt Liz—Jordan's mother had never been fond of heaping that sort of praise on her daughter, not wanting her to get bound up in her looks to the exclusion of all else—but for some reason, the praise meant a great deal more when it came from Hasan. A djinn, she thought, would be much more discriminating about such things. After all, now that Jordan had seen a djinn woman, she had a better understanding of the sort of standard she'd be compared to. Danya, even though she seemed like a serious bitch, was so beautiful she didn't look quite real, like a porcelain figurine come to life. Jordan was pretty sure that no one would ever compare her to a porcelain figurine.

In the end, though, what did it matter? If Hasan had been of the temperament to choose a mortal for his partner, he would have done so already. And apparently there were rules in place to prevent djinn from participating in the kind of intimacies the two of them had already shared, although she thought they really weren't guilty of all that much. A few stolen kisses. Were these elders such hard-asses that they couldn't let something so minor slip by?

Hasan moved away from the window and came over to the sofa, then sat down next to her. She liked the way the leather creaked from his weight, liked the warmth that seemed to flow from him. He didn't reach out to touch her, though, but kept his hands folded in his lap.

Jordan wasn't sure how she felt about that.

For some reason, tears stung her eyes. She blinked, kept her face angled away from him. Hasan already thought humans were weak, so the last thing she wanted was for him to see her bleary-eyed and weepy, especially when nothing had been decided between the two of them.

Or...had it? If he wanted to keep her around, he had to make her his Chosen. Danya had basically said as much, and the explanations Hasan had just given Jordan, those stories about the One Thousand and the various communities they'd set up around the world, also pointed out what appeared to be on irrefutable fact: A djinn could only be with a human if he—or she—made that person their Chosen. No loopholes, no workarounds.

"I was headed to Los Alamos when I came here," she said, not exactly sure where she was going with that remark, although she had a feeling it would place her on a path from which there would be no turning back.

"I guessed as much," Hasan responded. "It was the only logical destination for you."

Jordan knotted her fingers together. She wished she was still wearing the jewelry Hasan had loaned her the night before. At least that way she'd have something to fiddle with, something to focus on rather than his grave, handsome face, the way his shoulder-length hair brushed against his fine jaw. She wished she had the courage to turn toward him, to run her fingers through that heavy, glossy hair. But she didn't. She just barely had the courage to do what she knew must be done.

This had all been a fantasy anyway. An interlude. A handsome stranger, an isolated house. Never mind that the stranger was of an immortal race with a vengeful streak, someone who had the deaths of probably hundreds of people on his hands. She could never forgive that. She didn't want to forgive him, because in doing so, she might make it seem that those deaths didn't matter. Well, they did matter. Each and every one of them, those nameless victims of a cruel revenge.

Good thing all she and Hasan had done was kiss each other.

"It still is, isn't it?" she asked then. "I mean, the only logical destination."

For a long moment, he didn't reply. His fingers brushed the tops of his knees, restless. No jewelry for him—his beauty didn't need it, and the frame of his rich djinn clothing was enough. A faint gust of a breath, almost a sigh but not quite. "I suppose it is."

Why was it so hard to breathe? Her throat was thick, closed up, as though she was suddenly having an allergic reaction to a bee sting or something. That wasn't it, though; what choked her now was only those tears surging forth, weeping on the inside because she wouldn't allow herself to actually cry in front of him.

She pushed herself up from the couch. "Then I guess I had better pack my things."

"Jordan—"

She shook her head. "No, it's all right. I knew I couldn't stay—it was just...." Might as well stop herself there, since she didn't even know what she'd meant to say. Her brain was stuttering, trying to keep up, failing miserably.

Hasan rose to his feet as well. "I cannot let you walk all that way. Not with Farid out there, or those who might be in league with him. Let me take you."

"But you can't," Jordan protested. Somehow, it was worse that he was offering to help her. She wanted to be able to walk away, pack weighing on her shoulders but her head held high. In a few weeks or months, she might be able to forgive herself for beginning to care. "You told me yourself that Los Alamos is protected. You can't go there."

"Not all the way," he said calmly. His face was calm as well, features grave and perfect, like a statue come to life. "But I can take you to the borders of their protected territory. You can pass within the perimeter, and then I won't have to worry that Farid or anyone else might do you harm."

Did such concern mean that he cared, or was he only trying to spare himself the guilt of yet another death? It probably didn't matter one way or another. Besides, it was a very generous offer. She knew she should accept it. Hasan could blink her there, and then she would be with the Los Alamos group, among her own kind again.

It was where she belonged.

"Thank you," she said. "It would help a lot. I'll go get my things together now."

"Very well," he said. "I will wait for you here."

There really was nothing else to be said. She bowed her head, whether in resignation or acceptance, she wasn't sure, and turned away from him so she could go upstairs.

Thank God her back was to him. That way, he wouldn't be able to see the tears finally begin to track their way down her cheeks.

Chapter Eleven

THIS WAS ALL A MISTAKE. THERE SHOULD BE SOME way of taking it back. But he couldn't find the words to stop her, even as he knew in his heart this was the right thing to do. He'd vowed long ago that he would never commit to just one woman, and he certainly wouldn't change that vow for a human.

Jordan had wept; her eyes were reddened, her nose slightly puffy. Even so, she was almost heartbreakingly beautiful as she came back down the stairs, heavy backpack on her shoulders, hair tied out of the way so he could clearly see the smooth oval of her face, the determined little chin.

And now he had her in his arms again—not

to embrace her, as he probably should, but to carry her away from his home to a place near the perimeter of Los Alamos land. Actually, that border was now a good distance from the true border of Los Alamos itself, for in his reconnoitering, he'd realized that the community of survivors had expanded down into Española and some of the surrounding farmlands. Not to live, as far as he could tell, but to go down there during the day and work the fields, watch over the orchards and gather their fruit, so they would have enough to feed all the people they'd taken into their fold.

But they hadn't yet moved up into the canyon where the Rio Grande wound its way down from the higher country above. Here had once been tiny hamlets clustered near the bank of the river, and places where people cultivated small vineyards. Hasan decided it would be best to reappear there, in a wide spot in the road that had once been called Velarde, and where once there had been a busy wine-tasting room, a place where tourists had stopped on the way to Taos. From that spot, Jordan would only have to walk a quarter-mile or so to reach the first of the fields that the Los Alamos survivors cultivated.

When his feet touched solid ground again, he

held on to Jordan for a second or two longer than necessary. Only so he might recall the feel of her in his arms, the faint sweet scent of her hair. Had she noticed? He couldn't tell for sure, since her head had been tilted downward, as though she needed to focus on her grip around his waist so she might not slip off and be lost in that other space the djinn used to travel from place to place.

Then he let go, and she stepped away from him, using the pretext of straightening the pack she wore to keep from looking him in the face.

"Follow the highway," he said. "In a quarter-mile or so, there'll be a turnoff for a road numbered 582. Once you pass into the fields, you'll be in an area protected by Miles Odekirk's devices. Keep following that road, and eventually you'll come down into Española. I'm sure once you're there, you'll encounter someone from the Los Alamos group."

She looked down the road, her face in profile to him. Such a lovely profile, too, with its fine chin and straight nose. A breeze caught at the end of her ponytail, ruffling it. Down here, the air was warmer, the sense of onrushing autumn not so intense.

It took all the strength he had to remain where he was, to not walk to the place where she stood and pull her into his arms again, then take her back with him to Chama. But no, such thoughts were mere foolishness. He had no wish to be tied down to anyone, let alone a human who must become his Chosen. To spend the rest of eternity with one person? He could never agree to such a thing.

"Thank you, Hasan." Her voice was clear and strong, with no trace of the tears he knew she had wept not even an hour earlier. "I'll make sure to let them know of your kindness."

"There is no need for such a thing." In contrast to Jordan's words, his own sounded harsh, rough with an emotion he couldn't keep entirely at bay. "In fact, it is better if they know nothing of me."

Now she shifted so she was looking at him straight on. "Why not? It isn't as if they would go after you, would they?"

"No," he replied. "As far as I can tell, their main wish is to be left alone. But I didn't think you would want them to know about...." He stopped there, not sure that he wanted to try to describe what he and the young woman had shared.

A sad little smile touched her mouth. "It's all right, Hasan. I don't think they'll crucify me over a kiss."

And with that she turned away from him once again, and began to make her way down the two-lane road.

He stood and watched her go, his hands clenched into fists. Nothing would move him from this spot until he knew she was safe. Her slender form grew smaller and smaller as she walked away from him. The barrier was an invisible one, nothing that could be seen with one's eyes, and yet he was still able to sense the exact moment when she had passed through it, when she had come under the protection of Miles Odekirk's device, when science and technology were her new friends.

She was gone, and in their world now.

———

Don't cry, she told herself as she picked her way along the narrow road, probably already patched and bumpy even before the world ended, and now a mass of potholes and cracks. *Don't cry. You've cried enough already.*

And for what? It wasn't like she'd lost a relative, or broken up with a boyfriend of many years. She barely knew Hasan al-Abyad. Histrionics were entirely out of place here.

Even so, she had to blink fiercely, and sniffle

more than a few times, before the tears receded and she could see the landscape clearly. Down here, a hundred and fifty miles south of Chama, the aspens hadn't even begun to turn yet. The roadsides were riotous with desert broom and black-eyed Susans, their colors so warm, and yet still a signal that summer was gone.

Winter was on its way.

That didn't matter. By the end of the day, she'd probably be in Los Alamos. What it would be like, she had no idea. She'd never visited that part of the world. She knew her own impressions of the place were probably dead wrong. It was where they'd built the atomic bomb, and she imagined it as a sort of deserty spot with lots of ugly, drab 1940s-style buildings. Or wait…maybe she was thinking of the Trinity site. Wasn't that out near White Sands somewhere? Anyway, she figured she'd find out soon enough.

She wouldn't bother to reflect on the irony of creating all that destructive power, only to have a destroyer you didn't even know existed come along and really cause the end of the world.

The breeze here was mild, almost warm. It felt good, as did the sun that shone down upon her. Maybe it could help get rid of the chill that seemed to have descended into her bones, her gut, her heart.

No, don't think about that. Think about something else.

She passed empty houses, abandoned cars. Not a lot of trucks or SUVs, though, which she thought was strange in a rural area like this. It was so quiet that she could hear the Rio Grande rushing along in its banks, even though she couldn't actually see it at the moment.

This felt so exposed, walking along an empty road in full view of any djinn in the area. But no, there weren't any djinn, because Miles Odekirk had invented some kind of machine that kept them at bay. She thought of the ultrasonic bug zapper her mother had hanging in the patio of their Colorado Springs house and almost chuckled. Zap those djinn, just like pesky mosquitoes.

Jordan's smile faded soon enough, though. She really didn't want to imagine any harm coming to Hasan. What did Dr. Odekirk's device do, anyway? Hasan hadn't gone into any details. Was the field created by the machines fatal, or did it just make things so unpleasant that it wasn't worth it for the djinn to come around?

She doubted she would ever find out.

The road crossed the river to the west bank and began to run parallel to it. Now she could see the fields Hasan had spoken of, some of them left to run wild, some green with alfalfa, several of them filled with the dry ghosts of cornstalks, left to rot into the ground now that the harvest had been gathered in. This seemed like a lot of ground to cover, and Jordan wondered how many people actually lived in Los Alamos. Enough that they apparently needed all these fields. It would be good to eat vegetables again, maybe even a salad of real lettuce instead of that dandelion crap they'd been living on in Pagosa Springs.

Yes, there should be a lot to look forward to. Being with people again, people who could live semi-normal lives because they didn't have to worry about the djinn coming along and ruining everything. It would be quite a change from the life she'd led for the past few years.

Even so, she was saddened to see all the empty houses she passed by, mostly modest little one-story places probably built in the late '50s or early '60s, not unlike the home where she'd grown up. Her mother had been so proud of that house, so proud that she'd been able to afford it on her own, on just a waitress's wages and with a child to raise. The house still stood, of course, because the djinns' apocalypse wasn't the sort that leveled buildings or destroyed all the works of man, but Jordan knew she'd never see it again.

Something metallic caught her eye on the road ahead. At first she thought it was just another abandoned car with the sun glinting off its trim, but then she realized the object was moving. Not only that, but it was moving toward her. As she watched it come closer, she saw that it was a big truck—a Ford F-250, if she wasn't mistaken.

The truck slowed down as it drew near, then stopped altogether, the dust it had stirred up swirling around it like smoke. Its engine had a deep, throaty growl that seemed to find its way into her bones. She realized it had been more than two years since she'd heard a sound like that.

The door on the driver's side opened, and a man of medium height and build got out. He looked like he might be in his early forties, with sandy brown hair and blue eyes. And even though he was so perfectly ordinary in appearance, Jordan couldn't help staring at him, couldn't prevent herself from drinking in every detail, from the plaid shirt he wore, its sleeves rolled up to reveal tanned forearms, to the faded jeans and brown work boots. How could she not stare, when he was the first human being who wasn't in her little group of survivors that she'd seen in years?

It was true. There were survivors here. And they weren't djinn.

He was looking at her, too, studying her sturdy shoes and the pack on her back. Then he smiled. "Well," he said, "you must have come a long way to get here."

"I did," she replied. Her voice sounded a little throaty, but no doubt this stranger would merely think she was thirsty from walking along this dusty road. "All the way from Colorado."

His brows lifted. "That is a ways. How did you know to find us?"

"We—we talked to Dr. Odekirk on the radio, two years ago. But then we had to leave Colorado Springs, and the radio got broken, and—" Jordan had to stop herself there, knowing that if she started telling her story to this kind-faced stranger, she would probably dissolve into tears all over again.

"Hey," he said gently. "It's all right. You're safe now. I'm Brent Sanderson, by the way."

"Jordan Wells," she told him, and he held out a hand. She took it, was relieved by his firm grip, by the calluses on his fingers. That was the hand of a man who worked, and worked hard. So very, very human.

"Pleased to meet you, Jordan." He smiled at her, a friendly smile that had nothing in it but welcome. "You want a ride to Los Alamos?"

Why did the house feel so empty? It shouldn't feel empty. He'd lived here for two years without Jordan Wells anywhere around. She should have made it feel crowded, rather than the reverse.

Even so, the place seemed oppressively hollow to him. Well, it was a beautiful day. He might as well go out and enjoy it, especially since he knew that mild days such as this one would not last much longer. A few more weeks, and then the grass would be edged with frost every night, and the leaves would fall from the aspens, and the world would begin to close down, preparing for the long winter ahead.

Scowling, he went out the back door and headed up the hill toward the barn. If nothing else, he could let out those infernal goats, allow them to get their afternoon fill of grass before he locked them back up for the night.

Perhaps he shouldn't even bother. After all, the animals had survived on their own for months. Why should he intervene now?

Because of the wolves, he thought then. *The wolves are here, and winter is on its way.*

He could feel a frown beginning to etch itself into his forehead, and did his best to smooth his expression, even though there was no one around to see it.

Besides, he had promised Jordan that he would give the goats shelter. Would he go back on his word, so soon after she was gone?

Gone because you did nothing to stop her.

He reached the barn door and wrenched it open. At once the goats were there, pushing past him, happily finding their way to the grass, oblivious to his thundercloud of an expression. They milled about for a moment or two before they each located the perfect spot to have their lunch, and then set to.

Maybe he should get a dog.

Hasan ran a hand through his hair, pushing it away from his face. In general, the djinn did not keep pets, simply because the creatures' lives were so short in comparison to their immortal masters that sometimes it seemed as if they were here and gone within the blink of an eye. But still, a dog could be his companion for a while. A dog would help him forget about Jordan.

Oh, yes, I've heard that dogs kiss very well, he told himself, not bothering to contain the sarcasm in that inner voice. *That would be a very good replacement.*

What else could he have done, though? While he admitted perhaps it was for the best that he had not taken Jordan to bed, at the same time, he'd known he was walking down a dangerous road. Like an alcoholic human returning to the bottle, claiming that he could manage the addiction, he'd let himself grow far too close to that human female when he'd known the relationship could go nowhere.

Well, addicts could overcome their addictions, and he had no doubt that, like any other craving, his need for Jordan Wells would diminish over time, as long as he was resolute about keeping her from his mind.

The months and years would pass, and eventually he would not remember her at all.

At least, that was what he hoped.

Oh, yes, Los Alamos was so different from the way she'd imagined it that, if she hadn't seen the town limits sign they passed as Brent drove his truck up the steep highway leading into the mountain stronghold, she wouldn't have believed this was Los Alamos at all. All around were high plateaus with blazing aspens and dark pines and fir trees, while above brooded a dark peak that in the winter must be coated with snow. Houses on neat streets. A ball field where even now a group of kids were playing tackle.

The sight made tears start to her eyes once again. Kids playing outside, with no worry about being attacked...unless you counted getting pummeled by a truly spectacular flying tackle.

"It's a lot to take in, I'll admit," said Brent, who'd obviously noticed her reaction to the sights outside the truck's windows. "Especially if you've been in the wilderness for a while."

In the wilderness. That was a good description for it. She'd been wandering a long time. Pagosa Springs had always felt like a way station, even though she and her group had spent more than a year and a half there. It wasn't permanent, though. Pretty much everyone had lived like she had, with their bags packed, ready to go at a moment's notice. In the end, though, those preparations still hadn't saved them.

No, don't think about that. Jordan supposed she'd have to tell her story to someone at some point, but she didn't want to dwell on it now.

"Since you mentioned Dr. Odekirk, I figured I'd take you to see him first," Brent went on. Now they were passing through what looked like the main part of town, with neat little shops and offices bordering the streets on either side. There was even an enormous Smith's supermarket with actual cars and trucks in the parking lot, as though the people who lived here still used it as their center of commerce. She'd have to ask about that. Did they have electricity? What kept the food cold? Where did they get the gas to power their vehicles, including the ones that must bring the produce from Española up to the hilltop settlement?

"Is Dr. Odekirk in charge here?" Jordan asked.

"No, not exactly. Shawn Gutierrez—he's a former fireman—keeps things running day to day. But Miles Odekirk is our resident genius, and we wouldn't be here without him. I just thought you'd feel more comfortable talking to him to start."

Would she? Jordan didn't know. Maybe if she heard his voice, something familiar, then this wouldn't feel so strange. Since she could tell that Brent was trying to be helpful, she nodded and managed to smile. "Sure. I'm just glad that he's still around. That all of you are."

"Well, I can't say we didn't have a few times when it was touch and go, and a little too close to comfort for me, but in the end we managed to get through it all." Brent drove through what had once been the guard shacks that watched over the entry into the Los Alamos labs proper; now they appeared to be abandoned, as though the current residents of the town knew they didn't have to worry about anyone infiltrating the facility. Who would come here? All the survivors in the area already lived in town, and no djinn could get anywhere close.

Besides, it sure didn't look as if any full-scale research was going on at the labs. Brent guided the F-250 along an access road and then turned off into a parking lot, one that was entirely empty except for an older-model Subaru. They pulled up next to it, and he turned off the engine.

"Miles still works here," Brent said. "He and his wife Lindsay."

The mention of a wife startled Jordan. Not once during his interactions with the Colorado Springs group had Dr. Odekirk made any mention of a wife. Maybe he'd thought her existence wasn't relevant to their conversations. And also, what were the odds of a man and wife surviving together? Millions to one?

Her expression must have communicated something of her surprise, because Brent said, "They've been together for about a year and a half now. Their first child is going to make an appearance in the real near future, too, although that doesn't stop Lindsay from working with Miles. I swear, they're probably going to deliver that baby right here at the facility. Anyway, come along. I'll take you up to their lab."

He guided her into the building and into the stairwell. Jordan noticed that they had electricity here, although apparently not enough to power the elevators. They climbed four flights of stairs. Good thing Brent had given her a lift most of the way, because if she'd had to hike up this many floors after walking all the way from Velarde, she probably would have keeled over.

They emerged into a hallway that could have been from any vintage office building in the world—drab off-white walls, dingy beige linoleum on the floors. Here were more fluorescent lights overhead, as there had been in the stairwell. However, only every third fixture was lit, obviously another energy-saving measure. Which was fine—the lights provided enough illumination for her to see where she was going.

Brent paused at a door about midway down the corridor. It stood open, letting Jordan see that within was a largish space, with tables lining the walls and several more in the middle of the room. At one end, an enormous whiteboard covered the entire wall. That whiteboard had every square inch filled with complicated formulas and diagrams. She'd had to take some chemistry and physics to get her environmental studies degree, but she couldn't begin to guess what she was looking at.

Two people occupied the room. One was a tall man with brown hair and wire-framed glasses, thin-faced but not unattractive. The other was a woman probably three or four years older than Jordan, extremely pregnant, and also extraordinarily good-looking, with long dark blonde hair, the kind of warm-toned skin that seemed to have a perpetual tan, and striking green eyes.

Brent cleared his throat, because the couple were currently bent over a complicated wiring harness on one of the tables and didn't seem to have noticed that they had visitors. The woman looked up first, the small frown she wore erasing itself as she seemed to recognize Jordan's guide.

"Hey, Brent," she said. The man next to her continued with his work; the sharp scent of warm solder drifted toward Jordan's nostrils. The pregnant woman didn't nudge her companion, because that might have damaged the work he was doing, but she did lean in and say, "Miles, we have visitors."

"In a minute," the man said, his tone just this side of testy.

Annoyed as he sounded, Jordan still recognized his voice. The woman—who must be

Lindsay—had already called him Miles, so Jordan knew he must be the scientist in question, but even without that, she would have known who was speaking.

"Sorry," Lindsay said. "We just worked out this new configuration, and—"

"It's fine," Brent told her. "Lindsay, this is Jordan Wells. I found her coming down the 582 outside Velarde."

Lindsay's gaze sharpened. She might have the face of a cover model, but the brain behind that face apparently was no slouch, either. "You've survived all this time? On the outside?"

"Yes," Jordan said. "I was with the group in Colorado Springs."

That revelation made Miles Odekirk set down his soldering iron. Behind the glasses he wore, his blue-gray eyes were nearly as piercing as his wife's. "Colorado Springs? We lost contact with you twenty months ago. What happened? Did your equipment malfunction?"

"Not exactly. The djinn found us, and we had to run. We tried to bring the radio equipment with us, but it got broken. We ended up in Pagosa Springs, but we didn't have any way of communicating with you, of letting you know that some people had survived."

"How many?" Dr. Odekirk asked. He pushed

his glasses up with one long finger, although with his thin nose, they'd probably just slide back down again soon enough.

Jordan swallowed. "There were about a hundred of us in Colorado Springs. Only twelve made it to Pagosa."

The scientist and his wife exchanged a glance. Lindsay reached over and touched her husband's hand, as though letting him know she wanted to be the one to speak next. "How long were you in Pagosa Springs?"

"For a little more than a year and a half. But...."

No one said anything, only waited for Jordan to go on. They probably knew exactly what had happened, but they wanted to give her the time to get to it on her own.

"But the djinn eventually found us there. I ran—everyone ran. For some reason, they didn't catch me. I headed south. I didn't know what else to do. I knew that you were here...or at least, I hoped you'd still be here." Jordan's voice caught and she swallowed. It was all right. No need to break down now. She was safe. A gulp of air, and she went on, "I knew it was a long shot, but I had to try."

"You walked all the way from Pagosa

Springs?" Lindsay's voice wasn't so much disbelieving as surprised.

Jordan hated to lie to her—to all of them—but she wasn't ready to explain the few days she'd spent with Hasan al-Abyad. Maybe in time, but for now.... She nodded. "I hid in the trees when I could, in abandoned houses or barns or whatever else was available. I didn't see any djinn. Maybe they thought they'd killed everyone and didn't even realize I'd gotten away."

Through this recitation, Miles Odekirk had listened in silence, thumb and forefinger absently rubbing at his chin. "Did you see anyone at all? What about near Taos?"

Why he was concerned about Taos, Jordan had no idea. And why would he think she'd come that way at all? She would have had to jog miles and miles east to do so, and that would've added days to her journey.

It's because of where Brent found you, she told herself. *If you'd stuck to your original route, and walked the whole way instead of having Hasan take you to Velarde, you would've come down through Abiquiu and into Española that way, and there would've been no reason for you to be anywhere near the 582.*

"No one," she lied. "It's all empty. It's like the djinn came and went or something."

"Oh, they're still here," Miles said, although she didn't detect any condemnation in the comment. He was simply stating a fact, nothing more.

"And so are we," Lindsay put in. "Anyway, I'll bet Jordan is hungry and tired and would rather have the interrogation later after she's had a chance to rest."

"It's okay," Jordan began, but Brent only nodded.

"Lindsay's right. I can take her to see Shawn, get a place set up for her."

"Sounds great." Lindsay paused, one hand resting on her enormous belly. She really did look like she was going to pop at any second. No wonder Brent had opined that she might end up having the baby here in the lab. "And afterward, Miles and I can take her to Pajarito's."

"'Pajarito's'?" Jordan echoed, somewhat mystified.

"It's a restaurant here in town. We've kept it open so we would have a sort of gathering place, a spot that still feels like the old days. Anyway, it's mostly veggie stuff now, since livestock is too valuable for us to slaughter, but they still make a mean plate of truffle fries."

French fries. And a restaurant, a restaurant filled with people who were doing their damnedest to make sure the world didn't slide into oblivion.

It still hurt to think of how Hasan had let her go, but right then, Jordan felt a tiny spark of hope. Maybe she would survive this. Her heart would mend, and she'd go on.

It seemed like she'd come to the right place to heal.

Chapter Twelve

HASAN FELT DANYA'S PRESENCE IMMEDIATELY. Although djinn considered it very bad etiquette to blink themselves into another djinn's home without permission, that didn't mean they couldn't still precipitously appear on one's doorstep.

When she knocked, he was of half a mind to ignore her. She was not possessed of a great deal of perseverance or persistence, and so he guessed she would leave if he made her wait long enough. Then again, if he was so unconscionably rude, then she would become angry, and might send her minions against him. That sort of inter-djinn scuffle was not the kind of thing the elders would appreciate, but neither would they be likely to interfere. In general, they preferred to be hands off unless given no other choice.

Scowling, he pushed back his chair and went to open the door, leaving his half-eaten dinner behind him. There she stood on the porch, a gossamer veil of pale blue silk covering her white-blonde hair and drifting down to her shoulders. Hasan knew that covering was only for effect, as such a flimsy fabric would be of little use in warding off the chill of an autumn evening. Besides, djinn couldn't even feel the cold the way humans did. But that veil did look very lovely, just kissing her skin, its ends waving slightly in the breeze.

Once upon a time, he might have been affected by such artifice. Now it just annoyed him.

"What do you want, Danya?"

A perfectly arched eyebrow lifted. "Why, to come in and speak with you. There is no need for you to be so rude."

In answer, he stepped out of the way and swept one arm toward the living room in an exaggerated gesture of welcome. "Well, then. Do come in, Danya."

Her mouth pursed, but she gave no other response, besides doing as he had bade her and entering the house. He shut the door behind her;

a fire crackled in the hearth, and he saw no need to let in any more cold air than necessary, even if its presence wasn't enough to unduly trouble him.

"Ah, I've interrupted your dinner." She paused a few feet away from the dining room table and appeared to take in the single place setting at its head. "Dining alone?"

"Yes," he said shortly, moving past her so he could pick up his neglected wine glass. "Some claret?"

"That would be splendid. Thank you."

As soon as she had spoken, another cut-crystal wine goblet appeared on the tabletop. He picked up the matching decanter and poured a measure of claret into the glass, then handed it to her. "*Salut.*"

Danya raised her glass. "*Salut.*" After sipping at the wine, she said, "I will confess that I did not expect to find you like this, Hasan."

"Indeed? And how did you expect to find me?"

"Why, dining with your charming human pet, of course." Danya's silver-blue eyes, ringed in dark lashes, widened in what Hasan assumed the djinn woman thought was an expression of innocence. "You were so protective of her that it didn't even occur to me that you might send her away."

While Hasan knew that he owed Danya no explanation of what had happened, he also knew the easiest way to get rid of her was to give her some information. Not all, of course. But if she understood that Jordan was now gone, she would have no reason to come around here and bother him again. He had not spent a great deal of time with Danya, but he knew she had a jealous streak. She had not liked seeing her former lover with another woman...especially a human woman. No, she hadn't wanted him for herself, since she preferred someone who would worship her wholeheartedly, if even for only a short period.

"Would you like to sit?" he asked politely.

"Thank you, I would."

She pulled out a chair and sat down—it was not djinn custom for the men to pull out chairs for their women, for of course their powers tended to be equally matched—and Hasan resumed his own seat at the head of the table. Luckily, he had been nearly done with his dinner, and so he snapped his fingers and whisked the dirty plate and its accompanying silverware back to the kitchen.

"If you are hungry, I can get something for you."

"Oh, no," Danya said. "I have already eaten.

This wine is lovely, though." She took a large swallow, slightly larger than would be considered decorous, and put her glass down on the table-top. "So, do tell me. What happened with you and your captive human?"

"She wasn't my captive," Hasan countered, although that wasn't precisely the truth. At the beginning, Jordan most certainly had been his prisoner. A prisoner who was not confined to her room, and who had free run of his property, but they had both known he would not allow her to leave the lands that were his. A cell was still a cell, even if it encompassed acres.

A curl of Danya's full lips. "If you say so. Leaving that aside...it did seem that the two of you were quite cozy. What changed?"

Since Hasan hadn't yet wrestled that notion into submission yet, he wasn't about to give Danya a full or true answer. Even to admit that he wasn't ready to take a Chosen would be enough to tell the djinn woman he cared enough for Jordan to consider such a thing at all, and he did not wish to provide Danya with such intimate insights. "She was human. What other reason did I require?"

"Well, it certainly hasn't stopped our friends up in Aspen...or down in Santa Fe, for that matter. But of course, they were resolved from the beginning to have their little human charges, whereas I know you never subscribed to the notion that humans were worth saving at all. This is why I find it so...fascinating...that you could abandon your principles enough to allow yourself to be intimate with one of those creatures."

Creatures. Not so long ago, Hasan might have used the same epithet to refer to humans. Or rather, he might still find it appropriate in certain circumstances, but not for Jordan. No, she was far too exquisite to be called a creature.

"Momentary madness, I assure you. And when I woke from that madness, I realized the only thing I could do was send her on her way."

"Oh, surely not the *only* thing." Danya's eyes glinted at him over the edge of her glass goblet, which she'd once again lifted to her lips. "You could have gotten rid of her, just as you have so many other humans."

Never. Hasan knew he could not give that kind of an impassioned reply, and so he reached for his own glass of wine and allowed himself a sip. "I did not think it quite sporting, considering the circumstances. It was enough to crush her spirit by telling her that her infatuation with me was ridiculous, and that she needed to go."

There. He was rather pleased with himself

for offering those words, for they did make it sound as if the kiss that Danya and Farid had witnessed was far more Jordan's idea than his. Never mind that simply recalling the expression on her face as she turned away from him and began to walk toward Española was enough to make his throat constrict with remembered pain.

Apparently, Danya thought his comment convincing enough, for she leaned back in her chair and gave him a lazy smile. "Ah, so she threw herself at you. I suppose I can forgive her for that indiscretion, as you can be rather irresistible, Hasan."

"Oh, I think not," he said lightly. A gleam had entered Danya's eyes, one he did not overly care for. He did not wish to flirt with her, or try to rekindle what they had shared. That fire had died and could never return to life. He had already had enough of her selfishness, the way she measured others only in terms of their usefulness to her. "I think more that she mistook my kindness, and so believed there might be something between us."

"Misguided of her, especially when you consider that in her isolation, she can't have known about the Chosen, that some of our people have taken human lovers."

It wasn't worth pointing out to Danya that the

Chosen were hardly the first humans to be intimate with djinn. No, his kind had dallied with mortals for millennia—never in permanent relationships, of course, but in nights of passion that the humans often believed were only vivid dreams, or the work of lascivious demons. However, the kind of pairings the Chosen now shared with their human partners...those were entirely different, joinings that were meant to last for eternity.

Eternity. He wanted to laugh at their naïveté. They might be happy for a few years, or even decades, but the djinn had never been constant. Not when faced with forever. And that was also why he knew he must send Jordan away. He could see how the attraction they shared could be parlayed into a few seasons of passion. Eventually, though, he would have wearied of her, just as he'd wearied of every other woman he'd ever been with. Such an outcome was inevitable.

"No, you are right. She was young and innocent, and not terribly clever about such things. Truly, she had already begun to weary me."

"And where is she now?"

The question sounded almost innocent, but Hasan knew better. If he told Danya that Jordan was making her weary way south along the highway, he had no doubt that Farid would be sent to dispatch her. Of course Danya would not get her own hands dirty, but she would also have no compunction about getting her current lover to do the deed.

In this, however, it was easy enough to tell the truth. Jordan was in human territory, protected by the devices Miles Odekirk had invented. Neither Danya nor Farid could bring her any harm there.

"In Los Alamos," he said. Very well, that was a small lie, as he did not know for sure that Jordan would have yet reached that human stronghold. Although he had taken her most of the way, it was still a long walk from Velarde to Española, and longer still from there to Los Alamos. There had been no guarantee that she would encounter any of her own kind during that journey, although he'd hoped she might, for her sake.

Danya's nostrils flared in dislike. "Pestilential place. I'm surprised the elders haven't come up with a way to blast it from the face of the earth."

Not too terribly long ago, Hasan had been of the same opinion, although he'd never considered that the elders might try to do something about the human holdouts there. In general, they were far too hands-off for that sort of action. Now, of course, he could only be very, very glad that Los Alamos existed, for it could be a place of refuge for someone he'd begun to care about.

He allowed himself a small lift of the shoulders. "Perhaps. I am somewhat of the opinion that the elders believe if those humans were clever enough to come up with the means to protect themselves, then they should be left alone."

Danya's eyes flashed with scorn. "That does sound like the sort of capricious reasoning they enjoy inflicting on the rest of us. At any rate, it seems as if your little pet has found herself a new safe cage. I hope she enjoys it."

The implication being, of course, that living in such a confined place, surrounded by other limited beings, was a prison sentence of its own. Hasan wouldn't bother to argue with Danya. Let her think what she wished...especially if it meant she would no longer attempt to pursue any kind of petty vengeance against Jordan.

For himself...well, he hoped she would be happy.

She deserved it.

———

"God, for the day when I can drink beer again,"

Lindsay said, watching enviously as Jordan lifted her pint glass of brown ale and took a sip.

"I thought pregnant women could drink beer," she replied.

Miles frowned and pushed his glasses farther up his nose. He only had a glass of water in front of him, although Jordan didn't know if that was out of deference to his wife's condition, or because he simply didn't drink at all.

She had a feeling it was the latter. Even on short acquaintance, Miles Odekirk hadn't struck her as the type of person to worry about whether a certain behavior was polite or not. He was far too focused on his work.

The two of them made such an odd pair, the strikingly beautiful woman in her mid-twenties and the gawky scientist who had to be at least ten years her senior. Maybe once Jordan had a chance to know Lindsay a little better, she'd find the courage to ask exactly how the two of them had ever gotten together.

"Actually, the recommendation was beer for *nursing* women," Miles said. "And even that recommendation came under some fire. The risk/benefit analysis was somewhat flawed."

"Well, we'll discuss it again after this critter arrives." Lindsay winced, and put a hand on her belly. "Which, judging by the way he or she kicks, should be any day now."

"Go for next Tuesday, if you can," Brent put in. He'd tagged along because Jordan had asked him to. She wasn't even sure why exactly, except that it would have felt awkward for this group to only include her and the Odekirks. At least this way they were balanced. And Brent was the first person she'd met from this community. She'd only been here a few hours, and she wanted someone around who was at least semi-familiar to her. Anyway, she'd explained the request by saying that Lindsay and Miles might have a few questions about where Brent had found her, and luckily, he hadn't asked for any real details, had said it was no problem and he'd be glad to come along.

"Why Tuesday?" Lindsay asked, nose wrinkling. "Is this some silly horoscope thing?"

"No," Brent replied. He was too pleasant-faced to look outright offended, but he clearly wasn't thrilled by Lindsay's question. "That's the date I chose for the pool."

"The pool?" Miles looked confused. "What pool?"

"The baby pool," Brent explained. "A bunch of us have a little bet going to see when the kid shows up."

Even though Jordan didn't know most of the players involved, she couldn't help chuckling. "What do you bet? I mean, do you use money here?"

"No," Lindsay said. She didn't appear offended by the revelation that people were taking bets on when her baby would arrive—just the opposite, in fact. Her green eyes danced with laughter, even while Miles scowled and reached for his glass of water. "Pure barter system, although really, most everything just goes into a common pot. But people still have small items they can exchange, whether for other goods or for labor."

"Mitch put in that last six-pack of Guinness he's been hoarding," Brent said. "So it was worth it for me to try."

"What did you bet?" Lindsay asked.

"A month of shoveling someone's sidewalks and driveway this winter."

"Ouch. Then I hope you win."

"If I do, I'll give you one of those cans of Guinness."

"That was it," Jordan put in, as something she'd read years ago popped back in her head. "It wasn't regular beer—it was Guinness that was supposed to be good for nursing mothers. Something about the nutrients in the malt."

"Hmm." Miles didn't seem overly impressed by this addition to the conversation, but at least he didn't try to outright contradict her.

The food came then—the promised French fries, and also a very good green chile corn chowder. Serious comfort food, Jordan thought, so good that the absence of meat wasn't really that big a deal. Did they not do much hunting here? The forests above town looked as if they should have a decent deer population, and possibly elk, too. The Rio Grande wasn't that far away, either. A steady diet of fish could get old, but at least it provided necessary protein.

Maybe at some point she'd be able to ask. It was possible that the restaurant didn't have items like that on its menu because the supply couldn't be guaranteed. Anyway, she'd had plenty of meat and game bird and fish at Hasan's home in Chama. She used to go meatless all the time in college, often for as much as a week or more.

She didn't really want to dwell on the time she'd spent with Hasan, though. The best thing she could do was keep him pushed out of her mind. Eventually, her memories of him would fade, and he'd be only one out of a series of interludes in her life, nothing to get emotional about.

"Did Shawn get you settled in?" Lindsay

asked, once she'd put down her soup spoon and looked ready to take a break so she could talk.

"Yes," Jordan replied. "He and his girlfriend Katelyn were very helpful. They gave me one of the vacant townhomes in the Pine View complex, and said I should take a couple of days to get settled in before they put me to work."

"Oh, yes, everyone works here," the other woman remarked. She gave her husband a sly sideways glance and added, "Some of us more than others, I suppose. But they've got all these charts and tables and schedules to keep track of who's doing what, and where."

"What did you do before?" Brent inquired, shifting slightly in the booth so he could look at Jordan a little more directly.

Actually, everyone seemed to be looking at her, and she could feel an awkward flush rise to her cheeks. "Not much. I mean, I'd graduated a few months before the Dying, but I couldn't seem to find any work in my chosen field, so I was working as a waitress."

Lindsay gave a sympathetic nod. "I had a lot of friends in that boat. I think part of the reason I was hanging on and getting my master's was that I didn't feel quite ready to go out and face the cruel world. Then the djinn sort of took that worry out of my hands."

"I thought about getting my master's, but I really needed to get to work. Too bad no one wanted to hire me."

"Was it really that tough?" Brent asked. "I guess I had no idea."

Jordan figured he probably didn't. After all, he looked to be almost twenty years older than either she or Lindsay. He'd probably been settled and married, maybe had a family. His concerns would have been very different from theirs. "It wasn't easy. I had friends moving back in with their parents, or sharing houses and apartments. I was living at home when the Heat came along."

"What was your degree in?" Miles asked suddenly. During most of the previous exchange, he'd looked as if he wasn't paying any attention, but now the blue eyes behind the wire-rimmed glasses were focused sharply on her.

"Environmental studies, with a focus on renewable energy utilization."

"That would be very helpful here," he said, "since we run almost entirely on solar and wind power. Did you work directly with those systems?"

"No," she replied, and tried to ignore the look of disappointment that went over his sharp features. "But I've studied the theory. I just wasn't given a chance to get hands-on. I'm sure I could manage, though, once I was given the opportunity."

"Oh, they'll give it to you," Lindsay said, reaching for a French fry. "Probably more than you want."

"I want to pull my own weight," Jordan said earnestly. And she did. These people had been willing to take her in, give her a refuge, a new home. The least she could do was contribute as much as she could.

Besides, days of hard work wouldn't give her much opportunity to obsess over Hasan. That seemed like an excellent plan. Then she could start to figure out how she might fit in here. Moving on, maybe trying to start a relationship, now that she was someplace where she should be safe.

That might be harder than it looked on the surface, though. All of these people had been living together in Los Alamos for several years now. As far as she'd been able to tell, it seemed that most of them were paired off, like Lindsay and Miles, or Shawn Gutierrez and his girlfriend Katelyn. Even here in this restaurant, the diners appeared to be out as couples, or in groups of couples. People who seemed to be single, like Brent Sanderson, were definitely in the minority.

It's way too soon to be worrying about that

kind of thing, she told herself as she swallowed some beer, then reached for another French fry. *You've barely been here for three hours. Try to let the future be the future.*

Inwardly, she knew she was right. But still....

"Well, I know Shawn will be glad to hear that. Most people feel the same way, but you know how it is. In every group you always have a few slackers."

"What do you do when people don't want to pitch in?" Jordan asked, genuinely curious. Not that she claimed to be an expert on all things Los Alamos, but she hadn't seen any evidence of community policing during the brief time she'd been here.

"Public shaming works pretty well," Lindsay said. "A few times, people's food allotments were threatened. That generally gets most people to shape up. For the real hard cases, well...." She paused, then sent an odd little questioning look at Miles, as though she wasn't sure whether she should say anything else.

"Exile," Miles said calmly. "Which is basically a death sentence. No one can survive out on the road, not with the djinn still hunting humans." He cocked his head to one side, his gaze suddenly sharp. "Which begs the question how you managed it for so long, for so many miles."

A chill went through Jordan. The truth would have to come out at some point, but she really didn't want to talk about it right now. She shrugged, then realized that was an awfully nonchalant response to a situation that could be so deadly. "It wasn't easy."

"And it's nothing she needs to tell us," Lindsay put in. "At least, not after she just got here. There'll be plenty of time for that later."

Thank God. She didn't want to hide the truth forever, and she probably would feel comfortable talking about it at some point with Lindsay. Not in front of Miles, though. It was clear enough that he loved his wife, but Jordan didn't think her story of allowing herself to fall for a murderous djinn would find much sympathy with him.

She shot Lindsay a grateful look, then reached for her beer and allowed herself another swallow. Not too fast, though, or the drink would be gone, and she knew she wouldn't be able to order another. They had to ration the alcohol here, along with so many other things.

"And I'm getting tired," Lindsay announced. Her gaze slipped toward Jordan for just a second, as if she knew her dinner companion was just as weary but didn't want to admit it. "I think we should call it a night. Jordan, why don't you come by the lab tomorrow morning? I think there are a few things you could help me with."

"I don't see what—" Miles began, but his wife interrupted him with a gentle nudge to the ribs.

"Just little things. Does that sound okay?"

Jordan could tell that Lindsay wanted a chance to talk where it would be just the two of them. No doubt she'd arrange it so Miles was off working someplace else while they had their convo. "Sure. Shawn said the townhouse has a scooter in the garage that I can use, so it should be easy enough to get over there."

"Perfect. Let's try for around ten."

Lindsay sounded very confident. Whoever had tomorrow's date for the "baby pool" might very well be disappointed.

As for Jordan...well, she didn't know exactly what the other woman wanted to talk about, but she assumed she'd find out soon enough. She'd knew she'd better manufacture a few ready-made lies, though.

Just in case.

Chapter Thirteen

IT WAS FOOLISH FOR HIM TO DWELL ON HOW EMPTY the bed felt, because of course Jordan had never shared it with him. He'd actually never had a woman here at all; his time with Danya had been spent exclusively at her far more lavish home in western Colorado. All the same, he reached out with one arm to the open space to his left, as if thinking about Jordan might conjure her presence.

Of course she didn't appear. She was hundreds of miles away in Los Alamos, starting a new life.

Whereas he...Hasan didn't quite know what he was doing. This was not a new life for him, but merely a continuation of an old one.

Far away, eerie cries rose into the night. Not

wolves; in this case, the source of the sound was probably a pack of coyotes. He wondered how those predators would fare against the wolves that had begun to encroach on their territory. Would they fight, or simply slink away and try for better hunting elsewhere?

Should *he* have fought?

Annoyed, he sat up in bed. Across the room, a candle on top of the dresser flared to life, casting a faint, warm light, just enough to dispel the darkness. Sleep continued to elude him, and he knew better than to lie here and wrestle with his racing thoughts. Djinn could survive for long periods with little to no sleep, although eventually weariness would catch up them. Now, he didn't know what would be worse—to get up and have to face his own turmoil all through the darkest watches of the night, or try once again to lie down and shut his eyes, and force slumber to come through sheer force of will.

The coyotes yipped again, sounding more frenzied this time. Hasan wondered what they'd found. Merely a rabbit, or perhaps something a little more satisfying, like a yearling deer? He knew he needn't worry about the goats, as they had been locked up in the barn hours ago at the end of their afternoon feeding. There were probably a few more of their compatriots wandering around Chama's environs; he knew over the past few months he'd spotted more than the six he currently had under his protection. Perhaps tomorrow he should go out and try to round up the rest of them.

What else did he have to do with his empty days?

With one fierce movement, he threw the covers back and got out of bed, went to the window. The moon was high overhead, a little thicker than it had been the night before, but still not enough to cast much light. Even so, it illuminated the empty yard around the house just enough that he was able to see dark shapes moving across the open spaces.

Too big for coyotes. These had to be the wolves, coming to investigate the sounds they had heard, quite possibly thinking to take the coyotes' prize for themselves.

Before he'd even stopped to think what he was doing, he'd summoned his robes and his pants and boots, and had blinked himself outside. Cold air immediately hit the exposed skin of his chest and stomach, but he paid it no mind. Ahead of him were the wolves, moving swiftly and with purpose toward a stand of pine located a furlong from the house.

He followed them, moving silently as the

wind. None of them appeared to note his presence, which was as he had planned. His powers allowed him to push all trace of his scent far away, so the wolves would never know he was there.

In the center of the pines was a small clearing, and in that clearing a pack of some ten or twelve coyotes fought and snarled over the carcass of a young doe. Unfortunate, because now she would not have the chance to live and bear young, and keep these lands well-stocked with deer. But that was the way of things. Nature always found its balance—as long as no one interfered with it.

Because the coyotes were so preoccupied, at first they seemed to take no notice of the group of wolves approaching from the south. It was only when the larger predators burst into the clearing that the coyotes broke off from their feast and turned to face the newcomers. They circled the carcass of the doe, teeth bared, mouths dripping saliva.

For one long, agonizing second, the wolves paused. Not out of fear, Hasan knew, but to assess the situation. Perhaps it was right for them to interfere, as they were larger and stronger, and the more dominant species. But as he gazed at them, a fury kindled in him, anger that they would interfere with a kill the coyotes should be rightfully enjoying. The wolves were certainly capable of finding their own prey, but taking it from their smaller cousins was much easier.

As soon as that thought had crossed his mind, he knew he had to stop this. He raised his hands and summoned gusts of wind to assail the wolves, to drive them away from the coyotes. They howled in fear, bowled backward by the gale, one of them even striking the trunk of a tree. It fell to the ground, limp, but shook itself and got back to its feet. This did not bother Hasan too much; he did not wish to kill any of the wolves, only convince them that it was not safe for them to remain here.

Unfortunately, while disoriented by that first assault, they did not appear dissuaded, for in the next moment they surged forward again. And once more Hasan raised his hands, this time not as concerned with trying to keep them from harm. Several of the wolves struck the surrounding trees with such force that when they hit the ground, they stayed there, not moving.

The ones who were not harmed looked around, golden eyes wide and furious, wondering whence had come these furious attacks. Since the djinn had made himself all but invisible to them, they could see no reason why they were being assaulted like this. They began to back away from the coyotes, teeth bared, but their bodies hunched and low to the ground, a sure sign of their unease. In the next moment they were gone, leaving their fallen fellows behind.

Hasan went to one of the injured wolves and laid his hand on its head. The creature breathed, in harsh deep pants. It did not snap at him as he moved that hand down its body, felt its legs and ribs. The wolf whimpered but submitted to the inspection.

Only shaken and bruised. This animal would survive.

Similar inspections of the other fallen wolves proved more or less the same thing. Hasan made a scooping motion with his arms, lifting the three stunned beasts from where they lay and moving them through the trees and into the open meadow beyond. There, he set them down gently, and watched over them as, one by one, they rose to their feet and trotted off into the night, going in search of the rest of their pack.

Hasan remained where he was, focused on the wolves until the gray of their coats had faded into the darkness of the night. Once they were gone, he raised a hand and pushed his hair away from his face. From behind him came the sound of the coyotes feasting, low growls and snapping noises, probably from the deer's bones breaking as they tore her apart.

Why this reaction? Hasan couldn't say. If questioned on the subject, he would have responded that nature should run its course without interference from anyone, whether human or djinn. Something in him, however, had been stirred to action by the injustice of the wolves taking from the coyotes a prize they had rightfully earned.

Would he have acted this way even a week ago? Or had his encounter with Jordan changed him subtly, made him more likely to see the things in the world that needed changing? She had been so stubborn in her insistence that the goats must be protected, so unafraid of what he might say or how he might react to her demands. In that purity was a beauty which had nothing to do with the symmetry of her features, and everything to do with the fierce innocence of her soul.

He didn't deserve her. How could he be worthy of anything that pure, when he had the deaths of so many on his conscience? Never mind that at the time, he had not believed those he killed deserving of mercy. They were the ones who had nearly destroyed this world. Now, though...now he began to realize they were all individuals, people with their own hopes and dreams and fears. He had wiped them away, because they meant nothing to him.

But Jordan...Jordan meant something. Bitter irony that he should understand such a truth only after he had let her go.

He wanted her now more than ever, as he stood there in the cold night, listening to the coyotes feast. He wanted her in his arms, so she might dispel the chill at the very center of his soul.

But she wasn't here. She was gone, and all because of him.

As a djinn, he shouldn't have been able to suffer from the cold, and yet in that moment, his limbs might have been made of ice. He knew he should transport himself back inside the house, get out of this night air.

That would be too easy, though.

Instead, he began to walk back home, letting the cold and the discomfort be his penance.

Would it be enough?

No. He doubted anything he could ever do would be enough.

Jordan wasn't used to looking at a clock, or

keeping to schedules, but she did her best. Her new townhouse had come completely furnished, albeit stripped of any personal items that might have told her something about the person or people who'd lived here before the Heat stole their lives away. She could see why the people running Los Alamos might have agreed on such a policy, but at the same time, she wondered if it wasn't disrespectful somehow, that if those mementos had been left in plain sight, the survivors living here now might have been able to pay them silent homage every day, to recognize the lives they'd once led.

At any rate, the bedroom she now occupied had a wind-up alarm clock on the nightstand, and, as far as she could tell, it had been set to the correct time. The clock had roused her from a deep slumber precisely at 7 a.m., and afterward she had coffee and oatmeal—there was a box with little packets in various flavors. The oatmeal and the coffee had been left for her in the pantry, along with canned items such as soup and pork and beans and creamed corn. She also had work credits to use at Pajarito's if she wanted to go out, although after this settling-in period of a few days, she'd be expected to put in some actual hours to add to her balance.

That was fine. As she'd told the group at

dinner the night before, she wanted to pull her own weight. She wanted to work until she dropped from exhaustion, so she wouldn't have any time left over to think about Hasan. Maybe in a month...or a year...she'd have evicted him from her mind, would allow herself to truly start over.

Today, though, she had to see Lindsay Odekirk at ten o'clock. During Jordan's quick five-minute shower—all she was allowed, to ration water as well as the power required to heat that water—she tried to rehearse the stories she might tell, explanations for her survival that would seem plausible without being too over the top.

Anything to avoid explaining that she probably would never have made it here without a djinn's help.

Her bathroom had come supplied with toothpaste and a new toothbrush, soap, a comb, a hairbrush, and some drugstore-brand moisturizer. Did they give the same care package to everyone who came here, or had Shawn and Katelyn made sure Jordan had everything she might need? She didn't know, but she was grateful. It was so much easier to feel normal when following her regular rituals. Those rituals had been somewhat disrupted in Pagosa Springs, and more so at

Hasan's home in Chama, but as she brushed out her hair and then put on some tinted lip balm, Jordan thought she could easily fall into these civilized routines again. What end of the world? Nothing to see here.

As promised, the garage held a scooter, one of those little electric rip-off models from China that had been built to look like a Vespa. This one was aqua blue and white, very retro. As Jordan unplugged it from the wall socket, she wondered if the scooter had belonged to the people who once lived in this townhouse, or whether it had been put here when the larger vehicle that might have once inhabited this garage was taken away to be used by one of Los Alamos' current inhabitants. Shawn had told her that they'd get her set up with a car or truck before winter really rolled in, that most of the vehicles in Los Alamos now ran on ethanol produced from the crops grown down in Española.

For now, though, the scooter was more than adequate. Actually, with a corduroy jacket pulled on over the long-sleeved T-shirt she wore, it felt good to ride through the streets and feel the cool morning air on her face. People were already out and about, walking or biking or driving to their various assignments. A truck with an extended cab full of men passed her, heading down the hill. Going to harvest the last of the crops before the first hard freeze descended? Maybe, or maybe they were on a salvage mission to Española. It sounded as though there were still plenty of useful items to be scavenged from the abandoned town.

At any rate, everything around her spoke of a calm kind of energy, the energy of people who knew exactly what they were supposed to be doing. Jordan hoped to share in that energy soon. It would be good to have a purpose again. About all they'd been able to do in Pagosa Springs was try their best to stay alive. There wasn't any talk about rebuilding society, not when they knew it could all be taken away from them in an instant.

She rode up the town's main street—sooner or later she'd get all the street names figured out —and then followed it as it curved toward the Los Alamos National Laboratory facilities. Past the empty guard shack, and then on to the same building where she'd spoken with Lindsay and Miles the day before. The same somewhat shabby white Subaru was parked by the entrance, indicating that the couple was already here. Well, Jordan didn't find their early arrival too surprising. She'd already formed the impression that Miles would probably prefer to sleep here so he didn't lose out on any valuable research time, although she didn't know what in the world he might be working on. After all, his devices functioned as intended...obviously, or they wouldn't all be here.

With a mental shrug, she turned off the scooter and put down the kickstand, then climbed off. Since she didn't think she had to worry about theft, she undid the chin strap of her helmet and set it down on the scooter's seat rather than bothering to take it with her into the building.

Up the same four flights of stairs—couldn't they have chosen a lab on a lower level? It wasn't like they had to compete for office space—and then down the same hallway. When Jordan peeked in the doorway of the lab, she saw that Lindsay was in there alone, sitting down at one of the tables as she typed furiously away on the keyboard of a laptop.

It was such an ordinary scene, and yet something about watching the other woman working made Jordan's breath catch in her throat. She hadn't touched a computer since the terrible day she'd fled her house, the day when warnings had popped up on Facebook—one of the last sites to hang on until the internet crashed altogether—that the Heat hadn't been enough, that people were reporting sightings of terrible, beautiful beings intent on murdering every human unfortunate enough to cross their paths. The djinn wouldn't reach Colorado Springs for another month...probably because they were making a concerted effort to clear out Denver and its suburbs...but she hadn't known that at the time. She'd run from the house where her mother had died, wasted away to dust in her own bed, had run to the Mile High Inn, the bar and grill where she'd once worked. Why Jordan had gone there, she couldn't even say, except it had always been a natural gathering place. And that was where the first group of survivors coalesced, until their number was almost a hundred people.

"Hey," Lindsay said, closing her laptop. Jordan couldn't recall making any sound, but something must have alerted the other woman that she was there. "Are you okay?"

"Fine," Jordan replied. She knew she needed to get it together. Falling into unpleasant reveries about the past was not a good way to stay on her toes. "I suppose I was just thinking."

"Not about anything good, judging by your expression."

"Not really." She shrugged and came farther into the room. "Stuff from...right after. You know."

"Yes, I know." Lindsay seemed to check

herself, then added, "Well, that is, I know because of what the survivors here told me. I missed out on a lot of the nightmare right after the Dying because I was Chosen—you know, one of the survivors who got selected by a djinn for eternal life and love. Or something like that."

Wait…*what?* Jordan stared at her, wondering if she somehow hadn't heard that right. If Lindsay had been Chosen, then what the hell was she doing here in Los Alamos with Miles Odekirk?

"Yes, it's true," Lindsay said with a chuckle—followed by a wince as she put her hand on her belly. "Damn. Too bad there's no pro football anymore, because I think this kid would've had a great future as a field goal kicker. Go ahead and sit down, Jordan. Miles is off scrounging parts in the warehouse, so he'll be gone for at least a half hour."

"What if your field goal kicker shows up in the meantime?" Jordan asked, only half joking, as she pulled out a rolling office chair and sat down.

Lindsay pointed at a walkie-talkie that lay on the table a few inches away from her laptop. "Miles can be here in five minutes if I send out an SOS. I don't think we're quite there yet, though."

"Okay." Although Lindsay seemed relaxed enough about the same thing, Jordan couldn't help sending a wary glance at the other woman's oversized belly, a look that probably could have been interpreted as worry that the baby was going to pop right out at any second, like the alien in those sci-fi horror movies. "So...you were Chosen? But aren't you with Miles?"

A gust of a breath. For a second, Lindsay looked very tired, although she usually seemed like the perfect stereotype of a woman blooming with pregnancy hormones. "He...died. There was a group of rogue djinn. Real baddies."

"Worse than the regular ones?" Jordan wasn't sure she wanted to contemplate that prospect. Clearly, she'd missed a whole hell of a lot during the time she'd spent hiding in Pagosa Springs.

"Much worse." Her lips tightened, and Lindsay went on, "The regular djinn—the ones who wanted to wipe out mankind—considered these guys outside the pale, because they didn't want to abide by the elders' decree that the djinn of the One Thousand, the ones who wanted to save humanity, and their Chosen should be left alone. People were hurt. Some were killed. One of them was my partner, Rafi."

She spoke very calmly, as though the tragedy hadn't touched her all that much. Or was she only trying to push her feelings aside? Maybe she'd hooked up with Miles Odekirk as a way of forgetting, although Jordan couldn't quite prevent herself from harboring the uncharitable thought that it was a hell of a slide to go from a godlike djinn to a gawky scientist like Miles.

"I'm sorry," Jordan said quietly.

"It's all right. He...." Lindsay tapped her fingers on the table, then glanced over toward the window. Jordan wasn't quite sure what she might be looking for, because all you could see outside was the other buildings on the lab campus, and the outline of some far-off mountains. "How much do you know about djinn?"

"Probably not as much as you do," Jordan replied. It wasn't even that much of a lie. Yes, she'd spent some time with Hasan, but she was still left with the feeling that there were huge gaps he'd never filled in. "Mostly we tried to stay as far away from them as possible."

"Right." A slight swivel of the chair in which she sat, and Lindsay faced Jordan, one hand moving over her stomach in a gesture that probably wasn't even conscious. "Well, after the Dying, those of us who were Chosen had our djinn come to us and reveal who they were, why they were different. In New Mexico, we all first gathered in Taos, although the community ended up relocating to Santa Fe. Anyway, it was a shock to us survivors, as you can imagine. We were all grateful to be protected...and flattered, I suppose. I mean, here we were, regular mortals, and these godlike beings were coming to us and saying that they wanted us to spend eternity with them."

Jordan could see why that might be gratifying, in an odd way. To know that someone immortal and perfect had selected you, out of all the millions of survivors.... At the same time, the thought only awoke the pain she'd tried to bury, that no one had chosen her, that even Hasan had rejected her in the end. She cleared her throat. "I guess that would have been sort of world-changing."

"In a world that had already changed. Yes." Lindsay hesitated, then reached for the glass of water she had sitting by her on the table. "And for most people, it was a happy ending they hadn't expected."

"But you weren't most people?"

"Not really. I...." Another of those small winces that seemed to indicate the baby was moving again. "It was harder for me and Rafi. That is, he'd picked me, and I knew I was supposed to be swept off my feet, but it didn't feel that way to me, at least not after the first few weeks. We quarreled more than the other Chosen and their djinn ever did. He had this idea of who he thought I should be, and I wasn't that.

I mean, I was an engineering grad student. A geek. Not some wannabe goddess."

If memory served, there really hadn't been too many geeks who'd looked like Lindsay, but Jordan didn't bother to argue. If that was how the other woman saw herself, then that was her truth.

"And I realized after he was gone that he'd probably used his djinn glamour to soften me up in the beginning, to make me think I was in love with him, even though—"

"'Djinn glamour'?" Jordan cut in. She didn't think she liked the sound of that. "What are you talking about?"

"It's a subtle power they have. They can make you think that you want them, that you have the deepest connection in the world to them. I think more djinn used it on their Chosen than they wanted to admit, just to get things started when people were scared and worried and, frankly, kind of shell-shocked. You can't even tell what's happening. You think it's completely normal to fall head over heels like that."

Oh, God. Before she could stop it, one of Jordan's hands had gone to her throat. Was that what had happened between her and Hasan? Had he used his glamour on her? She couldn't think of a rational explanation for why she'd fallen so hard for him, and so quickly, but Lindsay's story provided the perfect explanation.

Hold on, she thought then. *If that's really what happened, then why did he let you go? If all he wanted was to throw his djinn "shine" on you and get you into bed, why stop before you'd done the deed?*

She didn't know. Maybe his conscience had gotten the better of him. Conscience. There was a joke. If he didn't have any compunction about killing hundreds—if not thousands—of innocent human beings, then she doubted he would lose any sleep about making a woman think she wanted to have sex with him.

Lindsay had been watching her intently, one perfectly arched eyebrow lifted slightly. "Jordan, are you okay?"

"I'm fine," she replied, forcing out the words even though she was anything but fine. "I just —I hadn't heard that before. It is kind of creepy."

"That's one word for it. Anyway, once Rafi was gone, I realized I'd never really loved him. He'd made me think I loved him. And then I was angry with him, and angry with myself for being angry at someone who'd died too soon." She gave a grim chuckle and added, "Well, too soon for a djinn. Who knows how many hundreds or thousands of years old he actually was? He would never tell me."

"But then you met Miles...."

"Well, I was working with Miles at first. He needed someone to help him, and I had more of a scientific background than anyone else in Taos."

That comment didn't make any sense. If Miles's home base was the labs here in Los Alamos, then what was he doing in Taos?

Lindsay must have sensed her puzzlement, because she said, "Let's just say the Taos djinn 'borrowed' Miles for some help with the rogue djinn. So we were working in the lab there together. Believe me, it wasn't love at first sight. We argued all the time."

"I thought that was a prerequisite, at least according to all the romantic comedies I've ever seen."

Lindsay grinned. "Well, all right. Maybe. He had his own demons to fight—he'd lost his wife and child in the Heat. It took him a while to figure out that it was okay to move on. But he did, and here we are." The grin faded, replaced by a soft smile as she touched her belly again. "This baby...it's our trust in the future. That everything will be okay. You know."

Jordan could only nod, although she wasn't

sure whether she shared Lindsay's optimism for the future. After all, they'd thought they were safe in Pagosa Springs, that they'd managed to finally evade the djinn once and for all, and she'd seen how that turned out. True, the situations weren't exactly equivalent, because the group in Pagosa hadn't had Miles's devices to protect them. Because of those devices and the cooperation that existed between the djinn of Santa Fe and the people in Los Alamos, the people here probably did think the future was now something to be looked forward to rather than feared.

Maybe someday she would feel the same.

Chapter Fourteen

HE WOULD SIMPLY HAVE TO FIND SOMEONE ELSE. No, not a mortal—he'd learned his lesson with Jordan. But a djinn woman, another individual who also found the prospect of heading into a long winter in an empty house unappealing. Danya was out of the question, of course. However, there were others who had been given lands in this part of the world, women who might be looking for companionship now that they had established themselves in their new homes.

Assuming that they hadn't already found someone to fill that particular void. While djinn relationships didn't last forever, they could span decades, which meant his chances of locating a woman he was attacted to and who was still available were considerably lower than they would have been if he'd made this determination as soon as he was given these lands. Now he worried that his plan might not be as easy to implement as he thought.

Bright sunlight streamed in through the windows. Hasan stood in the middle of his living room, arms crossed, and scowled as he took in his surroundings. Because he had still been consumed with tracking down the few survivors who remained in this part of the world, he hadn't spared much thought for the house he'd been given. The land was good, and he'd assumed that he would improve the house one day when he had time. Now, though, he looked at the place through the eyes of a djinn woman, and knew it would be found sadly lacking, small and cramped by his people's standards, no marble columns, no gold leaf, no reflecting pools or mosaics or tapestries. Just a mortal house, one that might have served its original owner well enough but certainly did not possess any amenities that a djinn would find appealing.

He had made some improvements to his own bedroom and left it at that. Those small changes would not be adequate, however. He would have to tear the entire place down and start over. For one of his people, it was not such a daunting task.

Earth elementals had the easiest time of it when faced with these sorts of challenges, but Hasan knew he could manage well enough.

But....

Even if he erased all traces of the current house and exchanged them for a palace of marble and stone, he could not erase his memories of Jordan here—Jordan sitting on the kitchen floor, her long hair slipping over one shoulder as she cradled the wounded goat...Jordan on the front porch, the light of the setting sun limning her delicate features in pure gold...Jordan at the dinner table, one corner of her mouth lifting as she teased him, oh, so delicately.

And that mouth on his, the sweetness of her lips, the lithe grace of her body pressed against him as he kissed her. He could reduce this house to rubble, and all those things would remain.

Yes, he wanted a woman, but not any woman. Only Jordan.

Once upon a time, Qadim al-Syan had quipped that Hasan's single-mindedness would get him into trouble one day. Now Hasan realized that his former friend's little joke was no joke at all, but a keen observation of a failing that could no longer be overlooked. He could try stopgaps and distractions, he could fill his days with empty activities, and in the end, none of it would matter. None of it did matter, if he couldn't have Jordan with him.

He let out a low growl of frustration, and went to the front door and wandered out onto the porch. A brisk, friendly morning greeted him, the sort of day that should have been filled with possibilities, but now seemed only one more in a series of days and weeks that must be endured.

It was his fault, he knew. Pride had told him that he could not care for a mortal, and he had believed its lies. But now that he knew he had made a mistake, what could he possibly do next? Jordan was gone, hidden behind a barrier as impassable as it was invisible. He had no way of getting word to her that he had changed his mind. And even if she knew somehow, would she even care, considering how he had sent her away?

Perhaps he should go to the djinn of Santa Fe and ask for their help. Yes, there was bad blood between him and Qadim because of how Hasan had treated Qadim's woman, but there had never been any quarrel between him and Zahrias, the leader of the djinn in the former capital of this region. And Hasan, although zealous in his quest to hunt down humanity's survivors, had not infringed on the rules that protected the Chosen, unlike those rogues who had been exiled to the outer circles. Qadim might disagree on that point, but in truth, his woman had not been Chosen when Hasan kidnapped her. In the eyes of the elders, he had committed no crime.

Ah, but Qadim and Madison now dwelt with the rest of the djinn and their Chosen in Santa Fe, and no doubt Zahrias would take their side against him.

No, Hasan would not ask for their assistance. He would do this on his own. It was better that way. Then he could hold up his head when he met again with Jordan. She would know he loved her enough to come after her without help from anyone else.

Love. Such a small word, one he had scorned in the past. Now he knew he could not afford to ignore the ache in his heart. He would seek her out, tell her the truth of his soul.

Even if it killed him.

———

Miles had returned to the lab not very long after Lindsay's revelations about her former djinn partner, and Jordan took advantage of his arrival to say that she didn't want to interrupt their work any longer, and she had some things to take care of at her new home. Another lie, but an innocent one. Anyway, she did have a bit more settling in to do, and besides, it was the sort of excuse that wouldn't raise any eyebrows. She thanked Lindsay for the chat, offered a muted hello to Miles—who looked more relieved than anything else, probably because he realized he wouldn't have to come up with a reason for kicking her out so he and his wife could get some work done—and headed out to retrieve her scooter.

It really was a beautiful day. Rather than return home right away, Jordan rode around town, coaxing the scooter up a few of the steeper hills, wandering through neighborhoods that looked like something out of a '50s sitcom. She supposed the architecture in the older parts of town made sense; after all, this place had been a working lab since the 1940s, and she had the idea that a lot of the scientists had stayed on and settled here after WWII was over. Why not? They still had work to do, and why not do it in a safe, isolated place with clean air and water?

And views. She paused at a park near the edge of one of the plateaus, and gazed out over the sweeping vistas to every side—dark pine forests, and golden sprays of autumn-toned aspens, and rocks in every shade from rusty orange-red to almost pale green. Her eyes traveled further, to the ribbon of green—now shaded faintly with gold from the cottonwoods beginning to turn—that was the Rio Grande as it cut through the valley where Española was located, all the way to the hills where the river emerged from its gorge, near where she and Hasan had parted.

A lump formed in her throat, and she swallowed. She didn't want to think about that moment, didn't want to think about the hard set of his mouth as he let her walk away from him. Problem was, the more she made herself not think about it, the more she couldn't seem to think of anything else. If there had been something she could have said to change his mind, she still couldn't think of it now.

"You're out and about," a half-familiar voice said, and she turned away from the view to see Brent Sanderson standing a few feet away. He held a black plastic trash bag in one hand and wore a vaguely apologetic expression on his face.

"I—I was just exploring. I wanted to get a look around."

"It's a good place to get a look, that's for sure." He remained where he was, and didn't try to come any closer to her. Maybe he'd gotten a good glimpse of her face and had realized she wasn't out here merely to take in the view. "Trash duty," he went on, hefting the garbage bag. "We tell the kids not to leave any litter behind in the parks, but they don't always pay attention. So I like to make the rounds every few days if I don't have too many cars to work on."

That's right, he'd mentioned something about working in the motor pool the day before, as he was dropping her off at city hall so she could meet with Shawn Gutierrez. Well, she supposed the motor pool was one benefit of the apocalypse—you could just bring your malfunctioning car to have one of your fellow survivors repair it, rather than taking it to a mechanic and wondering if there would be enough in your checking account to cover the cost of fixing the damn thing.

"That's nice of you," Jordan said, which she knew sounded sort of foolish. There wasn't much she could do about it now, though. "I noticed that everyone seems to have their own jobs to do."

"Oh, yeah." Brent set down the trash bag and came a little closer to her, but not so close that she had any sense of him invading her space. "Julia actually set a lot of that up before she went to live in Santa Fe, so mostly Shawn just has to make sure he keeps the schedules going."

Jordan knew he must be referring to Julia Innes, whose voice she had heard over the short-wave radio back in Colorado Springs. Jordan wished she could have gotten a chance to speak to the woman who'd once run Los Alamos; it would be another opportunity for continuity. Like Miles Odekirk, Julia could have offered another way to bridge Jordan's time in Colorado Springs to the life she found herself in now. "And squeeze in latecomers like me," she offered, smiling a little.

However, Brent didn't smile. His gaze moved toward the open countryside miles below, to the faint smudge that was Española, now empty, its only purpose to serve as a salvage yard for Los Alamos. "We don't get many latecomers," he said. "Not anymore. Not for months and months. You're kind of an anomaly." This time his eyes tracked back to her, too kind to be speculative, although Jordan could still see him wondering inside, trying to figure out how someone like her could have survived all those months after the Dying, could have crossed the empty, djinn-haunted miles to get here.

"Oh, I'm pretty ordinary," she protested. "Maybe just a little luckier than some."

"If you say so."

She really didn't want to disagree any more than that, because she'd be lying to him, too. Maybe she should just come clean and confess, tell the truth about Hasan. But wouldn't they recoil then, these nice, civilized people who were doing their best to re-create a world that was now gone? Wouldn't they look at her in disgust when they learned that she'd given her heart to a djinn —and not one of the friendly djinn in Santa Fe, but a being whose goal had been to make sure no human walked or lived or breathed outside that safe zone?

Hell, she couldn't even explain it to herself. She sure couldn't begin to tell them what she'd seen in Hasan, that he wasn't cruelty embodied. How could he be, when he'd driven off wolves to save her little goat, had dutifully gone with her into town to rescue the rest of the herd? If he was truly a soulless monster, he wouldn't have behaved in such a way. If he thought humans were so useless, he wouldn't have listened to her pleas...or kissed her and told her she was beautiful.

Brent had continued to watch her as she stood there in silence, his expression now curious. "Did you leave someone behind out there?"

Unshed tears burned in her eyes. She wanted to blame them on the wind. "Didn't we all?"

Hasan went to the barn and looked in at the

goats. He would let them out to eat their fill, then bring them back inside and set out as much hay and water as their accommodations would allow. Shut the door, but not lock it. He had to hope he wouldn't be leaving them alone so long that they would starve. However, goats were determined little creatures. If they got hungry enough, they could probably kick their way out of here. Once again they would be prey for the wolves and the coyotes, but better for them to take their chances in the wild than to remain trapped in the barn.

That was borrowing trouble, he knew. Miles Odekirk's devices and the field they generated wouldn't kill him. At least, that was the rumor amongst the djinn. They avoided the protected areas because entering them was painful, and, once inside, a djinn was stripped of his powers, no better than a human. Worse, really, because the energy-sapping power of the field actually weakened djinn physically in addition to blocking their elemental talents.

It would not be pleasant. But it also would not be fatal.

Unless, of course, the humans in Los Alamos made it fatal.

He would do what he could to shield Jordan, of course. If the field's effects weren't too detrimental, then he could pretend to be human. He would cast off his silken robes, and wear the uniform of a mortal man in this part of the world —jeans, a plaid shirt, work boots. With any luck, he could deceive them long enough that he might have a chance to speak to Jordan, to tell her that he had made a mistake and that he wanted her to come home with him. The mortals in Los Alamos would probably think she had come there following a lovers' quarrel, and not because she was escaping a djinn.

Surely once she saw his sacrifice, she would accept his apology, and would return to his house in Chama.

These pleasant fictions kept him occupied as he took care of the goats, then went back into the house to change his clothing. He did not even have to conjure the items he needed, as they existed here already, part of the wardrobe that had belonged to the home's previous owner. Yes, they needed a bit of pinching, pulling, and tucking to make them fit, as that mortal had been shorter and stouter than Hasan, but such minor alterations were child's play for a djinn. It was better to do this than conjure new clothing, because these garments had some wear to them, and therefore would be more believable.

Most human men in this region wore their hair short, but Hasan did not see any reason to carry the charade quite that far. He settled for pulling his shoulder-length locks back with a piece of string, and deemed that a good enough compromise.

Then it was time to bring the goats back inside, to take care of their food and water. They seemed to know something was happening, for they milled around him, blocking his route to the door, and the little one, the one he had saved from the wolf, butted its head against him. He scratched behind the animals' ears, knowing that Jordan would have wanted him to show them this little bit of affection. After a few moments, though, he let himself out, and made sure the door had caught securely, even though he didn't latch it.

Just in case.

The first part of the journey was simple enough. He went directly to the place where he had left Jordan, then retraced her steps so that he came to the edge of the djinn-repelling field in more or less the same spot.

He could sense the energy of the field, pulsing, daring him to enter. For the longest moment he stood there, feeling the hairs on his arms lift under the scratchy human-made shirt he wore. An odd little breeze danced down the canyon and pulled a strand of hair loose from the string that held it away from his face. He tucked the wayward lock behind one ear, then took a breath.

Time to go.

It was as though a thousand needles pierced his flesh all at once. He didn't quite gasp, but the air he had just inhaled escaped his mouth in a shocked little gust. Jaw clenched, he forced himself to take another step.

And then he was through.

The stabbing sensation was gone, although he could still feel phantom pinpricks all over his body. Worse, though, was the way it seemed as if some essential part of him had been stolen away, leaving him limp and shaken, barely able to stand upright.

This was the effect of Miles Odekirk's device. No wonder his kind had left the Los Alamos survivors alone. No djinn could prevail against a human while feeling so absolutely wretched, so completely useless.

Not entirely useless, though. He could still force himself to move forward, to put one foot in front of the other, even though it seemed as if he was wading through a river of mud. His breath came short and shallow, but he could breathe. He could do this.

Another step, and another. Hasan found if he focused on the movements of his feet, then the other discomforts tended to recede. Not all the way; he wasn't sure if he would ever be able to get a deep, cleansing gulp of air again, but he could function.

And curiously, as he made his slow but steady progress along the abandoned road, he found his mood improving. This was good, in its own strange fashion. Like the shamans and the wise men of old, he would cleanse himself in this barren landscape, would cast aside all the evils that had held him back—fear, and hatred, and resentment. When he finally reached Jordan, he would be purified, would be the man she deserved. At least, he hoped she would see it that way.

How long would this journey take, given his halting progress? He couldn't guess for sure, because of course his kind did not have to worry about such concerns. They could blink themselves from one place to another in an instant, and elementals of the air such as he could use the wind's currents to take them to scout a new location, if they were unsure of their destination. Either way, travel was not a laborious thing, one which could consume days and days.

Now, though, he would have to manage his best guess as to how much time might elapse before he reached Los Alamos. The thought of the climb to that hilltop town made him quail slightly, although he hoped he might encounter one of its residents before that point, could get a ride the rest of the way.

In which case, he had better prepare a story so he would have something to explain his presence when they began asking questions. His given name would be...Hank. It was the name of the man who had owned the house where he now dwelled; Hasan had seen it on various papers while he was clearing out all traces of the home's former occupant. And his surname? Hasan had never paid much attention to such things. He thought of the landscape around him, the country he'd just passed through. Not too far behind him was the plateau the mortals called Black Mesa. Very well...his surname would be Black. Hank Black. And he was...a rancher, with a spread up near Chama. Jordan had come across it while fleeing Pagosa Springs, and had stayed with him for a few days. In the end, they had quarreled, and she had left.

That all sounded plausible enough, as long as none of his story contradicted what Jordan had already told the people in Los Alamos. Explaining how he'd managed to stay alive all this time would take a little more work, but who was to say that other survivors didn't hang on here and there, in the world's more desolate corners? After all, Jordan's group had managed to live in Pagosa Springs for well over a year before they were discovered. A lone man in a house in the middle of nowhere...it wasn't so strange that the djinn might not have ever stumbled across him.

It helped to ruminate on these things as he walked, because that way his mind was focused on the tale he would tell, and not the way his heart seemed to pound in his chest, and how his legs and arms felt far too weak, as if his shallow breaths did not provide quite enough of the oxygen they required to keep moving. He had heard, however, that the djinn in Taos—now Santa Fe—had lived with these infernal devices operating day and night to protect them from the rogues who sought their destruction, and so he knew this discomfort would not kill him.

Even if he almost wished it would.

He passed a sign that told him Española was still five miles away. At this rate, there was no way he would be able to get to Los Alamos before sundown. Very well. His knowledge of this part of the world was scanty at best, but he thought Española was large enough that it must have had at least a few small inns, someplace where he could lay his head for the night. Yes, there would be plenty of abandoned houses, although he would consider them only as a last resort. He did not like the idea of sleeping some-place that had once belonged to a mortal. Contradictory, perhaps, when one could say the same thing about the house he now called his home, but he did not think it was the same at all. He had been given that land, that building. It was his. These places...no. They existed now only as monuments to those who had died within their walls.

The sun began to drop behind the hills, and the air grew chillier. Hasan tried to ignore the cold as best he could, although he berated himself for not bringing a jacket. Such human contrivances had never entered his mind, because in the past, heat and cold had had no effect on him. The device had taken that protec-tion away as well, it seemed. He didn't know whether that was by design, or whether all these debilitating side effects were just a happy coinci-dence. Put together, they almost...well, they almost made him human.

That thought made him scowl, and he crossed his arms and hunched his head against the wind, which came from the northwest, searching, cold. He was thirsty, too. Like a fool, he hadn't brought any food or water, not realizing how badly his body might betray him on this journey.

Off to one side, he noted a large structure, what appeared to have been some kind of over-sized center of commerce. The sign above the parking lot, now cracked and pitted from several years' worth of weather and neglect, proclaimed it to be Walmart.

Hasan didn't know what a Walmart was, but perhaps it might contain some of the items he needed. Or had it been looted?

If nothing else, going inside would give him some protection from the wind. He could shelter here for the night. Certainly no one had ever called this place home.

He shuffled his way across the parking lot and went inside. The interior of the building was dark and cavernous, and although his eyes strained against the gloom, he couldn't see all that much. Just another one of his talents that he wished he could use, for all djinn had the ability to see in the dark. Perhaps not as clearly as a cat, but well enough that they could get around without tripping over anything.

Hands outstretched to prevent himself from bumping into anything solid, he moved slowly, waiting for his vision to adjust to the change in lighting. He began to see the outlines of tables and racks, all of which must have once held a variety of merchandise. Now, however, they appeared to be mostly empty, although whether their ransacked state was due to looting that had occurred during the Dying, or because the Los Alamos community had done its own "shopping" here in Española, he couldn't say.

Perhaps this had been a mistake. A store like this would have been an obvious target. He would be lucky to find enough unsold clothing to gather together to create a makeshift bed, let alone any blankets or cots or other more useful items. As far as he could tell, the shelves in the grocery section were likewise empty.

It would have to be one of the abandoned houses after all.

Frowning, he turned back toward the entrance—only to be blinded by the beam of a flashlight shining directly into his face.

"Stop right there," said a rough human voice.

Chapter Fifteen

IT WOULD BE BETTER ONCE SHE WAS GIVEN HER work assignment, she was sure. Shawn and Katelyn probably thought they were doing her a favor by giving her a few days to settle in, but Jordan realized she didn't need nearly that much time. After telling Brent Sanderson goodbye, she'd gotten back on her little Vespa rip-off scooter and headed for home. Well, the home she'd been given. Maybe after she'd lived here for a few months, it would begin to feel like hers, but right now it seemed more as if she was staying in an impersonal residence hotel.

She needed to suck it up, though, because she couldn't ask Lindsay to act as her babysitter, not when she was due to become a mother any day now. This would get better. She'd start in with her work, get to know more people, start to rebuild her life. Then she'd be able to make plans, get together with friends at Pajarito's, just as she'd seen people doing the night before when she'd gone to the restaurant with Lindsay and Miles and Brent. Soon enough, the rough edges would be smoothed over, and she wouldn't even think about Hasan anymore, except possibly as an odd little interlude between the life she'd had in Colorado and the life she was living now.

In the meantime, she might as well make herself an early dinner. Nothing in the pantry looked all that interesting, but she made herself get out the can of pork and beans and set it on the counter next to the stove. Some scrounging in the kitchen's drawers produced a can opener; a minute later, she located a small saucepan in the lower cupboards.

And really, it was sort of a miracle to be able to turn on the stove and heat up the pork and beans and get out a spoon to stir them, to act as if it wasn't crazy that she could do something so ordinary two years after the djinn had ended the world. The tangy aroma of the beans drifted up to her nose, reminding her of the times when she was a kid and her mother had to work, so Jordan had been in charge of making her own dinner. Both she and her mother knew she wasn't old enough to be left home alone, especially at night, but her mom couldn't always afford a sitter. Jordan had been taught to be careful around the stove, to clean up after herself, to turn off the TV at nine and put herself to bed, to never answer the phone or the door.

The ringing of the doorbell startled her so much, she almost dropped the spoon she held. For a second, she couldn't quite orient herself, as if being lost in her memories had actually transported her back to the ten-year-old child she'd been, rather than the woman she'd become. Then she realized she was in Los Alamos, in the townhouse she'd been assigned, and that someone really was at the door.

She put down the spoon and hurried toward the front of the house, flicking on lights as she went, since by that point the sun was nearly down and the interior of her borrowed home quite dim. When she got to the front door, she turned the deadbolt and unlocked it, then opened the door.

Standing out on the front stoop were four men. Three of them she didn't know at all, although she thought she vaguely recalled seeing the tall, thick-set one—the one who appeared to have rung the doorbell—at Pajarito's the night before.

The fourth man...well, at first she didn't recognize him, either, because his night-dark hair was pulled back from his face in a severe ponytail, and he wore a plaid flannel shirt, worn jeans, and brown lace-up boots. Then she really looked at his face, at the fine, high cheekbones, the deep blue eyes under the level brows.

Oh, God.

It was Hasan. A pale and drawn Hasan, clearly doing his best to bear up under the continuous assault of Miles Odekirk's djinn-repelling devices, but definitely him. Just the sight of his face was enough to steal the breath from her lungs, although she knew she had to try to remain calm, to avoid showing how much his sudden appearance here had shocked her.

"Do you know this man?" asked the guy who seemed to be the leader of the little group. "We found him in the Walmart down in Española. Claims he's a friend of yours."

"I—" What the hell was she supposed to say? Clearly, Hasan was trying to pass himself off as a mortal, which meant he probably hadn't given them his real name. "Yes. Yes, he's a friend. We met up by Chama."

Her words seemed to mollify the thick-set man, because he appeared to relax slightly.

"That's what he told us. Said you had a difference of opinion, but he needed to come speak to you."

Difference of opinion? That was one way of looking at it, she supposed. She nodded. "Yes. I just didn't think—"

"Jordan, I am sorry about that," Hasan said. His voice was nearly as strained as his face, and she had to hope the men who'd found him had attributed his obvious weakness to the journey he'd just undertaken, rather than realizing he was worn out because of the way Miles's devices kept hammering away at him.

"It's all right," she said quickly. The important thing was to get him inside with her, and away from the men who'd brought him here. At the moment they didn't appear to see anything too suspicious about the situation, but she didn't know how much longer Hasan would be able to fool them. "Come in—let's talk."

Jordan stepped aside, giving him room to enter, and prayed he'd take the hint. He did, and had begun to step forward when one of the other men, a skinny guy who didn't look much older than Jordan herself, protested, "Maybe we should talk to Shawn first—"

"And what?" said the leader. "She says she knows him. It's not like they're going anywhere...right?"

"Right," Jordan said firmly. "If Shawn wants to come by and meet...."

One syllable formed in her head. She had no idea where it had come from, but she was grateful nonetheless.

Hank.

"...meet Hank, then he's welcome to. Although maybe not tonight? I can tell Hank is tired, and I was just about to get some dinner together—"

"That's fine," the leader of the group told her. "I'll let Shawn know that we have another arrival, and I'm sure he'll want to talk to both of you in the morning, but until then...have a nice evening."

He touched a finger to the bill of the baseball cap he wore, and then the trio turned away and went down the steps, heading toward a pickup truck Jordan noticed was parked at the curb. She gave a little wave and did her best to smile, then shut the door behind her and locked it.

There was Hasan. Standing still and quiet in the middle of the living room, watching her with wary but hopeful eyes...along with a sort of startled surprise that he'd been able to muster enough djinn energy to send that one all-important syllable to her.

She couldn't believe it. He'd come here—he'd braved Miles Odekirk's devices—just to see her.

What had caused such a change in him, she didn't know. Right then, she didn't care.

Without thinking, she went to him, put her arms around him. At once he was embracing her as well, although she noticed immediately how weak he felt, how his arms lacked their former strength. She pulled away and looked up at him.

"The devices—"

"Are most unpleasant. Do you mind if I sit down?"

"No, of course not. Here." She took him by the hand and led him over to the couch, watched as he settled onto it with a sigh, his eyes closing briefly. "Can I get you some water? It's about all I have, but—"

"Water will be fine. Thank you, Jordan." His eyelids lifted, and that steady blue gaze caught her, held her. "I am sorry that I am not quite myself."

"It's all right. Just rest. I'll be right back."

She went into the kitchen and got a glass from the cupboard, then filled it from the tap, since Shawn had assured her that the municipal water supply was perfectly safe, was fed by aquifers buried deep within these stony hills. Her hand shook as she held the glass under the faucet, and she willed herself to be calm. She still couldn't quite believe that Hasan waited for her in the living room. What kind of an effort had it taken for him to come here, to travel those weary miles while the anti-djinn devices sapped all his energy, all his strength? Especially since they'd passed the Walmart after Brent found her and was driving her up to Los Alamos, and she knew the store was much farther from her starting point than the distance she'd walked from the 582 before catching her unexpected but very welcome ride.

Hasan's eyes were closed again when she returned. She debated whether she should rouse him, or set the glass down on the coffee table and wait for him wake up on his own. The decision was taken out of her hands, however, because as soon as she began to place the glass on a coaster, his eyelids fluttered open, and he gave her a weak smile.

"Thank you," he said, and sat up and reached for the glass. His hand shook nearly as much as hers had only a minute earlier, and she wondered once again how he'd been able to conceal the true reason for his weakness from all those men.

She sat down on the sofa next to him. At once he reached over with his free hand and touched hers. His fingers were cold. They had never been cold before; he might be a wind elemental, but his touch had always been warm, no matter how chilly the air around them.

God, she needed to get him out of here.

He drank deeply of the water she'd brought, draining half the glass in one swallow. Then he put the tumbler back on its coaster. "I suppose you think I am mad."

"No," she said at once. That was the last thing she would have thought of what he'd done. Determined, bold, maybe even reckless...but not crazy. "I'm...surprised. After what you said—"

"I know. I had time to think." He shifted so he could see her more clearly. "I realized I had made a very grave mistake." A pause, and then he said, "I want you to come back to Chama with me."

Her breath caught. All right, she couldn't think of many other reasons why he would have come all this way, but still, to hear him state his plea so baldly caught her off guard. "Well, you need to go back," she replied, hoping she sounded calm and matter-of-fact. She wanted to ask how in the world he'd been able to mentally give her his alias, but right now they had more important things to worry about. "If you don't leave soon, this place will kill you."

"No, it will not kill me," he told her. "I may

wish to be dead because of this discomfort, but even that is not deadly. Just debilitating."

Those words reassured her a little, but she would be lying to herself if she didn't admit how much she hated to see him like this. He had always seemed so strong and sure, so in command of himself, that to watch him lean against the back of the couch, one hand lying limp on his knee, was to make her realize he wasn't quite as invincible as he'd seemed. For some reason, seeing him vulnerable like this made her love him even more.

"I cannot compel you, of course," he said. "Even if I were in full command of my abilities, I would not do such a thing. And now...." The words drifted off, weak, hesitant. "I doubt I could make myself do more than walk down the hallway. But I needed to tell you that I was wrong. I should never have made you go. I want you to come home with me. Please tell me that you will."

She'd hoped he might say such things to her, had uttered little prayers to whatever gods might be listening that he would realize he had made a terrible mistake. Even so, Jordan had to force herself to understand that this was real, and not a dream born of her need. And so she needed to make sure she gave him the right answer.

Actually, there was only one answer.

"Yes, I will," she said. Behind the weariness, his eyes lit up. She rested her hand on his, hoping that he might be able to take some of her warmth. Oh, dear lord, how she wanted to kiss him. He seemed so weak, though. She didn't want to force anything on him, thought it would be better if she let him make the first move. After all, he had a far better idea of how he felt than she did. Voice artificially brisk, she went on, "But we'll have to think of the best way to do it. I don't think we can just walk down the hill. Not in the condition you're in."

"I would argue with that statement, but I fear you are right." He shifted again, this time so he faced her. However, Jordan noted that he was careful not to move his hand from beneath hers. "Those devices...they were created by the very devil himself."

"No, not the devil. Just a man. A brilliant, odd man, but a man."

"Be that as it may. So how do you propose we slip away?"

Good question. If only she'd been given a real vehicle. Then she and Hasan could have taken their things and driven away in the night. It wouldn't even be stealing, not really, because she would have left a note telling the Los Alamos group where they could find their missing car or truck. But that little electric scooter could barely get around with her meager hundred and fifteen pounds on it. There was no way it could carry her and Hasan. Yes, you could argue that once you were out of this neighborhood, the way was mostly downhill...but not all of it. Española itself was fairly flat, and they'd be going back uphill once they were headed toward Velarde and the outer borders of the devices' field of operation.

"I'm not sure yet," she replied. "I don't have a car, only a scooter, and that won't work. Lindsay said something about giving me a vehicle once I had my work assignment, but that isn't supposed to happen for another day or so."

"'Work assignment'?" Hasan repeated, looking rather offended. "Can they not even treat you as an honored guest?"

"I don't think that's how it works around here. Everyone has to do their share to keep the community going. It's fair. I don't begrudge them that. But I do wish I had a car."

"I wish you did, too."

From the kitchen came the pungent aroma of scorched pork and beans, and Jordan stifled a curse. She withdrew her hand from Hasan's, but apologized as she did so, saying, "I had some-thing on the stove. I'd better go rescue it. Can you eat? It's not much—just beans—but I think it's better if you had something."

He offered her a weary smile. "Yes, some food might help. Thank you."

"You might not be thanking me once you've tasted it."

Her comment elicited a low chuckle. Feeling slightly heartened, she got up from the couch and went into the kitchen, then turned off the electric burner and moved the pot over to one she hadn't used. After locating some bowls in the cupboard next to the one that contained the glasses, she scooped an equal portion of pork and beans into each bowl, then got out some spoons. As meals went, it definitely wasn't gourmet, but she had to hope the beans would provide enough nourishment to give Hasan some extra energy.

She'd halfway expected Hasan to have closed his eyes and dozed again, but actually he was sitting up a little straighter and looking around the townhouse's cramped living room. "It's very small," he said, sounding a bit more like his old critical self.

Jordan repressed a smile as she handed him one of the bowls and a spoon. "Well, it was just me," she told him, and sat down on the sofa. "They probably didn't think I needed all that much room. Anyway, I'm sure all the best places have already been handed out."

"Perhaps." With a very small shrug, he took up his spoon and began to eat. From the way his brow furrowed, she got the idea that he wasn't a big fan of pork and beans, but he didn't comment on the food, only continued to scoop it into his mouth.

Even if she'd been capable of creating the kind of elaborate meals he'd fed her at his house in Chama, she couldn't have done so here, simply because she didn't have the raw materials on hand. Well, this was only temporary. They'd eat, and then he would rest, and in the morning she'd figure out how to get the two of them away from here.

Assuming he lasted that long.

"Can you—can you make it until tomorrow?" she asked. "I know you said it would be all right, but—"

"I will be fine. The effects of the field are uncomfortable, no more. The djinn in Santa Fe had to live with these same effects for days before the rogue djinn were finally defeated and the devices could be turned off."

Those words reassured her somewhat, but she still didn't want this to go on forever, or even more than a day. She'd have to get a car somehow. Unfortunately, a few rounds of playing *Grand Theft Auto* at a friend's house didn't exactly qualify her to steal a real vehicle. Anyway, she hated the idea of taking anything from the people here in Los Alamos. They'd shown her only kindness. But she was human, a fellow survivor, so of course they would be friendly to her.

Would they be so kind if they discovered the true identity of the man she was sheltering under her roof? Jordan wished she could say so with certainty, but she just didn't know the people here well enough to say. They'd all lost loved ones to the Heat, and possibly also to the djinn who'd hunted down the survivors. Jordan couldn't say for sure that they'd show Hasan any true forbearance, and she simply couldn't take that risk.

Lindsay might be a little more understanding, simply because she'd had a djinn lover. Or no, maybe that wasn't right. It sounded as though Lindsay's djinn had basically tricked her into thinking she cared for him. She might have a real reason to carry a grudge. On the other hand, her djinn lover had at least saved her from having to live through the ugly aftermath of the Dying, and so she might not hate Hasan for what he'd done, at least not in the way the other inhabitants of Los Alamos most definitely would.

"My love."

Jordan started and almost dropped the bowl she held. Not once had he ever used a term of endearment with her. She didn't doubt that he cared, but to hear those words from his lips....

"I've startled you, I see." With an obvious effort, he leaned forward and set his own bowl down on the coffee table. "I am sorry."

"No, don't be sorry. I—I liked hearing you say that."

The corners of his mouth curved upward. "I'm glad to hear it. But my love, I can see you wrestling with yourself. You do not have to concoct a grand plan this evening. Think on it, and we'll see what we can do in the morning. I feel better now that I am here with you, and have food in my belly. I will sleep."

"You'll be able to?" she asked. "Even with the devices acting on you all the time?"

"In sleep, I will be able to escape the weariness, if only for a few hours. It would be best."

She nodded. "The bedrooms are upstairs, though. Will you be able to manage?"

"If you help me."

Which she did, letting him hold her arm while they negotiated the staircase, his body not quite a dead weight as they went up, step by weary step...but almost. He was at the very limits of his endurance, she could tell.

The townhouse had two bedrooms, the master and one that appeared to be a guest room, with two twin beds and a single nightstand between them. Jordan knew she couldn't expect Hasan to cram his tall frame into one of those dinky twin beds, and so she took him to the master suite, easing him down onto the queen-size bed there. She unlaced the boots he wore and pulled them off, then hesitated.

"That will do," he said. "I can sleep in these clothes."

Color rushed to her cheeks, but she nodded. Of course he wouldn't be thinking about doing anything else, not with the state he was in. Once they were away and safely back in Chama...well, with any luck, they'd be able to make up for lost time. A small thrill went through her at the thought.

First things first, though.

"Sleep, Hasan," she told him. "I need to go down and do some cleanup in the kitchen, but I'll be right back."

"Very well."

The words had barely left his mouth before his eyes had shut. Jordan hoped he'd been right when he said sleep would provide a welcome respite. Maybe he could get some of his strength back, and then he'd be able to help with their escape the next day.

She tiptoed down the stairs, mind humming with plans. They had to get away from here. They just had to.

Jordan had come back upstairs soon enough, and disappeared into the bathroom for a little while. Hasan heard water running, and realized she was washing her face and brushing her teeth. He probably should have done the same, but he lacked the strength. At least djinn never had to worry about getting bad breath.

Or rather, they normally didn't have to worry about such things. With the devices disrupting his body in numerous ways large and small, Hasan couldn't hazard a guess as to whether he would need to worry about the same hygiene issues that humans did.

He lay next to Jordan, wishing with all his soul that he possessed the strength to reach out to her, to take her in his arms. But he didn't. He had to save all his energy for surviving, for existing from one moment to the next. That was why he hadn't kissed her, either, even though he'd wanted nothing more than to taste her sweet mouth again.

Soon, he promised himself. They would be away from here, and then....

And then, he wasn't completely sure. He wanted her. He understood that desire with every cell in his weary and aching body. But did he want her enough to commit to her for the rest of his unending days?

That was the real question.

Not one he had to answer now, however. He hadn't wanted to acknowledge the hidden worry that she might not desire him, that once she'd gotten away and was among her own kind, she would realize she had made a terrible mistake, had allowed feelings to develop for someone utterly unworthy of her.

An unfounded worry, clearly. She had taken him in without question, hadn't revealed his identity to the men who'd brought him here. If she'd truly turned on him, she wouldn't have reacted the way she did. That took strength, he realized, the kind of strength he was not sure he possessed. Nothing had ever been difficult for him—at least not until today, when he'd been forced to confront the loss of his djinn powers, the sapping of his body's strength. Jordan's strength was of a different kind, like the thin, flexible steel of a rapier. She might bend, but she would never break.

If he hadn't feared that his touch might wake her, he would have reached over to lay his hand on hers, just so he could feel the silky warmth of her skin, the faint throb of the pulse within her wrist. For now, though, he knew it was best to let her sleep, so she might have her full strength to meet the next day.

He must sleep, too. Strange how difficult that was, considering the weariness weighing down all his limbs. Perhaps the devices interrupted every rhythm in his body, even the ones that told him when it was time to sleep and time to wake. He must do his best, though. He did not know precisely what tomorrow would bring, and he had to get what rest he could. If God smiled on him, then perhaps this would be the only day he would have to suffer Miles Odekirk's devilish devices.

Only this one day, and then he could take Jordan home.

Chapter Sixteen

SUNLIGHT CREPT IN PAST THE MINI-BLINDS AT THE window, catching Jordan at exactly the wrong angle as she sat up in bed, then blinked. She put up a hand to block the tiny, offending rays, then glanced down at Hasan as he slept beside her. His eyes were shut, showing how thick and dark his eyelashes were as they lay against his cheeks, and his dark hair was scattered across the pillow.

She wanted to run her fingers through that hair, wanted to bend down and kiss him awake. He needed his sleep, though. Better to slip out of bed and go barefoot down to the kitchen. Maybe the scent of coffee drifting up the stairs would wake him gently, but if not, she would rouse him once she had breakfast going.

Which wouldn't be much. Yes, there was

coffee in the pantry—she opened the container and sniffed, and determined that it didn't seem too stale—and packets of instant oatmeal. Better than nothing, but....

It's enough to get you going, she told herself as she filled the coffeemaker's carafe with water and set it back on its heating plate. *Once you're back at Hasan's place, you can have him conjure you some eggs Benedict or a breakfast burrito or something.*

Of course, that little scenario assumed that they would be able to get out of here. As she leaned against the counter and watched the coffee begin to drip down into its carafe, she racked her brain for possible ways of obtaining a vehicle. Brent had said he worked at the motor pool. Maybe she could slip in there and spirit away one of the cars while the mechanics were working on something else. Surely they had to have the vehicles they weren't working on stashed somewhere around the property.

It's still stealing. And anyway, how would you be able to tell which cars had already been worked on and were just waiting to be picked up, versus the ones still waiting for repairs?

She probably wouldn't be able to tell. Also, it was a bright, sunny day. Her chances of slipping in without being noticed were pretty low, especially since she didn't know anything about the setup at the auto repair yard.

All right, scratch that one. Brent had seemed friendly, though. Possibly there was a way she could wheedle the loan of a car, as long as she was able to come up with a good excuse. No, he wouldn't go for that. He didn't know her well enough, might think she was planning to take off for some reason. Which of course was exactly what she was planning, but....

Or she could just tell them the truth. Hasan was no threat to them here while the devices were operating. Jordan toyed with that idea for a moment, then pushed it aside. The people here in Los Alamos were friendly with the djinn in Santa Fe. Maybe they would make a radio call to Santa Fe to check in, and then someone there would say that Hasan wasn't a member of their group, was in fact openly hostile to humans. Maybe Brent and Lindsay and Shawn were neutral enough when it came to dealing with djinn, but all it would take was one member of the Los Alamos community with a grudge that could only be settled by seeking personal revenge, and Hasan's life would be on the line. How on earth could she put the person she loved in danger like that? Better to slip away and hope for the best.

"The coffee smells good," Hasan said.

Jordan had been staring out the window at the small backyard as the coffee brewed. The sound of the djinn's voice made her jump slightly, but then she turned and smiled at him. "You should have called for me to come help you down the stairs."

"It was all right. I went slowly."

He moved across the room so he could take a seat at the little bistro set by the window. In the cheerful morning light, he did look a bit better. His mouth wasn't quite so taut and strained, and, while the dark circles under his eyes hadn't disappeared completely, they didn't seem as heavy. Now he just looked tired, rather than like someone who was about to keel over at any second.

"The coffee will be ready in a minute," she said, then went to fetch a couple of mugs down from the cupboards. "There's not much for breakfast except some packaged oatmeal, though."

"That will be fine. It's food."

Jordan wondered if he'd feel the same way after he'd actually consumed the stuff, but she refrained from comment. Instead, she looked back out the window, even though there was nothing to see out there except a slightly rusty charcoal grill and a dilapidated patio set made out of weather-aged redwood. Clearly, whoever had been in charge of prepping the townhouse for future occupation hadn't worried too much about the exterior accoutrements.

"I still don't know what to do about a car," she said, turning back toward Hasan. "About the best thing I can think of is to go to the city center and ask if I can be given my work detail today. Shawn had made it sound as if they'd provide me with a car once I had an actual assignment, so I think that might be the only way to accomplish this without turning into a car thief. And since I don't know how to hot-wire a car, I probably wouldn't be very good at that anyway."

"I don't want you to be a thief," Hasan said.

"Well, I'll still be taking a car. It's just that it won't feel so bad if someone else actually hands me the keys." The coffee looked as if it had dripped all it was going to drip, so she retrieved the carafe and poured some for Hasan, and then filled her own mug. "There's no milk, but I think I saw some sugar in the pantry—"

"This is fine. I need it to be as strong as possible."

Yes, she supposed he did. She watched as he raised the mug to his lips, then paused. "Is something wrong?"

"It's very hot," he told her, then set the mug back down. "Normally that would not be a problem, but now—"

Now, he had no tolerance. What other minor inconveniences that he never would have noticed while in possession of his djinn powers were now springing to the forefront, showing him just how weak he truly was?

She really had to get him out of here.

"Well, drink it when you're ready," she said, hoping that she sounded reassuring rather than just plain worried. "I'll go ahead and boil some water to make the oatmeal."

He nodded, and she went about the mundane tasks of filling the kettle and putting it on the stovetop, then fetching them some bowls and emptying a packet of oatmeal into each one. By the time she was done, the coffee had cooled enough that she could take a few cautious sips. Hasan followed suit, eyes closing briefly as he swallowed the harsh liquid. Definitely not the best coffee she'd ever made, but they weren't going for rich taste, just the effect it would have.

"And they would get the car back," Hasan pointed out, picking up the earlier thread of the conversation.

"True. Well, it sounds as if that's our plan.

After we're done eating, I'll take a quick shower and then head downtown."

Another nod, as though he didn't want to expend the effort required to give a verbal reply. Jordan noticed how he set down his mug of coffee after almost every sip, how his hands had begun to shake again. Whatever benefit he might have gotten from the previous night's sleep appeared to be slipping away quickly.

The kettle began to whistle, and she got up and lifted it from the burner, then poured enough into each bowl to get the oatmeal to a consistency somewhere between paste and glue. At least these were the pre-flavored kind—maple and brown sugar for her, cinnamon and spice for Hasan—so they shouldn't actually taste like glue. Much.

She gave him his bowl of oatmeal, then sat down and drank some more coffee before moving on to the food. It wasn't as bad as she'd feared, although the amount provided by each packet seemed pretty meager. She'd probably be hungry again well before lunchtime. That was okay; she and hunger were old friends. She could cope. However, the short time she'd spent with Hasan had already spoiled her. It had been such a refreshing change to have ample food, all of it delicious, and as varied as it was tasty.

"I can make another packet up for you, if you want," she told Hasan, who showed more enthusiasm for eating the food than he had drinking his coffee, and who was making the oatmeal disappear at a rapid rate.

"No, this should be fine. I don't want to make you waste more time taking care of me. The important thing is for you to go see Shawn and try to get a car."

Jordan wanted to protest, but she knew Hasan was probably right. A clock ticking on the wall opposite the stove told her it was now almost eight. Assuming the clock was correct—and she really didn't have any way of knowing for sure—the hour was still early enough, but not so early that people wouldn't already be working. Maybe. After all, she'd arrived here in the middle of the day, and so didn't have much of an idea as to how they structured their work schedules.

Better safe than sorry, though. She hurriedly ate her oatmeal, then excused herself so she could go take a shower. A fast one, fewer than five minutes, and she didn't bother to wash her hair, since she'd done that the day before. Less than half an hour had elapsed by the time she was back downstairs, dressed and ready to go.

It looked like Hasan had poured himself another cup of coffee, because it was nearly full again. He was staring out the window, expression far away, as she came into the kitchen, but he turned back toward her as she approached, and gave her a slight smile.

"The coffee is helping."

"Good. Hopefully, I won't be gone too long. Will you be okay here without me?"

"Yes. I'll be waiting."

She'd brought his boots with her so he wouldn't have to climb the stairs again. Now she set them down on the floor next to where he sat. "Here you go. I've already packed my things, so once I'm back, I'll just have to run upstairs and grab them. We can be out of here in less than five minutes. Sound good?"

"Yes."

Oh, how she wanted to lean down and kiss him, feel his lips again. He'd been oddly reticent, though. Ashamed of how weak he looked? No shame in that, not with Miles Odekirk's devices doing their best to suck every bit of stray energy out of him. But she realized she should respect Hasan's wishes, and so she only touched his shoulder briefly and said, "Hang tight. I'll be back as soon as I can."

Jordan went out to the garage and retrieved the helmet from where it was hanging on a peg. Someone had disengaged the motor for the garage door opener, probably because it used too much electricity, and so she pushed the door up on her own, wheeled out the scooter, and closed the door again. Maybe it would have been better to leave it open—she'd have to waste valuable time opening it when she got back—but no one else on the street had their garage door standing open, and she didn't want to attract any notice.

The breeze was cool, blowing down from the northwest again, although at least the sun felt warm, even through the long-sleeved T-shirt she wore. As she'd guessed, people were already out and about, most of them on foot, although she saw two pickup trucks, their extended cabs packed to the gills with men, heading out of town, up toward the mountains. What they were up to, she wasn't sure. Maybe going to cut down some trees, to begin stockpiling for the long winter months ahead?

Whatever they were doing, it wasn't any of her concern. She'd be long gone by then.

She hoped.

The parking lot at the city center held about ten cars and trucks. Jordan left the scooter in the motorcycle parking area and went inside the main building, then headed upstairs to the suite where she'd met with Shawn Gutierrez and Katelyn Fonseca the day before. To her relief,

Katelyn was sitting at the desk in the reception area, a walkie-talkie in one hand and an expression of concern on her pretty features. Like Lindsay, Katelyn was almost model-perfect when it came to her looks, a perfect match for Shawn, who was also very good-looking. From what Jordan had seen so far, the people in Los Alamos had a damn good gene pool for starting to repopulate the earth.

As Jordan approached the desk, Katelyn set down the walkie-talkie and made her best attempt at a friendly smile. "Hi, Jordan. I heard you have a friend visiting you."

Of course the men who'd dropped off Hasan would've reported his arrival. She was naïve to think that word wouldn't have gotten around. "Yes, Hank. We, um...met up in Chama."

Katelyn's smile turned sly. "I get the picture. How is he doing? Mitch said he seemed really tired."

"He's fine. He'd walked a long way after his supplies ran out. He's sleeping now." That all sounded mostly plausible, didn't it? Jordan had to hope so.

"Well, I'm glad the guys found him, then. So what can I do for you? I would've thought you'd be staying in with Hank."

"Oh, I'll check on him later, but I thought it

might be a good idea for me to get out for a while. That way, I wouldn't wake him up by accident. So, even though I know you and Shawn told me I had a few days to get settled in, I thought I'd still come by and ask if there was anything you needed help with."

At those words, an expression of relief passed over Katelyn's face. "Actually, there is. Lindsay started having some pains last night—"

"Oh, no," Jordan broke in. With the way Lindsay had looked and acted the day before, this news wasn't entirely unexpected, but still. "Did she have the baby?"

"No. Ellen—she used to be an RN and is the town doctor now, basically—anyway, she said that it still might be a few days, but that Lindsay had been overdoing it and needed to stay in bed until the baby was ready to come. So she's stuck at home by herself, probably going crazy with waiting. If you could go sit with her for a while, I'd really appreciate it."

"Miles isn't with her?"

Katelyn made a face. "Have you met Miles?" Obviously, she'd meant that as a rhetorical question, because she continued, "The last thing Lindsay needs is him fidgeting all over her, or worse, fretting about the work he's not getting done while he's there with her. He's better off working at the lab until he's really needed."

"I guess I can see that."

"Awesome. Their house is up on Barranca Road. Number 144. I'll get you a map."

Katelyn rose from her chair and went over to a file cabinet, then pulled out a piece of paper with a photocopied map of Los Alamos on it. "They made a bunch of these back when people were still coming here and needed to know how to get around. It's kind of circuitous, because you can't just cut straight across—all these plateaus and ravines. But if you go up to 501 and hang a right, then turn left on San Ildefonso, it'll get you there."

"I'll find it," Jordan promised, although inwardly she'd already begun to fret. She didn't need a car for this errand, which meant Katelyn wasn't going to give her one. And here she'd promised Hasan this wouldn't take very long.

Well, there wasn't much she could do about it now. Jordan glanced over the map one more time, then thanked Katelyn and went back out to the parking lot to reclaim her scooter. As she headed south on Trinity Drive, she tried not to curse, just because riding along on a scooter and mouthing obscenities under her breath was probably a good way to get a lot of unwanted attention.

The neighborhood became residential almost as soon as she turned onto 501, also known as Diamond Drive. It wound its way along, following the contours of the hills. Jordan passed a golf course, noted that the properties around her were growing steadily larger, more expensive.

The house that Miles and Lindsay occupied was also very large, on a lot that backed up to open hillside. Considering that he was the town's resident genius...and savior...Jordan supposed it made sense that he would have been given one of Los Alamos' nicest properties to live in.

She parked the scooter at the curb and walked up to the front door, trying not to be intimidated by the tall entryway, the manicured lawn. How did they keep the grass so perfect? Maybe one of the kids she'd seen playing ball the day before helped out; she certainly couldn't imagine Miles Odekirk pushing a lawnmower around. Or maybe they used goats as lawn-grooming devices, just as Hasan did. And how could they justify the water expenditure? Jordan certainly wasn't going to ask, but she couldn't help wondering.

Should she knock, or just go in? Katelyn had

made it sound as if Lindsay was more or less bedridden, so it wasn't as if she was in any position to answer the door. Jordan decided to compromise by cracking the door open—it wasn't locked—and calling inside through the crack, "Lindsay? It's Jordan Wells. Katelyn sent me over to check on you."

"In the family room," Lindsay called back. She didn't sound weak, or in pain. If anything, she sounded irritated. Jordan could only hope that irritation stemmed from being confined to a bed or couch, and not because of Jordan barging in on her.

She went inside, trying not to stare. The place was sleek and modern, the sort of house you could imagine belonging to a nuclear physicist. Did physicists make enough to afford this kind of home? Not that those sorts of concerns were a factor anymore. There were no longer any such things as mortgages. Still, this house was impeccably decorated, from the travertine floors and stacked-stone fireplace to the carefully painted art niches. It didn't feel like Miles. Maybe he'd lived someplace else here in Los Alamos, and then moved to this house after he got together with Lindsay.

The woman in question was reclining on a beige leather couch in the family room, a blanket covering her legs. A paperback book lay on her lap, closed. Her eyes met Jordan's, and the crease that had been working its way between her eyebrows seemed to relax slightly.

"So you got babysitting duty?"

"I wouldn't call it that," Jordan protested. "Katelyn thought someone should be checking on you. Actually, I'm sort of surprised your nurse would let you stay up here by yourself. It's kind of far from the center of town."

Lindsay pointed at the folding tray that had been placed next to the sofa. On it was a glass of water and a pitcher, and next to the pitcher was the same walkie-talkie Lindsay had in the lab with her the day before. "I've got it covered. Miles can be here in just a few minutes. Not," she added, taking the paperback and setting it down on the tray, "that I think this kid is going to be anything like that speedy. No, he's kicking around and fussing up a storm, but despite all that, I think I've still got some time."

"So Brent might still win the pool."

A lopsided smile. "Maybe. Although I hope things don't get stretched out that long. Anyway, go ahead, pull up a chair." She inclined her head toward a blond-wood side chair set up against the wall by one of the windows.

Jordan went and retrieved it, then put it down

by the couch, taking care not to bump the tray with the water and the walkie-talkie. "Can I get you anything? I see you have water, but—"

"No, I'm good. I had some toast earlier. It was about all I could manage to keep down. I keep getting these weird flashes of nausea. Too fun."

Since Jordan didn't know much about pregnancy or childbirth, she had no idea whether that was normal or not. Presumably, Ellen had been keeping track of these symptoms and hadn't been too concerned, or she would've had Lindsay moved to the hospital already. "Well, just let me know."

"I will." She shifted against the pile of pillows that held her upright against the arm of the sofa. "Miles told me that Mitch brought in a friend of yours last night."

Wow, news really did get around. But then, Lindsay was probably looking for anything that would keep her distracted. "Yes," Jordan said carefully. "Hank."

"I thought you were hiding something."

That comment made Jordan start, so much that she almost bumped her chair into the tray next to the couch. "What do you mean?"

"When we were talking at the lab. I got the distinct impression there was something you weren't telling me. I wasn't going to pry, because we'd just met. But...." Lindsay let the words trail off, then cocked her head and fixed Jordan with a steady look, even as she winced slightly as another kick sent its shockwaves through her. "Why wouldn't you want us to know you'd met another survivor?"

"Well, he...." Jordan hesitated, thoughts racing as she tried to piece together a plausible story. "He was dead set on staying on his land. He said he'd made it two years without the djinn finding him, and he didn't see any reason why that should change. That's actually why we quarreled. I wanted him to come down here to Los Alamos with me, and he wanted me to stay there. It wasn't like I could force him, so in the end I left on my own. But I guess he started to worry, started to feel guilty about letting me go, and so he came after me."

"Hmm." From the way Lindsay had responded, Jordan found it almost impossible to tell whether the other woman believed this tale or not.

Since she was already in deep, Jordan decided she'd better plow ahead. "He's resting now. It's not a fun journey, that's for sure, especially when you don't dare drive because it'll attract too much attention."

Lindsay nodded. "Yeah, we have spare devices

that people can take with them if there's some reason to travel outside the area protected by the field. That way, they can take a vehicle and not have to worry about whether the djinn have noticed them."

"You have a lot?" Jordan asked. "Of the devices, I mean."

"Thirty of them now. That's why we have most of Española covered, in addition to Los Alamos. We allow the field to die out about halfway down the 502, just so we don't get too close to Santa Fe. It's only fair, since the people there have helped us out a lot."

"I'm surprised."

A pause as Lindsay shifted her weight, clearly trying to find a more comfortable position, and then she lifted an eyebrow at Jordan. "Why should you be surprised?"

"Well...they're djinn."

"Djinn who have human partners. At first they were a little standoffish, but since then we've learned to work together. Everybody wins. That's why Miles is so dead set on trying to alter his devices so there's a way to let the good djinn into the protected areas while still keeping the bad guys out." She sighed and reached for her glass of water, took a sip. "He still hasn't been able to figure it out, though. I think the tough part is that he knows inventing the original devices was kind of a fluke. Lightning in a bottle. That sort of thing is very hard to replicate."

Jordan didn't know that about Miles's invention, but again, back in the early days after the Heat, the survivors in Colorado Springs had been more interested in knowing they weren't alone in the world and getting tips on how to avoid mankind's destructors than the nitty-gritty of how Miles Odekirk's devices worked. There hadn't been anyone in that group who could have built them, anyway.

"Anyway," Lindsay went on, "we've been making as many as we think we need. It's gotten easier and faster as time wears on. But re-engineering them to do something entirely different? That part's a lot rougher."

"I can imagine." Jordan knew she sounded absent, and she told herself that she needed to focus, to keep acting as if everything was normal. But it wasn't. How could it be when Hasan was a mile away, fighting with every breath to live with the effects of the devices that protected Los Alamos? She was supposed to be getting them a car so they could flee, not sitting here and chatting as if she didn't have a care in the world. There wasn't any way she could have turned down Katelyn's request to come here and check on Lindsay without looking suspicious, but still....

"Jordan."

"What?" God, she sounded guilty.

"What's going on? Really?" Lindsay pushed herself as upright as she was able, probably so she could better look Jordan in the eye. "We don't know each other that well, but I'm still getting the feeling there's something you haven't told me. Is it something about Hank? Was there another reason why you left, the *real* reason? If he's stalking you, or trying to hurt you in some way—"

"Oh, no," Jordan cut in quickly. "It's nothing like that."

"But there is something."

"Yes." She knew she should put on her big-girl panties and keep lying, do whatever she had to, if it meant keeping Hasan safe. She didn't want to, though. Not with Lindsay looking at her like that. No, they weren't friends, but there was something about the other woman's no-nonsense attitude and matter-of-fact way of looking at the world that told Jordan they could have been friends, if circumstances had been different. A deep breath, and then she said in a rush, "If I tell you, do you promise you won't tell anyone?"

Lindsay frowned slightly. "I can't make that

kind of promise. Not if it might endanger the community here, or—"

"No, there's no danger to Los Alamos or anyone in it. I swear."

A long pause. Lindsay fiddled with the blanket that covered her lap, callused fingertips playing with its frayed edges. She let out a breath and said, "All right, I promise."

Now it was Jordan's turn to hesitate. The secret was eating her up inside, but the lies were tearing at her even more. These people didn't deserve to be lied to. And, as she'd told Lindsay, Hasan didn't represent any danger to the community.

Also...and she hated to admit it to herself, but it was only the truth...she wanted someone to talk to, someone she could tell about Hasan, if only so they could tell her that she wasn't absolutely crazy for wanting to be with him. For loving him.

Fingers clenched on the knees of her jeans, Jordan said, "Hank isn't...Hank. He's a djinn named Hasan."

Lindsay's green eyes widened. "You're kidding."

"No. We did meet in Chama. I wasn't lying about that part. It's the land he was given. He found me in his house, searching for food."

"And he didn't blast you off the face of the earth right then and there? Most of the djinn who aren't part of the One Thousand aren't exactly what I'd call forgiving souls."

"No, he didn't. He did...he did make sure I knew I couldn't get away. But soon afterward we became friendlier—and he helped me save the goats—and I realized there was something between us. Not enough, though. Or at least, that's what I thought at the time. That's why I left."

Through all of this semi-incoherent explanation, Lindsay remained silent. Once Jordan was done, however, she shook her head. "I don't get it. I mean—don't get me wrong. You're very pretty. But usually 'pretty' isn't enough to stop a djinn."

Jordan knew that. She still wasn't quite sure what had caused Hasan to show her such mercy. All she could do was be grateful that he'd still possessed some inner grace, something that had prevented him from taking her life the same way he'd taken so many others. "I know. I kept thinking he was going to kill me. But...."

"But he didn't."

"No." Maybe that was enough. Maybe she shouldn't say anything else. She'd told enough lies, though—both to herself, and the people here in Los Alamos. "And it's not—it's not as if he hasn't."

"Killed people, you mean."

She couldn't meet Lindsay's eyes. "Yes," came out in little more than a whisper.

"So he's one of the djinn who hunted down the immune survivors."

"Yes."

"Well, shit." Lindsay pushed a lock of dark blonde hair away from her brow but kept her hand on her head, as if trying to prevent it from aching. "You know this, and still care about him?"

Jordan nodded because she couldn't quite trust herself to speak. Put that way, the whole situation did sound terrible.

"I should tell Miles..." Lindsay began, and Jordan's heart began to beat a little faster. Did she have the courage to snatch the walkie-talkie away from the pregnant woman, if she decided to reach for it? God, that was even worse. "...but I won't."

Jordan blinked at her, not sure she'd heard correctly. "You won't?"

"No. If this Hasan cares enough about you to come here, knowing he'll be in a place where his powers are stripped away and he'll have trouble just breathing, let alone fighting back, then clearly he must have changed in some way. You must have changed him."

"I don't know about that—"

"Well, I do." With a faint groan, Lindsay pushed herself up against the pillows once again. "I was with a djinn, remember? And my djinn—the one who made me his Chosen—he was all about trying to change me, to make me be the woman he wanted." Her brows pulled together, and she went on, "I told you about the djinn glamour. Has Hasan—"

"No," Jordan said quickly, then hesitated. Would she even be able to tell for sure if Hasan was using his powers on her? Maybe not, but she knew deep in her heart that he hadn't. There hadn't been one moment spent with him where she'd felt fuzzy or befuddled, or couldn't remember what had happened, except maybe the time when she'd gone upstairs after he'd kissed her. Even then, she knew the lapse was because her brain was trying to come to terms with what had happened. Other than that single instance, most of the moments she'd shared with Hasan were almost too painfully clear. "No, he didn't try anything like that with me. I didn't even know about this djinn 'glamour' until you and I talked yesterday. Really."

"All right, I believe you." Lindsay went quiet

then, as though she was thinking over what she should say next. "So...what's your plan? I can't imagine that Hasan would want to stay here. I saw the effects of dealing with Miles's devices when I was in Taos. Those djinn were suffering."

"He wants to take me back to Chama," Jordan told her. "Problem is, there's no way he can walk far enough to get away from the energy field, and I don't have a car. Just a scooter."

To Jordan's surprise, Lindsay grinned. "Well, that part I can help you with. When I came here, Shawn gave me a Volvo crossover vehicle, all-wheel drive. I never use it, though, because Miles insists on driving that damn Subaru of his all the time. The Volvo's in the garage now. The keys are hanging on a hook in the kitchen."

"I couldn't—" The protest was a hollow one, though. Jordan knew she'd begun to utter it only because that was what you did in situations like this. What she really wanted to do was run to the kitchen and snatch up the keys before Lindsay changed her mind.

"Yes, you can. Like I said, I never drive it."

"I won't need it after we get to the edge of the field. Once we're there, Hasan can blink us back to Chama. You can send someone to get it."

"Where?"

"On the 582, where it intersects with the main highway just below Velarde."

"It's a plan. So go on, get the keys. The rack is attached to the side of the cupboard near the entrance to the laundry room."

After sending Lindsay a grateful smile, Jordan got up from her chair and went into the kitchen. It was very clean and neat, with what looked like acres of granite countertops. As described, the keys dangled from a hook on a little wooden plaque with a hand-painted "KEYS" across the top. Probably a relic from the previous owners; it didn't seem like Lindsay's style. But there was a leather key fob with the Volvo logo, and an electronic key, one of the fancy kind that you didn't even need to put in the ignition.

Jordan lifted the fob from the hook and went back into the family room. Lindsay was lying back against the pillows, eyes closed.

"Are you okay?" Jordan asked, faintly alarmed. If the baby was coming, she'd have to stay here and wait until help arrived—and hope that no one noticed the missing key to the Volvo.

At once Lindsay's eyes snapped open. "I'm fine. Just tired, and wanting this to be over—and scared about it at the same time."

Jordan could only imagine. For herself, kids

and a family had been relegated to a far-off, misty future, not something she'd contemplated happening anytime soon. Lindsay didn't seem that much older than she; two or three years at the very most. And yet she was married and about to have a baby. "It sounds like you're in good hands with Ellen."

A tired little smile. "True. She's already delivered five babies. All healthy, everyone happy, no complications. Mine's been an uneventful pregnancy, so I don't have any reason to think it'll be different. And it does help that Miles has already gone through this. He'll know what to do."

That's right—the scientist had been married before, had a wife and child. It was still hard to imagine Miles Odekirk as a husband, let alone a father, but he did have experience that Lindsay lacked. That must be reassuring...even if Miles seemed to Jordan to be one of the least reassuring people on the planet.

As she nodded, Lindsay went on, "Anyway, I'm fine. Take the car and go."

"You're sure?"

"Positive. As long as it's okay for me to tell people the truth once you're safely away. I mean, I'll have to give some sort of explanation for why my car was abandoned on the highway up to Taos."

"Oh, that's fine. They won't—they won't try to come after us, will they?"

"No. I mean...." Lindsay let the words trail off and fell silent, as though weighing what to say next. When she continued, her brows were drawn together in a worried little frown. "I won't lie. There are a few people here who probably would want to come after you, try to kill Hasan, just to get some form of revenge. But...."

"But what?" The other woman's words had sent a hideous chill through Jordan, and all she wanted to do was get up and flee, get Hasan out of here, but she also needed to hear what Lindsay had to say.

"What would be the point? Killing one djinn isn't going to bring anyone back. Besides, the only way to effectively get rid of a djinn would be to bring one of our devices along so he'd have all his powers neutralized, and Miles doesn't exactly hand those things out like candy. We need every device we have. So I think you'll be okay."

While Lindsay's words couldn't rid Jordan completely of her worry for Hasan, she had to take them at face value. But she also knew she needed to go. Every minute they lingered here was an additional risk.

Still, Jordan hesitated. She'd been sent up here to keep an eye on Lindsay. It seemed terrible to run out on a woman who could go into labor at any second.

However, Lindsay didn't seem to harbor any doubts about her situation. She made a shooing motion with her hand and said, "Go. Get out of here. Help is just a walkie-talkie call away."

"You're sure?"

"Yes. Although if you keep standing there and arguing with me, you might just send me into labor, and then you really will be stuck."

Jordan couldn't help chuckling. "All right, all right." She began to head toward the kitchen, then paused. "Thanks, Lindsay."

"*De nada.* I want everyone to get their happy ending. Now shoo."

This time, Jordan didn't argue. She went into the kitchen and through the utility room, and on into the garage. As promised, a shiny dark blue Volvo XC60 sat on the far side. She went over to it, opened the door, and got in. A minute to adjust the mirrors and familiarize herself with the layout, and then she pressed the button to start it up.

If the car really had been sitting unused for a while, you'd never know it. The engine turned over right away. Thank God. Jordan reached up to push the remote, which was clipped to the visor, and the garage door began to open. Some paranoid part of her worried that she'd see Miles Odekirk's white Subaru pulling up just as she was leaving, but the driveway and the street beyond it were equally empty. She backed out, then closed the garage door. Obviously, no one was going to tell the Odekirks that they couldn't use their electric door, although whether that was out of deference to Miles's position in the community or Lindsay's advanced pregnancy, Jordan didn't know.

Not that it mattered. It had saved her some time, which was the important thing, especially because she had to stop, put the vehicle in park, then open the hatchback and retrieve her scooter, shove it inside. Thank God the scooter wasn't so heavy that she couldn't lift it on her own, and that the Volvo had enough room to accommodate it.

As she got back in and finished backing out of the driveway, Jordan wondered what she'd do if someone saw her driving Lindsay's car, tried to stop her, ask questions? She'd say she was going to the store to get Lindsay some ice cream. Wait, they probably didn't have ice cream here. Well, she'd think of something. What really mattered was that she had a car, and somehow Lindsay had understood, hadn't thought she was crazy for being in love with Hasan.

And soon, the two of them would be away from here, would be home.

Was Chama home? She didn't know for sure. But she would be there with Hasan, and that was the important thing.

Chapter Seventeen

ONE WOULD THINK THAT AN IMMORTAL BEING wouldn't have an issue with waiting, not when he had all of time to play with, and yet Hasan couldn't quite curb his impatience. He didn't possess the strength to pace about the little townhouse, but he did wait in the living room near the front door, one hand tapping on the knee of his jeans. It seemed as though Jordan had been gone a very long time. The really damnable thing was there wasn't much he could do about it.

Except wait.

A clock ticked away from somewhere within the kitchen, only serving to increase his agitation. Surely it couldn't take that long to go into town, get a work assignment and a car, and then come back here?

Feeling as though hundred-pound weights were attached to each ankle, he got up from the couch and went to the window, then lifted the unattractive plastic blinds slightly so he could peer through them. The street was empty, the only movement the leaves of the trees rustling in the breeze. At least he didn't have to worry about anyone coming up the walk and asking questions about his presence here.

Not yet, anyway. The men who had found him at the Walmart the evening before appeared to have accepted his explanations as to who he was and why he was here in Los Alamos, but perhaps as time passed, more questions would enter their minds, questions they'd want answered.

And here he was, utterly unable to defend himself.

No, he was borrowing trouble. These people had no reason to be suspicious of him, especially with Jordan out and about with them, ready to put in a good word. Yes, it would be difficult if he had to keep up this charade for any amount of time, but as things stood—

A dark blue vehicle pulled into the driveway. Hasan didn't recognize the car, but he was able to see Jordan behind the wheel. Relief rushed through him, making him feel weaker than he already was. He staggered back to the couch and sat down. He needed to conserve his strength, make sure he was ready to face whatever might happen next.

Apparently Jordan wasn't going to bother with pulling into the garage. She parked the car, and came up the front walk and into the living room. A small frown had been pulling at her brows, but it eased as soon as she saw him, and she smiled.

"I have a car," she said.

"I saw that."

"I'll just run upstairs and get my pack, and then we can go."

"What if someone sees you carrying it?"

"There's no one around. I don't know how many people actually live on this street, but whoever they are, they're gone now. Off at work, I suppose, or at least, doing the jobs they've been assigned." She came up to him, took his hand, gave it a small squeeze. "I'll be right back."

Then she was hurrying away from him, running up the stairs. In that moment, he envied her energy, the way she could bound up to the second floor of the townhouse as though it was nothing. Well, soon enough they'd be away from here, and he'd be himself again.

Once more he made his limping way over to

the window and peered out. As Jordan had told him, the street was deserted, and he felt some of the tension go out of his shoulders. He wouldn't be able to relax all the way until they were safely beyond the borders of Los Alamos, and farther still, to the edge of the field generated by Miles Odekirk's devices.

Jordan came trotting down the stairs, her pack bouncing on her back. When she came into the living room, she paused and pulled a key out of her pocket, then set it down on the coffee table. Hasan gave her a mystified look, and she explained, "It's the key to the house. I figured I'd leave everything unlocked. No one will disturb anything that's here, and it'll make it easier when someone does come around, looking for me. I don't know how many keys they have to this place."

That made sense. "I understand," he said. "Anything else?"

"No," she replied. "Let me just check outside real fast."

She opened the front door and paused on the front stoop. Apparently, she was satisfied with what she saw, because she went to the car and opened one of the doors to the back seat, then put her backpack inside. Now unencumbered, she came back to Hasan, offering him her arm. He began to protest, but she shook her head.

"We'll move faster with me helping you."

As much as he would have liked to argue, he knew she was right. Soon enough he would be restored to himself, wouldn't have to shuffle around like an invalid. He looped his arms in hers, and she guided him over to the car, opened the passenger-side door, and helped him slide in. After she shut the door, she went over to take her own seat, quickly settling herself in, one finger touching the button to start the ignition.

While they were backing out of the driveway, she put on her seatbelt and said, "Better fasten yours. Not that I plan to do any stunt driving, but you never know."

He did as she told him, wondering what would happen if he was injured while still in the djinn-repelling field's zone of effect. Would he have any of his djinn powers of healing, or would he be just as vulnerable as an ordinary mortal?

Hasan thought he would prefer not to find out.

Jordan had the car moving along at a good clip, but not so fast that their speed was likely to attract attention. Houses and autumn-hued trees passed by outside, until she pulled onto a main road and turned left, going away from the heart of town. So far they'd passed one other vehicle, a truck with a man and a woman in the front seat, but they hadn't appeared terribly interested in what he and Jordan were doing. And really, why would they be? This was a town of humans, a place where they'd been able to live safely for two years. They wouldn't suspect that they had a hostile djinn in their midst, let alone one who was being aided and abetted by a fellow human being.

Despite the lack of interest shown by the other inhabitants of Los Alamos, Hasan let out a small sigh of relief as they passed the town limits and began to make their way down the steep, winding highway that would take them into Española. While there were cars parked on the side of the road, the asphalt itself was clear, indicating that mortal work crews had dedicated themselves to the laborious task of getting all the abandoned vehicles out of the way.

Once they were down in Española, Jordan turned toward him and offered him a smile. "See, that wasn't hard, was it?"

"We are not out of the field yet," he said.

"I know, but we're out of Los Alamos, and that was where I figured we'd have the biggest chance of someone trying to stop us. The only people in Española are those who've been sent out on a scavenging party, and I figured it shouldn't be too hard to dodge a crew of four or five people—if they're even here at all. I don't know what their schedules are like, but I have a feeling they don't come down here every day."

Hasan hoped she was right. It would make sense to go out on one of these missions where they sought what usable goods were still left, then catalogue what they'd retrieved before they went out again. Were the mortals in Los Alamos that organized? From what he'd seen so far, yes, they were.

By all appearances, this was a ghost town. The streets had been cleared, but otherwise he thought everything must remain as it had been in the days that immediately followed the Dying. Storefronts boarded up, evidence of glass and other detritus still in some of the parking lots, even two years after that world-changing event. Pieces of paper so yellowed and shredded by the weather that they now looked more like dried leaves than artifacts of a civilization long gone. Yes, he'd seen much the same thing in the streets of Albuquerque—only in Albuquerque, Hasan's erstwhile friend Qadim had done his best to clean things up, especially in the area around downtown. He'd had a vested interest, since that barren cityscape had been his gift from the elders.

"Do you think they'll ever settle down here?" he asked as they passed a row of fast food restaurants.

Jordan shook her head. "I doubt it. After all, Los Alamos was a decent-sized town before the Dying, more than ten thousand people, I think. Even with some of the survivors starting families of their own, there probably can't be more than a thousand of them. They have a lot of room to grow before they have to start worrying about moving into Española."

Families. He supposed he shouldn't be surprised. Humans always had bred like rabbits. Djinn were much more careful about such things, planning carefully when to have children, if ever. Many djinn were like him and had no siblings at all, while others might have only one brother or sister. It was sufficient to ensure the continuation of the family name—for while djinn might be immortal, they were not indestructible—without putting an undue burden on the admittedly scanty resources of the otherworld.

He realized then that he'd never heard Jordan speak about her family. Perhaps her reticence stemmed from the pain of losing her relatives, but it did seem strange that she had never mentioned them.

"What of your family?" he asked, and she shot him a surprised look.

"'My family'?" she repeated. "What has that got to do with anything?"

"Perhaps nothing," he said. "But you did just say that the survivors in Los Alamos were starting families of their own, and so that made me wonder about your relatives."

Her fingers tightened on the steering wheel. "I didn't have much family to speak of. My dad left when I was a little kid, and my mother never remarried or had any other children. Her sister, my Aunt Liz, lived in Colorado Springs, too. We were pretty close. She got divorced before I was even born, and she also never remarried. So...no brothers or sisters, no cousins. My grandparents died in a car crash when I was six." She expelled a breath, her gaze studiously fixed on the road. Hasan could understand why she didn't want to look over at him; the portrait she painted was of a fairly bleak family history. "I probably had some distant relatives in Omaha, which was where my grandparents lived before they moved to Colorado Springs, but my mother never really tried to stay in touch. Too busy keeping a roof over our heads, I guess. What does it matter? Everyone's gone. *Everyone.*"

Better not to speak. He knew there was nothing he could say, after all. His people had done this, and he had been a willing participant. Yes, he had done his work here in New Mexico, and not anyplace she or her small family had lived, so he supposed he could argue he was not directly responsible for the deaths of anyone close to her, but that sort of rationalization would be disingenuous at best.

An ache within him, one he wished he could blame on the effects of the djinn-repelling devices. Those machines were not the source of his current discomfort, however. He wished he could ignore it, could pretend he felt nothing.

That would only be another lie. He knew exactly what the gnawing sensation in his midsection was.

Guilt.

Nothing he said, nothing he did, could change what had happened. He supposed he should be giving his thanks to God that at least he had met Jordan, had allowed her to thaw his heart. Was there any grace to be found in loving her? He prayed there might be.

"I'm not blaming you," she went on, apparently guessing at the reason for his silence. "Or rather, I won't blame you for their deaths. You're responsible for a lot, but not that."

"Thank you," he murmured.

"I'm probably just rationalizing. Anything to have it make sense for me to care about you. It's crazy." Still with her eyes straight ahead, not looking at him. By this point, they had left the ugly trappings of modern America behind them, and were driving through empty fields, the road bordered with warm autumn wildflowers, gold and orange. Her words hurt him, but he did not interrupt, knew that he needed to let her speak. "I mean," she went on, "I could have made a home in Los Alamos. It's the place where I should be. Instead, I'm going in the opposite direction, driving a fugitive djinn so he can get his powers back. And all because I think I'm in love with you."

Tears glistened in the corners of her eyes. Hasan could see them clearly because of the way the bright morning sun slanted in through the car windows. More than anything, he wanted to reach out to her, take her in his arms, weak and useless as they might be right now. But he also wanted her to keep driving. They were getting close now. A few more minutes, and they would be at the edge of the energy field, and he could be himself again.

"I'm sorry to have put you in this position," he said, and hated the words as soon as they left his mouth. They sounded stiff and formal, something one might say to a fellow at arms, or a business partner, but certainly not to the woman he loved.

Jordan lifted one hand from the steering wheel to wipe at her eyes. "It's more like I've put myself in this position. I could have tried to stop myself from falling for you, and I didn't."

Were feelings that easily ignored? Hasan didn't think so, but he also didn't try to argue with her. He understood—or at least, he thought he understood—why she would hate herself for caring for him. It was a betrayal of her very nature.

Some djinn might try to tell him that he had betrayed himself as well, and the rest of his people, but he didn't see it that way. For one thing, whatever atrocities mankind might have committed, whatever havoc humanity might have wreaked on this beautiful world it had been given, Jordan herself was innocent of all that. She had worked to make this earth a better place. She deserved nothing of what had happened to her. Nothing.

Especially not him.

"Here we are," she said, pulling over to the

side of the road next to a mile marker. "Can you feel it?"

"No," he replied sadly. It pained him to think of how the devices' dark energy destroyed anything djinn about him. "Not while I'm inside the field. Outside, when I have access to my power—that is a different matter."

"Then let's go."

She turned off the engine, and took a bulky electronic key from her pocket and laid it on top of the dashboard. Hasan sent her a questioning look.

"I'm just borrowing the car. Lindsay Odekirk loaned it to me. I told her I'd leave it here, and then she could have someone come and get it. But none of that is going to do much good if I take the key with me."

"She cannot come to fetch it herself?"

"Not really, considering she's going to go into labor any day now."

For some reason, that piece of information disquieted him. Hasan couldn't even say why, precisely, since Jordan had said that the mortals in Los Alamos had begun to have families of their own. Perhaps it was only the thought of Odekirk's bloodline continuing, that the man who had been such a thorn in the side of the djinn community would now possibly have a son —or daughter—to carry on his work.

"Ah," Hasan said. "I can see why she might have other matters on her mind."

For the first time, Jordan smiled. It was a tired little smile, but it still lit up her beautiful blue eyes and erased some of the weariness from her features. "Well, let's get going."

She undid her seatbelt and opened the door, and Hasan followed suit. A brief pause while she retrieved her backpack from the back seat, and then they were walking slowly down the road, retracing the steps they had taken only a few days earlier, albeit separately.

He might not have been able to sense the boundaries of the field while he was in it, but he knew the second he had crossed that invisible border. At once the weight dragging at his legs and arms was gone, and he could pull in a deep breath of the cool air, smell the scent of dry, warm grass. It was as though a cloud had lifted from the sun, and all the color had returned to the world again.

Without stopping to think, he plucked the pack from Jordan's back and dropped it to the ground, then pulled her into his arms. Ah, the sweetness of her lips, the softness of her hair as it brushed against his hands! He wanted to drink her in, savor her as he hadn't before, simply because he'd had no way of knowing how perfect she was until she was gone.

For the briefest instant, Jordan went stiff, as though from surprise, and then she wrapped her arms around him as well, opened her mouth to his, clearly as eager to taste him as he'd been to savor her. The lingering weakness in his body was gone, and he began to harden, needing her, wanting her. Damn these heavy jeans, the way they confined him. He needed them gone.

Well, such a thing was simple enough to accomplish, now that he was away from the djinn-repelling field. A mental blink, nothing more, and gone were the jeans and the flannel shirt and the work boots, and in their place were flowing silken robes in a deep azure hue.

Jordan gasped, then looked down at him. "I guess you really don't like human clothes, do you?"

"No, I don't." Another blink, and she was wearing a tight-fitting silk coat in a brocade of blue and deep rose, and matching pants and under-blouse. Jeweled slippers glimmered on her feet.

"You could give a girl some warning, you know." But she spoke with a twinkle in her eye and a smile on her lips. Clearly, she wasn't too bothered by the imposition.

"What would be the fun in that?"

She shook her head, and began to reply, but the words never left her lips. How could they, when in the next instant, he had transported her —and that damn backpack—to the living room of the house in Chama?

To her credit, she didn't try to chide him, only ran a hand through her wind-tousled hair and gave a quick glance around, as though to reassure herself of her surroundings. "Well, it all looks the same."

"Why wouldn't it? You've only been gone two days."

"Have I? It felt longer than that." She came to him and slipped her arms around his waist. "I— I'm sorry for what I said earlier."

"There's no need for you to feel sorry. I understand why you might feel that way. In fact, I would be more surprised if you did not."

Her body sagged against him as she leaned her head against his chest. "Thank you. I mean... oh, hell, I don't even know what I mean, or what I'm thinking anymore."

"You've had a busy time. It is understandable."

She didn't reply for a moment, but pulled

away so she could stand there and watch him carefully. Hasan did his best not to blink or look away, although it felt odd to be subjected to such scrutiny. Then she said, "What do you want most right now?"

He didn't hesitate. "You."

A slow smile spread over her lips. "The feeling is mutual. So...."

"So," he repeated. Now that they were here together, with nothing keeping them apart, he experienced an odd hesitation. They had made no promises to one another, except to admit that they both cared for each other. What did that mean, exactly, though? She was not his Chosen. She was only a mortal human.

Whom he loved. Whom he wanted so much that he did not know if he could wait another second to have her. They could figure out the rest of this later.

In the meantime, he had to make her his.

Chapter Eighteen

As soon as Hasan approached her, took her in his arms, she knew what was going to come next. Her heart pounded in her chest, but she wouldn't stop him. She had no idea where any of this would end, but she had enough regrets. Too many empty months, too many cold, lonely nights.

All right, it wasn't nighttime, was blazing bright daylight on a perfect October morning. That didn't matter, though. What mattered was the way Hasan lifted her from the floor as though she weighed nothing, carried her up the stairs to his room. He could have blinked them both there, she knew, but she guessed that he wanted to do it this way, wanted to prove to her that he'd regained all his strength.

Truly, this was a much better place for them to make love for the first time, rather than the cramped bedroom of that shabby townhouse. The drapes had been pulled shut, but the window beneath them was open, and the shimmering silk shivered in the breeze. The hangings on the bed also moved with that gentle wind, as though enticing her to lie down within their depths.

Not that she needed much of an enticement, not with Hasan setting her down on the bed's billowy softness. The mattress cradled her like nothing she'd ever experienced before, welcoming her. And there was Hasan, pulling the jeweled slippers from her feet, right before he lay down next to her and drew her close, mouth claiming hers again, bodies pressed to one another. She could feel his warmth, the heat of his flesh, through the silken garments she wore, and a delicious shiver passed over her.

"Cold?" he murmured.

"No. Just the opposite."

"Ah."

Then he was kissing his way down her throat, his fingers working the silver buttons of the long fitted coat she wore. It parted, revealing the thin silk of the undershirt beneath. His breath was hot as his lips traveled across her chest, and he pulled the undershirt down so his mouth could close on her breast, tongue tracing its way around her nipple.

She gasped, heat flooding her, pulsing warmth growing between her legs. It had been so long since she'd felt like this, she'd halfway worried that her body wouldn't remember what to do. But it was responding to Hasan's touch like a flower waking after a long winter's sleep, opening to him, ready. His fingers found the drawstring of the blousy pants she wore, tugged it loose so he was able to slip his hand inside.

Oh, God. He was touching her, stroking her, and she was already so wet for him, so ready. He made a guttural sound in his throat, as though pleased to find her so responsive. She wanted to respond to him, to show him how much she wanted him.

Her hands slipped over the heavy muscles of his chest, caressing. The silk trousers he wore did nothing to conceal his arousal, and she liked that as well, liked that he was reacting to her in such a way.

She wanted more, though. She wanted to feel him the way he was feeling her. Since his pants were constructed in much the same fashion as hers, it was easy enough to locate the drawstring that held them tight to his narrow waist, and yank at the cord.

They didn't slip down right away, of course. Not with his massive erection holding them up. He paused for a second in stroking her so he might ease them down past his cock, and then they fell in a slither of silk to the floor.

Oh, dear God, his body was amazing. Her hand slipped over his shaft, feeling how rock hard he was, how smooth his skin. He moaned softly, even as his mouth found hers again, lips demanding, needing to taste her.

As she needed to taste him. Had she ever lost herself in a kiss like this? She didn't think so. At the same time, he kept caressing her, strong fingers finding the spot where she needed to be touched, where she hadn't been touched in so very long—

The orgasm took her by surprise, hitting with the suddenness and ferocity of a lightning strike during a summer monsoon storm. Her back arched, and she had to keep herself from biting down on his lip, from screaming her ecstasy into his open mouth. He held her close, stroking her hair as the climax shuddered its way through her body.

"I love you," he murmured, shifting so his body covered hers.

For a moment, she flashed back to the night they had met, when he had pursued her, had held her down. This wasn't so different—the weight of his body against hers, although now he wasn't trying to keep her from running away.

Oh, no. She would never run away from him again.

He pushed into her, and she wrapped her legs around him, driving him deeper. Yes, he was big, but she knew she could manage. Really, she was so aroused, so wet, that he slipped in with no resistance, filling her in a way she'd never imagined was even possible. They rocked together, falling into a shared rhythm, one that gradually increased its pace, until she knew she was going to come again, that every cell in her body was about to thrill to the same burst of ecstasy.

A cry escaped her throat, and Hasan let out a brief, hard breath, right before he tensed, then spilled into her, filling her body with his heat. She welcomed that release, so glad she'd been able to make him feel that way. As he relaxed and lay on top of her, however, a stray, unwelcome thought slipped through her mind.

Oh, shit. We didn't use protection.

There wasn't anything she could do about it now, but inwardly she berated herself for being so careless. You'd think her friend Suzanne's near-miss back in Pagosa Springs would have made her a little more careful.

Well, she'd just gotten over her period when the djinn had attacked and she'd run for the hills, so maybe she wasn't yet in the fertile part of her cycle. Hard to believe all that had happened only a little more than a week ago, harder still to believe that she now lay in the arms of one of those djinn, someone who should have been a hated enemy but instead was the man she loved.

Hasan rolled off her, reached out to cup her cheek with one hand. He must have sensed her worry, because he asked, "Jordan, is something wrong? Did you not want that?"

She had to chuckle. "Oh, no, I wanted it. I just —I just should've thought about having you use protection."

"'Protection'?" he repeated, a puzzled frown pulling at his dark brows.

"So I wouldn't get pregnant. I mean, it sounds as if humans and djinn can reproduce, so—"

"There is nothing for you to worry about," he cut in, then took one of her hands and held it to his lips so he might press a gentle kiss against her palm. "There are no such things as 'accidents' with djinn. We decide when we want to have children. It cannot happen without conscious effort."

Although relief flooded through her, Jordan still tried to figure out how that might work. "So, what—you just tell your little wigglers that today's the day, and then it's a done deal?"

"Perhaps not exactly in that manner, but yes, more or less. We are certainly not ready to become parents, and so I made sure it wouldn't happen."

"Ah." She knew she should be glad that he'd been proactive about the whole thing, but something about the "not ready to become parents" remark rubbed her the wrong way, as though he didn't think they were serious enough for such a thing to happen.

Which of course they weren't. They might have declared their love for one another, and they might have just had sex, but they were a long ways off from discussing any kind of a future, especially one that included children.

"Does this bother you?"

"No," she said at once. The last thing she wanted was for Hasan to think she was disappointed in him, or in what they had just shared. It was rather a lot to process. "It's nice to know that I won't have to worry about a baby. We've got enough on our plates, right?"

"Yes," he replied, although there was something almost hesitant about the word.

"Speaking of which," she said. "Our breakfast was almost nonexistent, and you just worked up my appetite. Could you conjure something for the two of us?"

"Of course. I will admit that I am rather hungry."

She smiled and leaned over to kiss him. Not a long, drawn-out kiss, but just a quick touch of lips against lips, enough to show that she was glad of the intimacies they'd just shared, and had no worries for their future.

Whether he believed it or not...that she didn't know.

───────

Jordan seemed subdued, but Hasan didn't press her to explain herself. Their relationship would be forever different now, and she must find her own way in working through that change. They climbed out of bed and got dressed again, then went downstairs. He conjured eggs Benedict and home fries because that was what she asked for, and they ate slowly, enjoying their food.

It was only after their late breakfast—or early lunch—was done that he worked up the nerve to broach the subject he knew they must discuss. When two humans or two djinn were intimate, they might go on with their lives as though nothing momentous had occurred, but such was not the case when a djinn and a mortal lay together...at least not now, in this world after the Dying, where there were strict rules about such things.

He brought her out to the porch so they might sit on the bench there and catch some of the early afternoon sun, now falling full on the front of the house. Jordan took her seat next to him and lifted her face to the breeze, which was not strong enough that it could take away from the warmth of the sun. She looked very beautiful like that, eyes half shut so her thick lashes almost lay on her cheeks, glints of gold showing in her loose hair.

"I spoke to you a while ago of the Chosen, of who they were," he began, and her eyes opened, focusing on him intently.

"Yes."

"I want you to be my Chosen, Jordan."

She went very quiet, gaze fixed on him. Perhaps she breathed, but he couldn't discern any rise or fall of her breasts. It seemed that his words had shocked her into a stillness beyond silence.

They had come as rather a shock to him as well. How many of his djinn brethren would laugh at him, if they learned of his abrupt about-face? That Hasan al-Abyad, hunter of mortals, had lost his heart to a human woman, wished to make her his partner for eternity?

Even he could recognize the irony of the situation.

"That means...." The words trailed off, as though she couldn't quite find it within her to give voice to the thought.

"It means that we would be together forever, my love. We would be bonded, soul to soul. You would never age, would remain as you are now. You would never become ill, and would be able to recover from all but the most grievous of injuries."

"How...?" She moistened her lips, then went on, "How is that possible?"

"Because when we are joined, you take some of my strength, some of my djinn energy. Not so you would have my ability to call the wind, or to travel instantly from place to place. Magic flows in my veins, as it does not in yours, because you are human. But the connection will give you some of a djinn's physical advantages."

Another long silence. She looked off into the distance, at the stands of gold-crowned cotton-woods that bordered the river. The wind caught her hair, ruffling the fine strands around her face.

Hasan let himself admire the fine, delicate outlines of her profile, even as he willed himself to remain quiet, to allow her to think. It seemed he had caught her off guard, but surely she must have known that something like this might be coming. Or perhaps not. He had spoken to her of the Chosen, true, but that was before he realized the depth of his feelings for her. Very likely, she had not believed she would be put in the position of having to decide whether she could accept such a proposition.

This was unusual, he knew. The djinn of the One Thousand had made their decisions and claimed the humans they selected, and the humans had to go along with those choices, for good or ill. Whether they all ended up happy, he had no way of knowing, because he had held himself apart from those djinn and their humans, thinking them foolish and misled, and straying far from the true path he himself followed.

Unlike them, he was offering the woman of his heart a choice. It was, he thought, a great deal to ask, to share eternity with someone you had barely known for a few days. And yet that was the only path she could take, if she wished to be with him. On that point, the rules were very clear.

And if she turned him down, did not believe their new and fragile love was something that could stand the test of time? He would have no choice but to return her to Los Alamos, for that was the only place where he knew she might be safe. That would be a great irony, to give his heart to a mortal, only to find she did not want it after all.

Jordan turned back toward him, and reached out so she might take his hands in hers. The touch of her flesh was enough to rekindle the heat within him, but he knew he must not allow himself to react. There would be many opportunities for them to make love to one another...if she said yes.

Her fingers tightened on his. "I want to be your Chosen, Hasan. What do I have to do?"

"Nothing but what you have already done, my love." He raised her hand to his mouth, kissed the delicate but strong fingers. "And I must tell the universe that Jordan Marie Wells is my Chosen, and that she is forever bonded to my heart, forever under my protection."

The wind swirled around them. An acknowledgment of the words he had just sent out into the world? Perhaps. The thing was done. He could sense it, sense a sharpened awareness of her presence, of every breath she took, every shift in expression.

"Was that it?" she asked. "I don't feel any different."

"No, you would not, I expect. You will notice the change if you experience a mishap where you might otherwise have injured yourself, or if you get soaked going out in a rainstorm and yet never catch a cold...or look in the mirror year after year, and continue to see yourself as you are now. As I said, it is a subtle thing, this change that has now been wrought."

And because he could not hold back any longer, he pulled her to him, kissed her there in the sunlight, feeling the bond between the two of them strengthen. She responded with eagerness, mouth open, body pressed against his.

Hasan was just contemplating whisking her away, back up to the bedroom, when their kiss was interrupted by a loud *bang,* followed by some very angry-sounding bleating. At once Jordan pulled away, her eyes wide.

"What in the world was that?" she asked.

"The goats," he replied, realizing what must have made the noise. "I left them shut up in the barn, so they might be safe, but I think that they have heard us, and are not very happy about being kept inside when they know we are here to let them out."

"Then I guess we'd better go take care of them," Jordan said. She let go of his hand, but gently, and got to her feet.

With a resigned sigh, Hasan rose as well. He would have much preferred to take her back to bed, but there would be time enough for that later.

All of eternity, in fact.

———

Jordan hurried up the hill toward the barn, Hasan a pace or two behind her. Although she could sense his disappointment, he hadn't made any protest about coming up here to rescue the goats. And really, as much as she wanted to go to bed with him again, she thought that having a little breathing space wasn't a bad idea. She needed some time to process what had just happened.

She was no longer an ordinary human. She was Chosen.

Hasan had explained something of what that meant, but Jordan had a feeling it would take her some time to really wrap her head around the notion that she was no longer aging, that she would be perpetually twenty-five, in a future that had no real end. She would have been crazy to turn him down, and yet...what if they started to get tired of one another after fifteen years, or twenty, or even a hundred? Hell, her own father hadn't even lasted for five.

No, better to push those thoughts away. Hasan was definitely not her father. She knew she still had a lot to discover about the djinn who'd somehow fallen in love with her, but casual with his affections he most certainly was not. He would not have asked if he hadn't truly believed that his love for her was strong enough to last through uncounted years.

She pulled on the handle for the barn door, and it opened. Hasan had left it unlatched, probably thinking that the goats could kick their way out if he stayed away too long. Clearly, they'd entertained the same idea, because they came milling out as soon as the door opened, the wood showing new gouges where they'd given it a few experimental blows.

Quickly stepping out of the way, she watched as the goats hurried into the field, taking up positions almost at once as they began cropping at the grass. Looking at them, Hasan smiled—a real smile, with no irony or sarcasm in it. She loved the way that smile lit up his dark blue eyes, showed off the flash of his perfect white teeth.

Yes, right then she thought she could survive eternity with him quite well.

Jordan went over to him and slipped her hand in his, leaned her head against his shoulder. He gave her fingers a gentle squeeze, as though he, too, recognized this moment of quiet happiness for what it was.

"There are more of them than there were," she remarked, watching the goats.

"Yes," he said. "I knew we hadn't found them all, and so I went out and rounded them up after you left."

He didn't say anything more than that, but she thought she understood. She might have pressed him to track down the goats and make sure they were safe the first time around, but after that, he'd felt duty-bound to make sure their brothers and sisters were also taken care of.

It was small things like that, she thought, that had made her fall in love with him. Some might say it was only physical attraction—and God knows, Hasan was handsome enough—but she knew it was more than something so superficial. An odd gentleness lurked within him, one she would never have expected to find, given his history. While she wouldn't make excuses for the things he had done, she thought she under-stood...at least a little. His actions had sprung from a deep anger at what mankind had done to this world, a desire to put things right. And while Jordan knew she herself could never have acted in such a way, she thought she recognized the crusading streak that had spurred his actions.

"We will have to leave, you know," he said quietly, and she startled and looked up at him.

"'Leave'?" she repeated. "What do you mean?"

"I mean that you are now my Chosen, and since we have bonded, we must go to live with the other djinn in Santa Fe."

"But...aren't these your lands?"

"Not anymore. It is part of the compact the One Thousand made with the elders. Those djinn and their human lovers must live apart from the rest of our kind, have their own communities."

A pang went through her as she looked at the sun-warmed meadows, the blaze of aspens in the distance. "I'm sorry."

"Don't be. It is an easy sacrifice, if it means I can be with you."

A wave of warmth went through her as she looked up at him. Love, yes, but more than that—a sort of affection she didn't think she'd ever felt before. She began to go up on her tiptoes, so she might kiss him on the cheek...

...only to feel a rough arm go around her throat and yank her backward, even as a pale-haired djinn woman materialized a few feet away from Hasan and gave him a mocking smile.

"Hello," said Danya. "Am I interrupting something?"

Chapter Nineteen

THEY'D ARRIVED SO SUDDENLY, HASAN DIDN'T have time to react. A muffled little cry from Jordan as the hulking Farid grasped her by the throat and pulled her away was Hasan's only warning. That, and Danya appearing before him, wearing a languid, scornful smile.

"Let her go," he rasped, and took a step forward.

Danya lifted her eyebrows and shot an uninterested glance at Jordan, whose eyes were wide with fear, pleading for him to rescue her. "Don't be tedious, Hasan," she said. "Really, I'm doing you a favor. What do you think would happen to your reputation if word got out that you were consorting with one of these creatures? You would never hear the end of it."

"I am not 'consorting,'" he spat. "Jordan is my Chosen now. You have no right to touch her."

This revelation made Danya pause for a moment, but then she lifted her shoulders in a negligent shrug. "A convenient story. Was there anyone here to witness you making her your Chosen?"

"Of course not. That is not necessary. The elders will recognize my bond with her."

"Oh, I suppose they would...if they were here. But since they are not, it will be your word against mine...and Farid's. Isn't that right, darling?"

The hulking djinn nodded, arm still wrapped around Jordan's throat. "Yes. No one will know."

Hasan's hands tightened into fists. He knew he would have to be careful here, however. In a contest of sheer strength, he would most certainly lose. Also, if he initiated a physical confrontation, he couldn't know for sure that Danya might not join in, thus making any show of force even more lopsided. He guessed that she would prefer to stay on the sidelines, so to speak, and watch her former and her present lover battle one another, but he couldn't be sure of that.

Willing himself to remain calm, Hasan said,

"Danya, such jealousy is unbecoming of you. Jordan is not your rival. Indeed, you gave every indication of being glad to see me go. So why should you care what I do now...or with whom I do it?"

During this little speech, the djinn woman's expression shifted from irritation to amusement. "Oh, my dear Hasan—surely you don't believe this is about you? I am most certainly not jealous, so please dismiss that notion. You always did have too high an opinion of yourself."

"Then again, I must ask—why interfere? What possible difference does my relationship with this human make?"

Danya glanced from him to Jordan. Even with Farid's arm wrapped around her throat, Jordan appeared more angry than frightened. Hasan could only pray that she wouldn't try anything foolish, that she would let him manage his fellow djinn. He knew his lover was intelligent and resourceful, but those qualities weren't quite enough to allow her to prevail against two immortals who outmatched her physically in every way.

"You should know the answer to that question very well, Hasan," Danya said. She played with the silver bangles she wore, the tinkling little metallic sound they made somehow discordant, annoying. He recalled how that was a nervous habit of hers...and how much it had come to irritate him. "You made your opinion of humans and their works quite clear. Indeed, it is one that you shared with many of our people, myself included. So I am doing this for your own good, in order that you might abandon this madness which seems to have seized you. The time to select a Chosen is long past. If you had cared that much, you would have counted yourself among the One Thousand. You did not, however, which means that, deep in your soul, you care little whether humans live or die. This female has taken your fancy, it seems, but it can only be a passing fancy, nothing more. If I remove her from the world, you will come to your senses soon enough."

"I fear you have misread me," Hasan returned. He wanted to shout at Danya for her arrogance, her presumption in believing she knew his soul better than he did himself. Losing his temper would accomplish nothing, however, save perhaps to make Farid act by snapping Jordan's neck and ending this once and for all. "I will not deny that I sought vengeance for our people, and for the damage done to this world, but Jordan is innocent of all that. Indeed, she devoted her life to making sure that damage did not continue."

This plea did not seem to move Danya. She lifted an ironic eyebrow, wound a lock of moonlight-pale hair around a finger, then lifted her shoulders. "So you say. If that is the case, then good for her. But her services are not needed, because we djinn are the masters of this earth now, and we know it is safe, with the humans gone."

Hasan did not reply immediately. In truth, he was not sure how he should reply, since it seemed that no matter what he said, Danya would find an argument to counter his words. Perhaps it was time to strike at Farid, and hope that the element of surprise would be enough to allow him to prevail.

He realized that Jordan was staring at him, ignoring the two djinn. Was she pleading with him to do something? No, he didn't think so—her expression was quite blank, and she didn't look frightened at all. Then he saw her gaze slide away, past him to where the goats happily munched on the frost-yellowed grass, apparently unconcerned by the confrontation taking place a few yards away from where they stood.

Why on earth was Jordan looking at the goats? Her attention returned to him, but only for the barest trace of a second. Again she glanced over at the goats, and gave the faintest nod of her head.

Of course.

Hasan had to keep himself from smiling. By all appearances, the situation was more than dire, and so to begin grinning for no reason was certain to invite Danya's suspicion.

He had a feeling that the beautiful djinn woman, so concerned with her appearance at all times, would not like what was about to happen next.

A quick mental push, not unlike the one he had used to get the recalcitrant goats rounded up and moving in the direction he wanted. This time, however, he was much more forceful about reaching out with his djinn powers. He didn't want to guide the goats; he wanted to startle them.

It seemed he succeeded in that goal, because at once the animals let out a series of surprised bleats, and took off running...right toward Danya.

She barely had time to look over at them to see what the commotion was all about before they barreled into her, knocking her to the ground. A frightened shriek escaped her throat. Farid, who clearly let his cock do the thinking for him, lunged forward to help his fallen lover, letting go of Jordan.

That was the opening Hasan had hoped for. He blinked himself to Jordan's side, took her in his arms. She let out a relieved little gasp and clung to him. "Thank God," she whispered.

The goats milled about, making it more difficult for Farid to reach his lady love, who was shoving ineffectually at the goats, her shimmering silken garb now smudged with dirt. Then, clearly frustrated, she pushed out with her hands, sending a tremor through the ground. The goats, startled by this development, leaped out of the way, bleating as they tried to find someplace to stand where the earth was still acting as the earth should—by staying in one place and not moving about. The animals bolted toward the house, leaving Farid to take Danya's hand and help her to her feet. She brushed at the dirt on her clothes, a fierce frown marring her perfect brow.

"That was a low trick!"

Hasan gave her a mocking little bow. "Was it? I would think you would be pleased, because this little demonstration has shown that Farid cares more for your safety than he does for carrying out your vengeance. Truly, you have found a love for the ages."

She opened her mouth to make some kind of a retort, then shut it with an audible snap. Hasan fancied he could hear her teeth grinding from where he stood.

Farid began, "Danya—" and she whirled on him.

"Don't say anything," she hissed. Her baleful pale gaze transferred itself to Hasan, and she added, "You think you have won? Very well. Take your insipid little Chosen and be gone from this place. You no longer have any right to be here."

"No, I do not," he agreed, his tone mild. "In fact, Jordan and I were discussing the move to Santa Fe when you so rudely interrupted us. Now I will ask you to be gone, Danya—with the reminder that attempting to bring harm to a Chosen is one crime the elders do take quite seriously."

She did not appear to have a reply to that remark, and so she shot him and Jordan one last ferocious glance, then locked her arm with Farid's. The two of them disappeared with another rumble of the earth, strong enough that Jordan stumbled. Hasan's arm tightened around her, and she looked up at him, a grateful smile touching her lips.

"Wow," she said. "You might have warned me that your ex-girlfriend was that evil."

"I had no idea she would be *quite* so evil," he replied. "I suppose I should be flattered. However, it seems your little ploy with the goats thwarted her. One thing about Danya—she is very aware of her own importance. Being knocked into the dirt by a herd of farm animals is something that would take her a long time to live down, which means she will take pains to make sure no one learns of what happened here."

"What if we tell the djinn in Santa Fe?"

He bent and kissed Jordan on the cheek, marveling at the silky soft texture of her skin. "They live their lives apart from the rest of the djinn, so the story shouldn't travel very far. And if it does...."

"Yes?"

"I won't shed too many bitter tears."

Jordan chuckled then, and slipped her hand into his. "Well, if we're really going to Santa Fe, I suppose we'd better get moving."

————

She could tell that Hasan was somewhat

saddened by having to leave, although he did his best to seem cheerful as he gathered his belongings together, deciding what he wanted to take and what he could leave behind. How they were supposed to transport everything, Jordan really didn't know. Yes, Hasan could "blink" everything to its new destination, but he had to know what that destination was first. And that, he told her, would be up to Zahrias, the leader of the djinn in Santa Fe.

"There are of course many unoccupied houses in the city," Hasan said. "But it is not as simple as just choosing one and moving in. We will have to let Zahrias tell us where to go."

Jordan didn't know if she particularly liked the sound of that. On the other hand, according to what she'd heard in Los Alamos, Zahrias was now married to Julia Innes, which meant he must be somewhat sympathetic to humans. Otherwise, why would he be leading a community of djinn and Chosen?

There was another matter to consider as well.

"What about the goats?" she asked Hasan as she peeked out the living room window to see how their little herd fared. As far as she could tell, they'd recovered from Danya's display with the earthquakes, but Jordan noticed they were still sticking closer to the house than they usually did.

Hasan came over to the window and looked out at the goats. "I cannot blink that many at once," he said. "Perhaps we should move them the human way."

"The human way?"

"In a trailer, using one of the trucks left behind here in Chama. How long would such a drive be?"

She had to stop and try to recall the maps she'd pored over as she planned her escape route from Pagosa Springs to Los Alamos. "A couple of hours, I think. It's really not far. But we'll have to go slower than we could have back in the day, just because of all the abandoned vehicles on the roads."

"That will be no problem," he said. "If you are willing to drive, then I can move the vehicles out of the way as we come upon them. Yes, it will slow us down a little, but probably not as much as you fear."

That was a relief. She'd never towed a trailer before, but with Hasan watching out for her—and with no worry about other drivers on the road, or merging into traffic, or any other common issues with driving back in the day—it should all work out fine.

"I'll drive. It'll be fun. I guess we'd better find a trailer, then."

"There is a truck in the garage here. We can use that to locate the trailer."

Jordan followed Hasan out of the house to the detached garage, which was cavernous, clearly built to accommodate a full-size RV, although at the moment it contained only a half-ton Dodge pickup truck. The truck was covered in dust, but otherwise looked practically brand new. Once again, she wondered about who had owned this property before the Dying. Someone with a lot of disposable income, that was for sure.

Despite its basically new state, the truck didn't want to start. Not that strange, considering how long it had been sitting in the garage, untouched. However, all Hasan had to do was place one finger on the battery, and the Dodge started right up, its big engine sending out a deep rumble that Jordan could both hear and feel.

It was a little intimidating to drive something so powerful. Back before the Dying, she'd gotten around in a twelve-year-old Toyota Corolla. Hasan gave her an encouraging smile as he climbed into the passenger seat, and she pulled in a breath and put the truck in reverse, backing out of the garage so she could follow the dirt track that led to an access road about a quarter-mile away from the property. After that, they were in "downtown" Chama within the next few minutes. Jordan stopped in the middle of the road, considering the best way to go. She didn't know much about what lay north of town, if you followed the 17 on its way up toward Antonito, just over the Colorado border. On the other hand, she'd passed several ranches on Highway 84. That seemed the safest bet.

She turned right, heading north.

"Where are we going?" Hasan asked.

"There are farms and ranches in this direction. One of them must have a livestock trailer."

He nodded. "That does make sense."

Had Hasan ever ridden in a vehicle like this before? He'd mentioned coming to this world to taste its food and see its sights, but maybe he never had any reason to get in a half-ton truck. He did seem interested in their progress, watching the landscape move past as he sat much higher than he had in Lindsey's borrowed Volvo, occasionally glancing at the dashboard and all the instrumentation there. Because this truck had been fitted with all the bells and whistles, it had navigation and satellite radio, dual-zone climate control, the works. Of course, the nav and the satellite radio were useless without the necessary technological infrastructure to back them up, but it still looked rather impressive.

They came to a narrow lane that led to what had once been a prosperous ranch, with white-painted wood fencing around multiple corrals. Or rather, the fences had been painted white once, but were now an off shade of gray, the paint peeling and flaking away. Jordan wondered what had happened to the animals that were once kept here. Had they gotten out of their corrals, or had they been trapped here?

She really didn't want to imagine that scenario, and so she pushed the image out of her head. After all, the goats in Chama seemed to have done pretty well. No reason why the horses and cattle couldn't have fared the same.

The lane went past a large, handsome house done in the New Mexico territorial style, with a steeply pitched metal roof and wide porches. It was almost as nice as the house where Hasan had taken up residence, and she wondered why the elders had sent him there rather than this property. Of course, having the river so close by did make the Chama home that much more attractive.

As she'd hoped, there was a large barn behind the house, and when they got out of the truck to poke around inside, they found a long trailer that would have accommodated at least six horses, probably more.

"This will be sufficient?" Hasan asked, looking it up and down.

"More than sufficient, I think. We can put the goats in here and all our things, and probably have room to spare. We need a hitch, though."

"A hitch?"

"It's an attachment that lets you hook up a trailer to a tow vehicle. The truck is set up for towing, but no one installed a hitch. I'm hoping there'll be one here somewhere."

"Ah. I fear you will have to look for it, since I doubt I would recognize a hitch if I saw one."

Jordan knew she'd recognize it, but as for being able to determine that it was the right size to fit in the receiver on the Dodge—that was an entirely different story. A quick survey of the stall where they'd found the trailer didn't turn up any hitches, and there weren't any in the tack room, either.

They left the barn and went in search of the garage, which turned out to be tucked in behind the house. There they found a heavy-duty Ford pickup, clearly the vehicle the owners of this ranch had used to tow the trailer. It did have a hitch, and after a few minutes of puzzling out how all the connectors worked, they had it uninstalled, Hasan carrying it propped up against one shoulder like a makeshift club.

Apparently all vehicles of this towing capacity used a standard size of hitch. They were able to install it without a problem, and a few minutes later, were on their way back to Chama.

They put their belongings in the compartment closest to the truck's cab, and then rounded up the goats and coaxed them into the trailer. None of the animals seemed very thrilled to be put in that enclosed space, but at least they didn't balk. Hasan closed the door to the trailer and latched it, then looked around...at the house, at the aspens glowing golden in the distance.

Jordan put a hand on his wrist. "You going to be okay?"

"Of course," he said at once. "It is only a house, and not even one that I built. I shouldn't have any attachment to it, but...."

"But?"

His blue eyes sought hers. "But it is where I fell in love with you. For that reason, it is dear to me."

She wrapped her fingers around his. "I'll be with you, no matter where we go. We can make more memories in our new home."

"You are right, of course." He pulled her close, and leaned down to kiss her, but gently, with none of the wild passion he'd shown earlier. That was all right; Jordan almost welcomed the tenderness more, because it seemed to show her more than anything else how much he had changed, how much he had allowed his heart to open to hers. As he lifted his mouth from hers, he pushed a strand of hair away from her face. "Let us go."

Nothing else to say, really. These were the rules, and they needed to follow them. Jordan knew she didn't want to face another confrontation like the one she and Hasan had just survived. If they stayed here, they'd only be risking further encounters with Danya and Farid...and, for all Jordan knew, these mysterious "elders." She'd just as soon avoid dealing with them at all.

So she got into the driver's seat and buckled her seatbelt, then waited for Hasan to do the same. It was harder than she'd thought to maneuver the truck and the long trailer behind it onto the lane that joined up with the highway, but after a few false starts, she was pulling away from the house. She could see it in the rearview mirror, looking somehow forlorn, although they'd taken care to lock it down as best they could—the windows shut, all the food removed from the kitchen, the lights turned off. It was too much to hope that someone else might come along and make it their own. Jordan had traveled all the long, weary miles from Pagosa Springs to this spot, and she knew better than anyone else how empty this country was. There simply weren't any people left.

Tears burned in her eyes, and she told herself not to be foolish. She'd spent only a few days here. Yes, as Hasan had pointed out, this was where they'd discovered their love for one another, but there would be another house, another place to share their lives.

If he noticed her distress, he gave no indication of it. He stared out the window, watching the landscape passing by. Memorizing it, so he wouldn't forget the time he'd spent here? Jordan didn't really know how it worked with djinn. They lived such long, long lives. Did their memories pile up and up as the years passed, eventually crushing the older ones until they were no longer recognizable, turning carbon into diamonds?

Although the roads here hadn't been cleared the way they were in Los Alamos, it wasn't as difficult for her to avoid the abandoned vehicles as she'd feared. In almost every case, there was enough room for her to wind around them, even with pulling the trailer. And in those few instances where they wouldn't otherwise have been able to squeeze past, Hasan lifted a hand, and a wind came from nowhere to push those offending cars and trucks and SUVs out of the way.

In less time than she'd imagined, they were winding down past Abiquiu. Georgia O'Keeffe country, with the spare, stark juniper trees and the cliffs in a rainbow of colors, and the flat-topped peak of the Pedernal, O'Keeffe's favorite mountain, looming blue-purple off in the distance. And from there to Española, where of course the roads were completely clear, thanks to the work of the crews in Los Alamos. Jordan wondered if she and Hasan would come across any of those crews today, and what on earth she would say if they did have such an unfortunate meeting.

However, their luck held, and they made it through town without incident, following the highway as it became the 285 and bent slightly east, heading down toward Santa Fe. They passed empty casinos, their parking lots emptier than she'd expected. Maybe the Santa Fe djinn had done their own prospecting here. She couldn't begin to guess, because she knew so very little about the place where she was heading, or the people who lived there. Julia Innes would be among them, but even so, she was little more than a name and a voice.

The highway climbed up past the turnoff for the Santa Fe Opera, then dipped down toward the town itself. On the left was a national cemetery, rows and rows of identical white headstones flickering at the edge of her vision. The Heat had claimed so many more, but they had no graves, no markers to remind the living of those they'd lost.

"Do you know where I should go?" she asked Hasan as they passed a huge empty field where wildflowers grew. Driveways abruptly dead-ended there, telling Jordan that something else must have occupied the space, although no other evidence remained to tell her what it might have been. "I mean, where do the djinn live?"

"In the heart of town, I believe," he replied. "If you follow the signs directing you to the Plaza, then they should take us where we need to go."

"Okay." She slowed down, because once they crossed Paseo de Peralta, the road narrowed and began to curve, and she didn't want to tax the truck hitch. At least the roads here were just as empty as they'd been back in Española.

As they approached the intersection of Guadalupe Road and San Francisco Street, however, Jordan found herself jamming on the brakes. Standing there in the middle of the road was a forbiddingly handsome djinn, his arms crossed, flickers of flame dancing in the air around him.

It looked like they'd found the welcome committee.

Chapter Twenty

HASAN HAD BEEN EXPECTING THIS, AND YET HE still couldn't prevent a quiver of unease in his gut as he sat next to Jordan, facing Zahrias al-Harith, leader of the Santa Fe djinn, and his Chosen across a polished wood table at what had once been the La Fonda Hotel. Julia Innes' expression was far more welcoming—she was a strikingly beautiful woman—but even her smile couldn't soften the frown that Zahrias wore.

The main reason for that frown was probably the person Hasan had very much hoped to avoid —Qadim al-Syan, his erstwhile friend. Sitting next to Qadim was Madison, his Chosen. She appeared more intrigued by this turn of events than anything else, but if looks could be daggers, Hasan knew he would have been pierced multiple times by the knives Qadim was throwing at him.

Oh, he had reason. Hasan had to admit to himself that he had not behaved particularly well when it came to Qadim and Madison. Driven almost mad with anger at what he'd seen as a betrayal by his friend, Hasan had kidnapped Madison, believing that taking her away would make Qadim come to his senses and realize his foolishness in giving his heart to a mortal. Of course, the opposite had happened, and clearly the passage of nearly a year hadn't done much, if anything, to lessen his former friend's resentment over what had happened.

"This is unacceptable," Qadim said, glaring at Hasan and quite pointedly ignoring Jordan, who sat in her chair with her hands folded in her lap, every inch of her slender body stiff with worry. "They don't belong here."

"That is for me to decide, Qadim," Zahrias returned. He appeared more irritated than anything else; little flames danced around his head and then winked out of existence, a sure sign that he was distracted. "Am I not the leader here?"

"You are," Qadim rumbled. "But I am a resident of this place. Have I no say?"

"Of course you do," Julia said. Her voice was

low and soft, but something about the way she spoke made one want to sit up straighter and pay attention. "But maybe I should remind you that at first I wasn't exactly thrilled about you coming to live here, either."

"That was different."

"Not as different as you might think," Zahrias remarked. "I shared Julia's reticence. However, I realized that we could not shut you out, not as someone who had taken a Chosen. You had as much right to be here as anyone else."

"That is precisely it," Hasan said. Qadim's dark eyes flared with anger, but Hasan went on, "We are only following the rules. Once I had made Jordan my Chosen, I knew I had no choice but to bring her here. We could not have remained where we were, lest we draw down the anger of the other djinn, or of the elders. It is our right to be here."

"In a djinn community, yes. But why must it be this one? You," Qadim demanded, pointing an accusing finger in Jordan's direction. She jumped slightly, and Hasan reached over and laid a reassuring hand on her leg. "Where do you come from? Chama, where Hasan resided?"

"No," she replied. "I was born in Colorado Springs. And I came down into Chama from Pagosa Springs."

"There," Qadim said, his tone triumphant. "You see? The 'rules' always stated that we djinn must settle in the community nearest to where our Chosen lived. This woman is from nowhere around here. Go live with a djinn community they must, but it should not be this one. There is one in Colorado, is there not?"

"In Aspen," Zahrias said.

"Well, then," Qadim said, as if that settled everything.

Madison had been listening to all this with a slight frown, clearly absorbing but not wanting to get in the middle of the discussion. Now, however, she leaned forward, her head with its magnificent mass of curly red hair tilted to one side. "I might not be remembering clearly, but I'm pretty sure Santa Fe and Aspen are almost equidistant from Colorado Springs. Or at least, back when I was a kid and my family went visiting places, it sure felt as if it took as long to drive from Santa Fe to Colorado Springs as it did to get from there to Aspen."

Zahrias nodded, as if considering her words. "We need a map."

"There are probably still some at the concierge desk," Julia said. "I'll go take a look."

Offering Hasan and Jordan a reassuring

smile, she got up from the table and left the conference room.

With Julia gone, it was as though a leavening influence had left the room. Qadim tapped the tabletop impatiently with his fingers, brow knitted together. Hasan noticed that Madison had a hand on one arm, clearly hoping that her touch would prevent him from doing anything rash. Not that Hasan was too worried; Zahrias would stop the earth elemental if he attempted anything physical.

It didn't seem as if Jordan was too reassured by the presence of the djinn leader, however. She kept shooting him surreptitious little glances from under her lashes. Was she worried that Zahrias would rule against them, that he would send them back on the road, goats and all? That would be a very long drive, so he could not blame her for being concerned. It was probably more than worry over the journey, though. At least she knew Julia peripherally, and if the Santa Fe and Los Alamos communities were as close as they seemed to be, more connections existed there—including Lindsay, the wife of the scientist Miles Odekirk—than Jordan would have in Aspen, where everyone would be strangers.

Julia returned, holding a folded piece of

heavy paper in her hand. She spread it out on the table so everyone could get a closer look.

"If you look at the legend, you can see that it's about 250 miles from Colorado Springs to Aspen," she said. "And about 320 miles from Santa Fe to Colorado Springs. So technically, the Aspen compound would be closer."

"You see?" Qadim crossed his arms across his chest, looking very satisfied with himself. "I told you that she had no business being here."

"However," Julia went on, "anyone who's driven these roads will tell you that it takes less time to get from Santa Fe to Colorado Springs than it does to get from Colorado Springs to Aspen, so you could also say that Santa Fe is closer when it comes to travel time."

"Semantics," Qadim said. The frown was back. "This splitting of hairs was not what the elders intended when they said that each djinn must settle in the community closest to his or her Chosen."

Zahrias had been studying the map intently. Now he straightened, and leveled a steady glance at Qadim. "Perhaps." He lifted the map from the tabletop and refolded it before saying, "I need to think on this carefully. Qadim and Madison, you may return home. I'll inform you of my decision."

"But—" Qadim began, and Zahrias raised an eyebrow.

"That's fine," Madison said. She slipped her arm through Qadim's and stood, forcing him to rise as well. "Come on, Qadim."

He still looked thunderous, but he appeared to understand that any further arguments would only paint him in a poor light. The two of them left the room, and Julia let out a sigh.

"I had a feeling he was going to dig in his heels," she said.

"I cannot blame him," Hasan told her. "If our situations were reversed, I probably would feel the same way."

She gazed at him, expression frankly speculative. "You know, Hasan, you're really not what I was expecting."

"I've done my best to mellow him out," Jordan remarked, and Julia chuckled.

"It seems to be working." She turned to her partner, who still stood next to the table, the folded-up map in his hands. "Well, Zahrias?"

For a long moment, he didn't speak. He stared down at the map he held, then looked out the window, which opened on a street that once had probably bustled with people shopping and sightseeing, but now was quite empty. "It would be easier to send you away," Zahrias remarked. "I have a contentious enough group here as it is, what with Jasreel and Aldair, and the bad blood between myself and Qadim."

Hasan tried to ignore the dread rising within him, Jordan's suddenly pale cheeks. "I will apologize to Qadim, if you think it will do any good."

"I don't know if it would," Zahrias replied, his tone heavy. "Earth elementals tend to be the worst at holding grudges. But I can tell that Julia thinks you should stay."

"I didn't say anything," she protested.

His mouth lifted in a thin smile. "You didn't have to, my love."

"Well, I do think it would be better," she said. "Especially since Lindsay reached out to me, let me know what was going on."

"Lindsay?" Jordan broke in. "Is she all right? I felt terrible leaving like that, but she said I should go—"

"Lindsay is fine," Julia said with a smile. "She went into labor almost as soon as Miles came home that night, and she had a baby boy early the next morning. Rumor has it that Miles actually stayed home from work to be with them."

"And they're really fine?"

"Yes. And she told me she knew exactly why you had to leave. No one's blaming you for that."

Jordan didn't precisely smile, but the look of

gratitude on her face was clear enough for everyone there to see.

Zahrias spoke then. "You will stay, I think. Qadim will have to overcome his anger, lest he choke on it."

Hasan reached over and took Jordan's hand in his. She clung to him, her tight grip telling him of her relief. "Thank you, Zahrias," he said.

"Oh, I am not being quite so magnanimous as you might think, Hasan. This town is a large one. Our group has settled in close to the city center, for there were plenty of homes here that were adequate to our needs. I think, however, that it would be better if you put some distance between you and Qadim, just to be safe. On the western edges of our territory is an area that was once called Las Campanas. You should make your home there. As I said, it is still inside the borders of our territory, still on land that no other djinn will contest, but it will take you somewhat outside Qadim's orbit."

"It needs to be someplace where we can keep our goats, though," Jordan said, her tone somewhat anxious. "A property with some land around it."

An almost mischievous expression spread over Julia's elegant features. "I think I have just the place."

It turned out that Julia had compiled a list of houses in the area that had been up for sale at the time of the Dying—"easy enough to do, based on brochures and one-sheets at real estate offices," she explained. She'd sketched out a quick map and some directions to a house she thought would work. "If you don't like it, though, just let me know. I tend to hang out here at La Fonda during the day because it's a central location where people can find me. We used to have meetings at the house, but Zahrias decided he didn't want people showing up all the time for trivial things."

Jordan assured Julia that she was sure the house she'd selected would be fine, although now, as she drove northwest out of the heart of town, she couldn't help experiencing a few butterflies in her stomach. What if the place turned out to be not that great? She and Hasan were already here on sufferance, so the last thing she wanted to do was make any waves.

Hasan was looking around with interest, surveying the street they turned onto after she pulled off the highway. The lots here were large and far apart, the landscape studded with junipers and piñon pine. They kept going, the truck and trailer chugging their way up the hill as the road shifted from pavement to gravel.

Eventually, they came to a gated property with the correct address. The gate stood open, so there was no impediment to continuing on their route. Here the trees clustered more thickly, offering privacy. And there was the house, a low adobe-style structure. Sprawling.

No, *huge*. As Jordan scanned the property, she realized there were actually two houses—the main house, and then a separate guest house that she estimated was still twice the size of the modest one-story where she'd grown up. Another building...the stable, with a large corral beyond it. All walled in, which meant the goats would be safe from any marauding coyotes.

"I think," Hasan murmured, "that this should be sufficient."

"I think so, too," Jordan replied. "But let's get those poor goats out of this trailer, and then we can look around."

She pulled up next to the stable and put the truck in park. Hasan got out immediately and went around back to open the trailer, using his own special form of djinn persuasion to get the goats moving through the gate that opened into the corral. Not that they needed much coaxing— they saw the dry grass that waited for them and practically tripped over each other to get out there and start eating.

"Well, that should keep them occupied for a while," he said, coming over to her so he could take her hand. "Shall we go inside?"

"Yes, let's," she responded, and tried to quell the nervousness rising in her.

Hasan guided her across the open gravel area that separated the house from the stable. As they approached the front door, she could see the garage off to the left; they'd need to pull the truck in there once they got the trailer uncoupled and safely stowed in the stable.

But then she abruptly stopped worrying about the truck, or the garage, because they were going up the steps into a sort of enclosed front patio, with slate flagstones on the floor, and then up more stairs into the house itself.

"Holy shit," Jordan murmured. "This is a *house?*"

"It would appear so," Hasan said. "A very large house."

She had a hard time taking in the scale of the place. Room flowed into room, and the ceilings were enormous, held up by pillars carved by master craftsmen in the shapes of twining leaves and flowers. Really, it looked more like a hotel, or a resort—not that she'd ever been anywhere as remotely fancy as this. Multiple fireplaces, including one in the master bedroom. Secret patios hung with wisteria, although of course the vines weren't blooming at this time of year. A stream wandered its way through the grounds, lending the quiet whisper of the water to the sound of leaves rustling on aspen and oak. The presence of the stream reassured her. After having the sound of the San Juan River in the background all the time she was in Pagosa, and the Rio Chama at Hasan's house, she would have missed that low murmur of running water. Now she knew she would always have it with her.

"They just...gave this place to us?" Jordan asked at last.

"Yes, because they had no use for it. As Zahrias said, the rest of them live much closer to town."

Where there were also probably plenty of beautiful homes, although she had a hard time imagining that any of them could come close to this one.

Hasan appeared to be worried by her silence —which was really no more than awestruck wonder from staring at her new home—because he said, "Will you be all right, living far away from the others? I do not want you to feel like an exile simply because Qadim and I are feuding."

"Oh, no," Jordan said immediately. She went to Hasan and put her arms around his waist, felt a rush of warmth go through her as he held her close. "I would have been perfectly happy to stay with you in Chama, and that was much more isolated. And this thing with Qadim...I'm sure you'll work it out eventually."

"I hope so."

"I know so."

"You do?" He slipped one finger under her chin so she looked up at him. "Why are you so certain?"

She had to pause for a moment to analyze her thoughts. Yes, Qadim had sounded very angry—and had good cause to be, from what she'd been able to tell. "Because," she said simply. "Because you hated humans, and yet here we are. People can change...even when they've been around for a few thousand years."

For a long moment, Hasan didn't reply, only gazed down into her face. Then he bent and kissed her, gently still, but with a long, lingering heat beneath that touch of mouth on mouth, one which told her he would take her to that magnificent bed in the very near future.

"Yes, my love," he said. "People can change."

The End

Awoken is the last full-length novel in the Djinn Wars series. A holiday novella will be available in early December 2017.

Look for the spinoff series, Djinn Dominion, in spring 2018.

Want to make sure you don't miss any new releases? Sign up at www.christinepope.com to get on Christine's mailing list!

Also by Christine Pope

THE WATCHERS TRILOGY

(Paranormal Romance)

Falling Dark

Dead of Night

Rising Dawn

THE WITCHES OF CLEOPATRA HILL

(Paranormal Romance)

Darkangel

Darknight

Darkmoon

Sympathetic Magic

Protector

Spellbound

A Cleopatra Hill Christmas

Impractical Magic

Strange Magic

The Arrangement

Defender

Bad Blood (August 2017)

Deep Magic (October 2017)

THE DJINN WARS

(Paranormal Romance)

Chosen

Taken

Fallen

Broken

Forsaken

Forbidden

Awoken

Illuminated (December 2017)

THE SEDONA FILES

(Paranormal Romance)

Bad Vibrations

Desert Hearts

Angel Fire

Star Crossed

Falling Angels

Enemy Mine

TALES OF THE LATTER KINGDOMS

(Fantasy Romance)

All Fall Down

Dragon Rose

Binding Spell

Ashes of Roses

One Thousand Nights

Threads of Gold

The Wolf of Harrow Hall

Moon Dance

The Song of the Thrush (November 2017)

THE GAIAN CONSORTIUM SERIES

(Science Fiction Romance)

Blood Will Tell

About the Author

Christine Pope has been writing stories ever since she commandeered her family's Smith-Corona typewriter back in the sixth grade. Her work includes paranormal romance, fantasy romance, and science fiction/space opera romance. The Land of Enchantment cast its spell on her while she was researching her Djinn Wars series, and she now makes her home in Santa Fe, New Mexico.

To be notified about new releases by Christine Pope, please go to www.christinepope.com and sign up for her newsletter.